CANVAS OF DECEPTION

A Levi Yoder Thriller

M.A. ROTHMAN

Primordial Press

Copyright © 2025 Michael A. Rothman

Cover Art by Jason Gurley

This is a work of fiction. Names, characters, businesses, places, events, locales, and incidents are either the products of the author's imagination or used in a fictitious manner. Any resemblance to actual persons, living or dead, or actual events, is purely coincidental.

All rights reserved.

Paperback ISBN-13: 978-1-960244-85-7
Hardcover ISBN: 978-1-960244-86-4

CONTENTS

Chapter 1	1
Chapter 2	20
Chapter 3	32
Chapter 4	45
Chapter 5	62
Chapter 6	75
Chapter 7	90
Chapter 8	108
Chapter 9	125
Chapter 10	136
Chapter 11	146
Chapter 12	161
Chapter 13	173
Chapter 14	189
Chapter 15	205
Chapter 16	219
Chapter 17	242
Chapter 18	252
Chapter 19	266
Chapter 20	277
Author's Note	289
Preview – Multiverse	294
Preview – New Arcadia	308
Addendum	329
About the Author	340

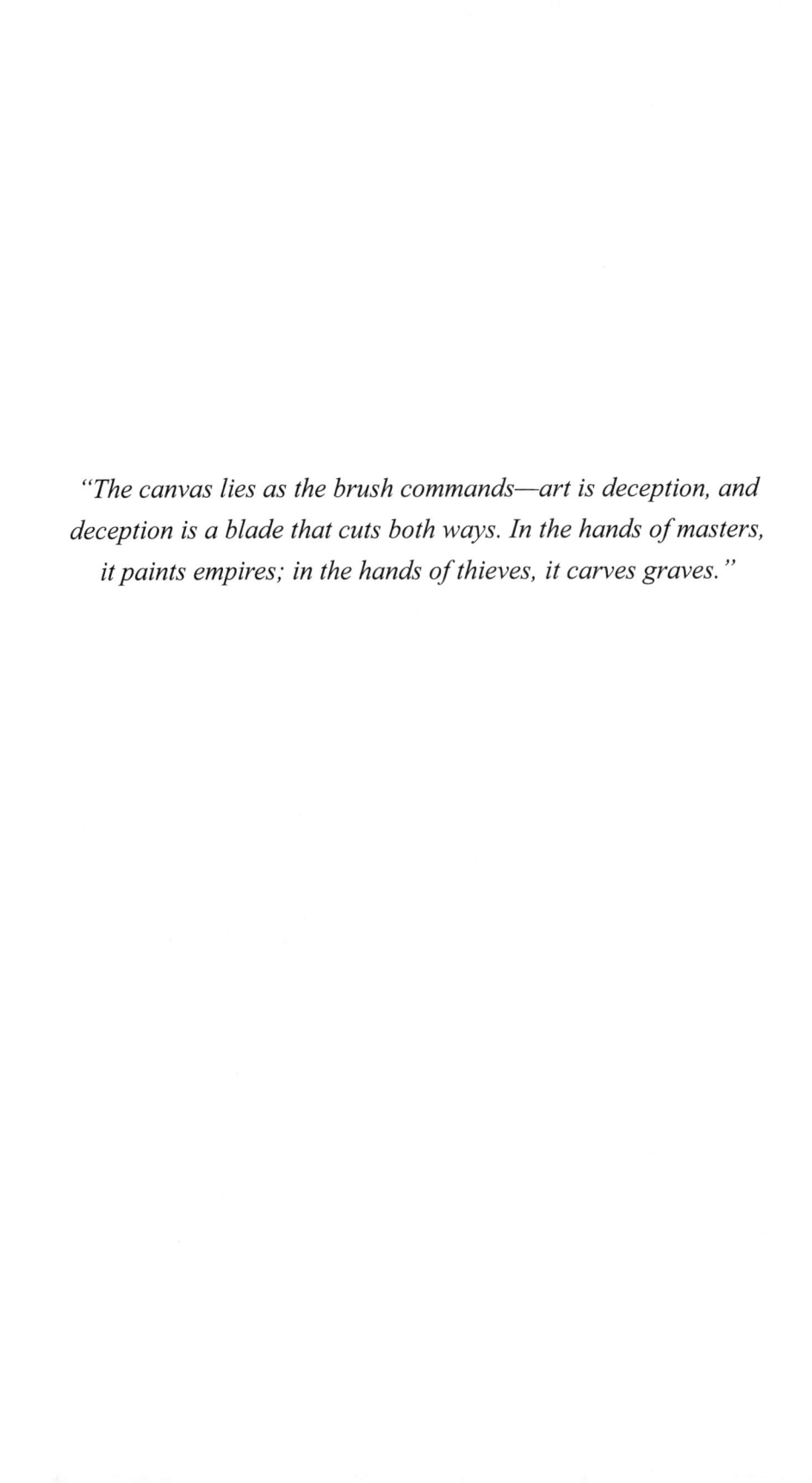

"The canvas lies as the brush commands—art is deception, and deception is a blade that cuts both ways. In the hands of masters, it paints empires; in the hands of thieves, it carves graves."

CHAPTER ONE

Paris, August 21, 1911

A hush fell over the Louvre's grand halls, the usual bustle of Paris nightlife reduced to a distant murmur behind centuries-old stone walls. Vincenzo Peruggia adjusted the white smock draped over him, the same uniform the museum's maintenance staff wore. Perspiration slicked his palms; he wiped them against the rough fabric of his smock before tugging his cap lower. A toolbox dangled from one hand, adding to his unremarkable appearance among the scattering of workers shifting ladders and scaffolds.

The aromas of floor wax and aged timbers mingled in the still air, carried on the faint metallic echoes of tools clanking in the distance. With the museum closed to visitors for the night, only a skeleton crew remained. Vincenzo's pulse thudded with each deliberate step toward the *Salon Carré*, where the Mona Lisa hung. He forced calm into his features, willing himself into total focus. Any wrong movement—any slip of the mask—and he'd be caught.

He found the painting exactly as he remembered: smaller than most visitors imagined, its softly muted palette and mysterious smile almost eclipsed by the surrounding masterpieces. For a moment, he let his gaze rest on that legendary face. The enormity of what he was about to do pressed in on him like a weight.

He lowered his toolbox and knelt. Earlier reconnaissance had told him the frame was fixed by simple wooden brackets and tiny nails. Carefully, he wedged a narrow tool into the seams, prying the panel free with scarcely a whisper. No one seemed to notice him; he was just another worker on the night shift.

Under his smock, Vincenzo wore a large apron. With painstaking care, he eased the Mona Lisa from its frame, leaving the gilded wood behind. The painting, set on a thin wooden panel, was compact enough to tuck beneath his apron without bending or damage. His fingers trembled as he buttoned his smock, concealing the priceless treasure.

Picking up his toolbox, he made his way down the corridor. High ceilings loomed above, and the countless masterpieces lining the walls seemed to glare at him in silent judgment. Footsteps echoed from somewhere behind, and a distant guard offered a disinterested nod—his attention already lost in the headlines of a newspaper. Politics and wars, Vincenzo thought, so trivial compared to what was happening at this very moment.

He descended the museum's sweeping main staircase, its grandeur magnified by the hush of the late hour. Each step he took down the cold stone steps rang in his ears, a private thunder.

Near the exit, a lone guard stood yawning by the heavy oak doors.

"Quiet night?" the guard asked, stretching.

"Always," Vincenzo replied, managing a smile. His faint Italian accent went unnoticed as he gestured to his toolbox. "Just returning these to the workshop."

The guard waved him through with only a cursory glance.

Outside, moonlight bathed the Louvre's imposing facade. The city of Paris exhaled around him—distant clatter of hooves on cobblestones, the rare automobile rattling by, the soft murmur of street vendors still plying their trade. He kept walking, back straight, eyes forward, until he was swallowed by a narrow alley. There, under the comforting shadow of a tall brick wall, he let the tension slide from his shoulders. Church bells chimed the hour, their toll echoing across the Seine.

He pressed a hand to his smock, feeling the steady beat of his heart and the cool surface of the stolen Mona Lisa beneath. A trembling laugh escaped him—pure relief and triumph. Then, with a last glance toward the pale moon, Vincenzo Peruggia disappeared into the labyrinthine streets of Paris.

The greatest art heist of the century had just been accomplished.

Port Of Baltimore, Maryland – Today, 9:00 a.m.

The fog wended its way between the buildings lining the water, drifting like a many-armed specter as it wrapped around the warehouse, its tendrils coiling over the pier. Farther out, a ship's engine droned—a low, monotone buzz—blending with the gentle wash of water against pilings. Inside, flickering fluorescent lights hummed overhead, casting twitchy shadows across the stained concrete floor. The air reeked of salt, damp wood, and a sharp tang of rust that prickled the back of the throat.

Two silhouettes in dark coats slipped between towering crates, their footfalls absorbed by the cavernous stillness. Wisps of breath curled in the cold air, vanishing into the gloom.

The taller of the two—a man whose coat carried the heavy scent of tobacco—aimed a flashlight down the aisles. The beam jumped over rows of nearly identical crates, each labeled with stenciled markings. His light paused on a sign at the end of one aisle: *B-14*.

"This way," he muttered, turning in.

They moved deeper into the warehouse. The temperature seemed to drop with every step. The flashlight exposed chipped paint and gnawing rats darting under pallets. At last, the beam settled on a crate larger than the rest, bearing fresh Cyrillic markings.

"Just like Frankie said."

He handed the flashlight to his partner, who shone it on the crate while the taller man rummaged for a crowbar. With a grunt of effort, he pried the lid free. Wood splintered, nails shrieked in the silence, and a spill of straw cascaded to the floor.

Inside, cocooned in bubble wrap, lay a rectangular shape.

"Looks like what we came for," the man said, breath clouding in the cold air.

The flashlight beam trembled slightly as his partner watched. A blade appeared in the taller man's gloved hand—quick, deft, practiced. He sliced through layers of protective plastic. The bubble wrap sloughed off to reveal not just a painting, but a strange secondary wrapping: a bag-like shell of plasticized steel mesh, tightly drawn shut with a thick braided cable. At the closure point sat a small, rectangular metal box, smooth and featureless except for a flat, matte panel about the size of a thumbprint.

The smaller man—wiry, sharp-featured—stepped forward. He adjusted thin spectacles on his nose. "What the hell is that some kind of lock?"

The taller one shrugged, then pressed his thumb against the panel. A dull buzz emitted from the device—but nothing else. No click, no release. Just silence.

"An electronic lock?" the smaller man ventured.

"Well, I know what to do with locks." The taller man reached into his coat and retrieved a bolt cutter, the kind meant for heavy chain. "Either way, I'm not standing around guessing whether or not we got the right package."

With a hard crunch, he snapped the cable. The mesh sprang slightly open, releasing a muted tension.

The mesh fell away, revealing a painting in a gilded frame.

Setting aside the larger flashlight, the smaller man pulled out from his pocket a pen-shaped light and played a violet beam across the surface of the canvas. His movements were methodical, a studied awe creeping into his face.

The taller man shuffled closer, eyes narrowing. "Is that what I think it is?"

"It can't be…" The smaller man's words trailed off, almost reverent.

"So it's a fake?" The taller man's tone grew dangerously low.

"Wait," the smaller man hissed. The UV light settled over a corner where the shadows and highlights blended with unnerving realism. *Sfumato*—the smoky transition of tones—so refined it made him swallow hard. "This technique… if this is authentic, it should be under bulletproof glass at the Louvre. Not in some warehouse."

He ran the beam over the ornate edge of the frame. A slight metallic *tick* cut the air.

Both men stiffened, breath catching mid-inhale.

The taller man's hand fell to the pistol tucked in his coat. "What the hell was that?"

A wavering distortion shimmered over the painting's surface. Then came a hiss, sharp as broken glass. The taller man staggered backward, hacking a wet cough. His legs buckled as he wheezed, his hands scrabbling desperately for grip on a breathable pocket of air.

The smaller man gasped, eyes bulging as he clutched his throat. His flashlight rattled across the floor, its frantic beam slicing irregular patterns on the walls. He choked, nails carving furrows into his neck. Blood dotted his fingertips as his body lurched in ugly spasms.

A spume of saliva and crimson ran from the taller man's mouth as he too convulsed. Within seconds, both lay still.

On the concrete floor, the gilded painting clattered with a

final, echoing thud. Its carved frame gleamed under the flickering lights—silent, deadly, and perfectly still.

A moment of unnatural quiet followed, punctuated only by the dull hum of a ship's engine outside. That distant machine carried on, indifferent to the two cooling bodies sprawled at its periphery.

In the half-lit shadows, the painting remained where it fell, its presence a dark omen of something far more dangerous than art.

Manhattan's Upper East Side – The Helmsley Arms

Levi Yoder pushed through the ornate glass doors of the Helmsley Arms, letting the swirl of cool, conditioned air wash over him. The lobby was polished to a shine—white marble floors gleaming under crystal chandeliers, the faint smell of pine cleaner and leather drifted up from the lounge chairs. It felt like stepping into another world: old money, old families, old debts.

Dominic Russo—barrel-chested, slicked-back hair, and a thick mustache that might have been fashionable in a bygone era—sat behind a small security desk to one side. He called out in heavily accented English, "Levi! Over here! I gotta message for you."

Levi raised the paper shopping bag in his hand. "Dom, my friend, I come bearing gifts."

With a grin, he pulled out a smaller bag with the logo from

Nonna's bakery printed on it and left it on the desk. "Fresh cannoli for you guys working the shift."

Dominic tapped his own chest. "I shoulda known you wouldn't forget the big guy." A flash of gold from his tooth caught the overhead light. "But listen, Frankie said that the Don wants you upstairs. I'm guessing it's something important."

Levi glanced at his phone. *One missed call.* Must've been during his subway ride, the signal was always spotty. He tucked the phone away. "Noted." He offered Dominic a friendly wave, heading toward a bank of brass-paneled elevators.

A UPS driver hustled in, arms loaded with packages, and Dominic redirected his attention, barking instructions. The elevator doors slid open with a soft chime, and Levi stepped inside, pressing the button for the top floor. As the car rose, he flexed his shoulders, trying to ease a vague sense of tension. The missed call was from Vinnie himself, and he hated talking on the phone. Something was definitely up.

Two men the size of refrigerators stood sentry at the penthouse's carved double doors. The moment they saw Levi, one murmured into a mic tucked in his cuff. Then he cracked the door open, nodding Levi through. "Levi, the Don said to grab a seat. He'll be right in."

Inside, the spacious parlor was a striking blend of old-world opulence and modern touches—leather sofas, antique tables, a crackling fireplace that infused the air with the scent of seasoned wood and faint smoke. Off to one side stood a large marble statue, an exact copy of the Venus de Milo, its timeless grace commanding attention.

Levi crossed to the fireplace, his gaze drifting to the mantel and landing on a framed photo that tugged at his heart.

Memories played in his mind like a silent reel. The picture showed a younger Levi, a younger Don Vincenzo (Vinnie), a blonde who would become Vinnie's wife, and there was Mary—Levi's own wife, gone these many years. Lipstick prints smudged the glass in two spots: one above Levi's head, one above Vinnie's. The photo was taken at Jennings Beach—wind-tousled hair, sunburned noses, Mary's black hair whirling around her carefree grin.

It hurt to see the old photo. Not only because he'd never quite gotten over Mary's death, but it was a reminder that Vinnie and he were the same age, and they looked it. Now, as Levi stood there, he realized Vinnie looked noticeably older: gray at his temples, deeper creases around his eyes. Yet Levi somehow looked a decade—maybe two—younger. He knew perfectly well why that was, but admitting it even to himself made him uneasy and his chest tightened with the guilt he felt over it.

"Levi!"

Vincenzo Bianchi's voice boomed from the private entry to the parlor. He strode in, arms spread in greeting. Despite the silver threaded through his hair and the lines etched on his face, his presence was formidable. Levi turned, mustering a smile as Vinnie wrapped him in a hearty hug, patting him on both cheeks in the old Italian style.

"Damn," Vinnie said, stepping back to give him a once-over.

"You look better every time I see you. Not sure what you're doing, but it's working."

Levi offered a small shrug, though the remark stung more than he let on. "You needed to see me?"

Vinnie looked at the shopping bag Levi carried and peered inside. "Ah, you went to the old neighborhood." He patted Levi's flat stomach. "You eat enough of Nonna's desserts and maybe you'll finally get a belly."

Levi chuckled, shaking his head. "It's not for me. Alicia's getting into town tonight and I figured something sweet might be nice."

"She's a good kid," Vinnie said, nodding. "Smart, resourceful. I remember when she was just a little thing. She always acted a decade older than she was." He gave Levi a knowing glance. "Kinda like someone I know." He jerked his head toward an ornate desk at the far end of the room. "Come on. Let's talk."

Levi followed, the fireplace's warmth making the wide room feel cozy even as he sensed tension radiating from Vinnie. Something was wrong. Once they were settled—Levi on a leather chair, Vinnie behind the desk—the Don poured himself a hefty measure of amber liquor from a cut-crystal decanter.

"It's been one of those days," he muttered, tossing back the drink and refilling the glass. "I don't normally hit it this hard, but sometimes, well…" His voice trailed off, and he leaned both elbows on the polished wood. "Two of our men—Vito Maniscalco and Carmine Ricci—are gone."

Levi's stomach clenched. "Dead?"

Vinnie nodded, jaw set. "It happened this morning. They went to pick up a shipment from the Red Hook warehouse—

something from that Russian contact you helped us make a connection with."

Levi pressed his lips into a thin line and returned the nod. He immediately recalled the mental image of Oleg Zharkov, a young Russian mobster he'd met a long time ago. He was one of the ones who'd benefited from the fall of the Iron Curtain and had contacts in both the Russian government and the seedy underbelly that ran things over there.

"Well, I'll cut to the chase…" Vinnie swirled the amber drink. "It looks like your boy Zharkov was connected to a few people who knew where certain 'interesting items' got stashed behind the Iron Curtain—stuff the Nazis looted during the war."

"And Zharkov's crew found it?"

"Exactly." Vinnie jabbed his index finger in his direction to emphasize the point.

Levi's eyes widened at the enormity of what Vinnie had just said. Everyone knew that the Nazis had stolen half of Europe's art treasures; few were ever recovered.

"The idea was that our organization would act as an intermediary of sorts."

Levi nodded, knowing exactly what the Don was saying. The Bianchi family would be fencing whatever it was. Buying and selling what the law would normally consider stolen goods.

"We'd help bring some of this stuff back, give it some verifiable provenance, and then we'd all make a killing from it." Vinnie paused; a bitter expression crossed his face. "Today was the first shipment, and I've got two dead men and a crated painting. It's at a safe house nearby."

"So, do you think…" Levi paused, measuring his words. "Do you think the Russians played us?"

"It's possible," Vinnie said, his voice carrying an ominous tone. "Or maybe the Russians have nothing to do with this and we got burned by someone else. All I know is that there's no way two of my men both decided to have heart attacks in the middle of a pickup. I need you to go figure out what's what with the shipment, you *capisce*?"

"Sure, no problem. What about Vito and Carmine? Did they really have heart attacks?"

"We don't know yet," Vinnie said with a dismissive wave. "One of our guys at the Medical Examiner's office is going to get back to us the moment they know what's up." He pointed at Levi. "You go talk with Frankie. He'll tell you where the painting's stowed and if you need to go to the warehouse to track stuff down, he'll give you the info you need."

"Vinnie, I'm guessing you need some answers right away, right?"

The Don hesitated for a second, his lips tightly pressed together, then shook his head. "I know your baby girl's coming tonight, you can—"

"Don't worry about Alicia. In fact, I was going to ask if you don't mind my taking her with me. You know she's been training with the Feds and stuff, and I'm pretty sure she's getting sick of those Outfit guys. I know she's been itching to maybe start her own investigative practice, so I think shadowing me a bit might be good for her, and she might prove to be handy."

Don Bianchi tilted his head and gave Levi a knowing grin.

"She's a good kid, Levi. Smart, that one—but I don't need to remind you that she's not part of our thing."

"Of course she isn't, and I don't want that kind of life for her. Like you said, she's a good kid. I heard about some of the stuff she did with Tony and I'd like to see that kind of spunk with my own eyes, if you know what I mean. It's hard for me to imagine my baby girl doing that kind of stuff, but if Alicia's up for that kind of grit, then maybe she could become useful in ways I didn't expect. This feels like the right time to see what she's capable of."

The Don was silent for a moment, then gave a single nod. "Fine. You go talk with Frankie first and get the lowdown on where the package is. Give Alicia my best, go ahead and poke around, do what you gotta do. I don't need to know any more until you have some answers."

Levi stood, buttoned his jacket, and gave his best friend a nod. "I'll let you know when I've got something solid."

"Nobody takes out two of our men. Levi, I need some names." The Don gulped down his second drink, never letting his gaze leave Levi. "You got my permission to do whatever it takes, and I don't care where it leads." He motioned dismissively toward the parlor's entrance and poured himself a third drink.

The flicker of fluorescent lights filled the hidden workroom behind Gerard's, illuminating the rows of shelving stacked with electronics and assorted equipment. Levi leaned back in his chair, waiting for Alicia's arrival. A faint scent of cooking oil and beer lingered in the air, a reminder that the neighborhood bar was just twenty feet on the other side of the work room's entrance.

A beep sounded at the workroom's only door, and Levi stood, a smile spreading across his face as his adoptive daughter, Alicia, stepped inside. She had no idea he would be there; he wanted it that way, knowing that this was a pivotal moment in her life—and he wanted to witness her reaction in person.

"I hear congratulations are in order. You've finished your first solo mission," he said, opening his arms for a hug. "I'm proud of you."

He saw the crack in her composure immediately—the slight tremble in her lips before she stepped into his embrace. When she began to sob, he held her tightly, wishing he could shield her from all harm. Yet from the moment he'd found the young Asian girl on the streets, he knew she was different: thoughtful but streetwise, always finding a path through her troubles.

"I didn't know you were in town," she said through her tears, her voice muffled against his shoulder.

"I just got in." He eased back, placing his hands on her shoulders, and studied her face. "Do you know what you're going to do?"

Alicia wiped her tears roughly with the back of her hand, clearing her throat, obviously embarrassed by her show of vulnerability.

Denny, Levi's longtime associate—a man he trusted implicitly—handed her a box of tissues before wandering toward the far end of the room to give them space. Levi noticed how tightly

Alicia clutched the tissues, as though trying to hold herself together.

"What do you mean?" she asked, dabbing at her eyes.

He pointed to a chair beside the table where his briefcase lay. "I know you've been questioning your future—especially with the Outfit. You're on the brink of becoming a full member. It's a big decision, one I understand all too well. Mason's offered me full membership before, and I've always turned it down. I prefer my freedom. I don't like being tied to anyone—not even them."

"You're already tied to another outfit, in a way." Alicia gave him a lopsided grin.

She wasn't naïve. Though Levi had never openly admitted his connection to *la Cosa Nostra*, she'd been around enough of his associates—past and present—to piece it together. She recognized the whispers of the Mafia.

Levi let the comment pass, remaining focused. "What are your plans?" he asked again.

Alicia pursed her lips, her expression thoughtful. Levi saw the gears turning in her mind as she considered his question. He admired that about her—how she didn't rush to speak, how she absorbed and weighed every possibility first.

"Dad, to be honest, I like the idea of being flexible and having freedom—kind of like you describe—but I'm just not sure. I mean, if I wanted to go it alone, I don't even know where to start. I don't understand the economics of it yet."

Levi nodded. "That's a fair concern."

She hitched her thumb in Denny's direction. "He helped me *so* much while I was overseas, for all I know I owe him tens of thousands of dollars."

"Millions!" Denny's voice rang out, followed by a wheezing laugh.

"See?" Alicia shrugged with a faint smile. "Millions. Other than the money I got up front for the mission, it's not like I have a huge savings. And where would I get clients? I just don't—"

"Alicia, hold up a second." Her father motioned for silence. "Denny's obviously kidding about 'millions,' but set aside the money for a moment. Honestly, I wasn't sure whether you would be cut out for this kind of work. Sometimes, things can get ugly."

Levi glanced in Denny's direction. Though several aisles of shelving separated him from the electronics whiz, Levi lowered his voice. He trusted Denny, but *family* matters were a different story. Turning back to Alicia, he leaned closer and spoke in a whisper. "Tony told me what you did at Don Vianello's place—the move with the phone, using the assassin's sister to get leverage. Could you do that in real life? If the situation called for it, would you be able to hurt someone?"

Alicia's eyes widened. She started to speak but clamped her mouth shut, frowning as she weighed her answer.

Her hesitation spoke volumes.

When she did respond, her voice was steady but tinged with emotion. "I don't think so. If someone deserved it, maybe. But torturing someone who was innocent? No. I couldn't do that. I don't care how much money is involved."

"Good." Levi smiled, feeling the tension slip from around his neck and shoulders. He hadn't been certain how she'd answer. "Neither could I," he said, leaning back. "You're smart, Alicia—great instincts. And from what I've heard, you do well under pressure. So, I'm going to make you an offer."

He flipped open the briefcase, the lid snapping back to reveal neat stacks of crisp hundred-dollar bills. Her eyes widened, the reaction instant and unguarded. Though she quickly eased her shoulders, the moment of tension betrayed her surprise—shock rippling through her like a current she couldn't fully suppress.

"This is your seed money," he said. "It's yours regardless of what you decide, even if you don't want to go independent. You and your sisters don't know this, but each of you girls has a briefcase like this as an inheritance when you turn thirty. I think if you want to start your own thing, you can get this a bit early. It'll give you time to figure out the economics of it all and work your own deal with Denny and possibly some other people I might introduce you to. What do you think?"

She gasped softly, staring at the money. "What about the Outfit?"

"Don't commit to them full-time," Levi said, waving away the idea. "Do contract work, like I do. Mason won't like it, but I'll help make him see it in a positive light. That way, you can live in both worlds." He nudged the briefcase toward her. "So, what do you think?"

Alicia's smile lit up her face—the same smile she'd shown him when he first informed her that he was adopting her. He saw the decision solidify in her eyes even before she spoke.

"I think this is what I want," she said softly. "I want to go independent. And... thank you, Dad. For everything. I love you."

A rush of warmth surged through Levi, although he kept it hidden behind his calm exterior. Nothing more needed to be said; she knew how he felt.

She stood, leaned over and kissed the top of his head, like

he'd always done to her. "I'll call Mason tomorrow and tell him I want a change to my contract."

"Good. Then it's settled. I've got something for us to do." Levi stood and gave her a lopsided smile. He glanced behind her and held a puzzled expression. "Where's that cat of yours? I thought he was always by your side."

She glanced in the direction he was looking and shook her head. "A neighbor borrowed my cat carrier and the folks on the Acela don't like it when I carry him in my arms. It's not like he's going to hijack the train or something. Anyway, he's with the neighbor. Bagel likes harassing her dog and—hey, what did you mean by you have something for us to do?" She tilted her head and gazed at him with a suspicious expression. "You mean, tonight?"

Levi nodded. "If I remember correctly, you took some art classes when you were at Princeton, right?"

"Yes…" She said the word very slowly, her suspicion slowly turned to a look of amusement. "Why do you ask?"

Levi turned away and called out to Denny, "Alicia and I are taking off. I might need you later tonight. You going to be around?"

"You know me, I'm always around. ♪ Just call my name and I'll be there ♪."

Alicia groaned as Denny sang part of his response. "I suspected you were cheesy, but I never suspected you'd be quoting a Mariah Carey song."

"Mariah? Oh, you're such a young thing, that's the Jackson 5, and don't you forget it."

"Okay, enough with the music trivia." Levi snorted and

shook his head. "Just keep your phone on and we'll talk later." He motioned for Alicia to follow as he headed to the workroom's entrance.

Just as Levi was about to open the door, he looked over at Alicia and asked, "By the way, how's your Russian?"

CHAPTER TWO

A cold wind rolled through Manhattan's canyons of glass and steel as the dark sedan pulled up to the curb. Their Uber had arrived. Alicia slipped into the back seat first, met by the sharp tang of disinfectant, stale cigarette smoke that clung to the car's interior, and the sound of an eighties rock ballad playing softly through the car's speakers. Her father, Levi, followed, nudging the door closed with a muted thud. Outside, a thin mist had begun to gather around the streetlamps, making the city lights waver in the haze.

"Turn up the music, would you?" Levi asked, leaning forward to catch the driver's eye in the rearview mirror. His voice was smooth, threaded with quiet authority. The driver responded with a curt nod and flicked the volume knob. An electric guitar riff erupted from the speakers, reverberating around them in pulsing waves of bass.

Levi lowered his head, leaning close to Alicia. "Keep your

voice down," he whispered, his breath warming her ear despite the chill of the winter air. The scent of his cologne—a mix of spice and leather—drifted toward her, familiar yet strangely unsettling. The driver craned his head slightly, as he pulled away the curb. He muttered something under his breath, but the volume of the music provided a shield of noise.

Alicia shifted in her seat, the worn leather squeaking beneath her. She brushed her fingertips over the small tear in the seat cushion—an old habit to calm herself—while she waited for her father to speak. It was obvious to her that that wheels inside that head of his were turning, his eyes flicking back and forth between her and their surroundings. Neon lights from passing storefronts flickered across her father's sharply tailored jacket, revealing the lines of worry etched into his features. He was tense about something, and that set her on edge. She'd rarely ever seen him as focused.

"There's two dead men," he whispered, barely audible over the pounding guitar and the muffled thrum of city traffic. "Vinnie told me that they were found dead in a warehouse over in Baltimore, no obvious signs of a struggle."

Alicia caught a flicker in her father's eyes, a hint of unease that made her own pulse skip. She inhaled, catching the pungent mix of a nearby hot dog stand and melting snow wafting in through the half-cracked window. "Okay," she responded under her breath and leaned in closer. This conversation had become deadly serious.

Levi pulled in a deep breath and let it out slowly. "Let's just say that the only thing near them was a shipping crate. It arrived from Russia, evidently from a new business acquaintance, but an acquaintance that hasn't yet earned any significant level of trust if you know what I mean."

She nodded, fully aware that her father was leaving out details that almost certainly had to do with his mob connections.

"Anyway, we're heading to my place so we can prepare, but Frankie's put the crate with its contents in a place where we can go study it. I want you to have your forensic thinking cap on for this."

A burst of drums shook the car's speakers, covering the hitch in Alicia's breath. Her mind whirled. Russia. Artwork. Dead men. "What was inside the crate?" she asked quietly.

"A painting. Supposedly," Levi said, hesitating. "That's all I know—Frankie didn't have much more he could share, I doubt anyone's seen this at all other than the two dead guys, so we need to be careful."

Alicia whispered, "Dad, do you think the crate or what's inside had something to do with their deaths?"

He shrugged. "When you don't have enough information to come to an educated conclusion, then you have to assume the worst." Her father glanced at the driver, whose focus was on the traffic ahead of him, and cocked an eyebrow as he asked, "What to you would be the worst-case scenario?"

With her mind her mind racing, Alicia pressed her lips together and let her imagination run through the possibilities. "Did you say the crate was already opened before by the guys who got killed?"

"I didn't say that, but that matches what I was told."

Alicia's gaze narrowed and she shook her head. "Maybe there's some kind of booby trap they set off on the crate? Maybe something about the painting—could it be covered with some kind of nerve agent?"

Her father shrugged. "None of those possibilities have been eliminated."

A chill raced up and down Alicia's spine. "Maybe that's our first move... full hazmat gear and go in assuming we're dealing with something nasty on the crate or painting? I think that's the approach I'd take."

"Okay." He nodded without giving anything else up on what he thought of the idea. "We'll do as you suggest."

"Um, Dad... do you have that kind of gear I'm talking about? You know, stuff like level A, or at least level B hazmat suits?"

Her father chuckled and gave her a wink. "You'd be surprised what kind of toys I have stashed away."

The shabby Uber turned onto Park Avenue, the grandeur of the Upper East Side looming ahead. The rhythmic clack of tires on slick asphalt thrummed through the vehicle.

They pulled up to the curb in front of the Helmsley Arms. The hush that fell when the driver switched off the music felt deafening. Alicia's heart pounded in the sudden silence, mixing with the hush of the city night.

"We're here," the driver announced as a large figure approached the rear passenger-side door.

The door unlocked with a mechanical snap and someone opened the door, letting in a gust of cold air scented with wet concrete and the faint sweetness of roasted nuts from a distant cart.

A familiar face peered into the cabin and Alicia smiled. "Hey, Tony!"

"How you doing, princess?" Tony Montelaro spoke with a New York accent. He stepped back letting her father out, they greeted each other with a pats on each other's shoulders.

Her father nudged Tony and said, "Give the driver a little something for an added tip. Alicia and I have some business to attend to."

Alicia hopped out of the car and caught up with her father. High above them, the spires of towering penthouses disappeared into a swirl of fog. Even in the bustling heart of Manhattan, the shadows seemed to stretch, thick with secrets and there something about the nighttime that sent a thrill up her spine.

A thin mist clung to the narrow alleyway, reflecting the pallid glow of a single overhead lamp that sputtered in protest. Levi led Alicia along the cracked pavement toward a nondescript steel door set into the side of an old, gray building. From a distance, nothing about it seemed remarkable—just another neglected basement entrance lost in New York's labyrinth of side streets. But the way Alicia's eyes flicked around told him she was paying careful attention to their surroundings.

Reaching the door, he swiped a plain white plastic card over a recessed panel. For a heartbeat, nothing happened but the faint hum of electricity in the walls. Then came a subdued beep, and a heavy click reverberated through the steel frame. Alicia glanced at him, eyebrows slightly raised, and Levi gave her a wink. He could tell what she was thinking without her saying a word. She wasn't stupid, he knew that she knew that he was involved with the Mafia. She also knew without him having to spell it out that this little adventure of theirs had the Bianchi family written all over it. When most people, even his brilliant daughter, thought of the mob, they didn't picture electronically secured entries or any sort of modern technology.

They would have been mostly right about twenty years ago, but since then, things have changed. And Levi had helped facilitate some of that change.

They both slipped past the now-open door. The corridor beyond descended into the basement, its walls a dull, institutional white. Lights flared on in timed increments as they walked, revealing concrete floors that appeared newly polished, yet somehow still smelled faintly of age and industrial cleaner. The moment they passed a section, the lights behind them snapped off, plunging that area back into darkness. It was impossible not to feel the hairs on his neck prickle, as if the building itself monitored their every step.

Around the next bend, they came to another door, electronically keyed like the first, but significantly heavier—almost vault-like. Levi punched in a code, then swiped his card again. This time, the lock made a deeper, more deliberate clunk, a sign of the thick soundproofing he knew existed inside. Over the years, this room had been used for all sorts of clandestine activities, including the occasional interrogation.

They emerged into the hidden safehouse proper—a cramped, low-ceilinged chamber that reeked of stale air, as though nobody had opened it in months. Levi breathed in deeply and he tasted something in the air. It wasn't the coppery scent of blood, which this room had been splattered with in the past, but it was something else. The overhead fluorescents buzzed, flicking to life, revealing the space that would serve as our makeshift lab for the evening.

Alicia unzipped the duffle bag she'd been carrying. "Dad, I can smell something in the air. Let's not get any closer before we get dressed."

She handed him the bundle containing a head-to-toe hazmat suit with its own air supply and he began putting it on.

Levi grabbed a clear plastic bag, put his phone inside it, and set it on the ground. He watched Alicia as she donned her suit, all the while her eyes swept the room—methodical, precise, like a forensic scientist on a mission. He felt a flicker of pride as she checked and double checked the seals between her gloves, boots, and the suit.

She turned to him and made a twirling motion with her finger. *"Turn around so I can buddy check you."* Her voice crackled from the tiny speakers built into the hazmat suit.

They both checked each other's suit, passed each other's mutual inspection, and Levi motioned toward the far end of the room where they both could see a medium-sized crate. "Okay young lady, it's all yours. Your move."

Alicia nodded behind the clear facemask and Levi followed her as she walked deeper into the soundproof room. There was a single work table in the center, its metal surface dented and pockmarked. Atop it rested the real reason they were there: a battered wooden crate. Stenciled in black Cyrillic lettering across the front were the words *Red Horizon Transport*. The edges of the crate were splintered, with nails protruding at odd angles. Alicia ran a gloved fingertip across the letters, quietly swabbing them before transferring the sample into a small Ziploc bag. *"I'm going to take samples from everything."*

"Topside surface," she murmured, her voice crackled through Levi's speaker. She labeled the bag with a Sharpie in neat handwriting. Levi glanced down at her determined posture. Her quick, confident movements reminded him of how much she'd learned during her time with the Outfit.

The overhead light was weak, casting a pale circle over the crate. Levi felt a sense of grim determination as he reminded himself that two men that he knew had died because of this shipment. He grabbed the crowbar from the duffel and said, "I'll help open the crate."

Whoever had resealed the wooden box had done it in a completely haphazard way with nails halfway protruding from the wood and others bent in half—it was clearly a rush job.

Careful not to disturb Alicia's methodical routine, Levi worked on backing out the nails, all the while being careful not to let any of the sharp edges puncture his suit. He pulled on the last nail, wood squealed against wood, setting his teeth on edge. As he lifted the lid, he spied something inside that had been wrapped in multiple layers of bubble wrap.

"Let me unwrap it so I can take samples along the way." Alicia advanced on the box with caution, swabbing each layer of wrapping before peeling it away. Her gloved hands moved with the practiced confidence of someone handling a live explosive. Levi reached in to help steady the painting, the plastic squeaking under his grip. When the wrappings finally fell away, the painting caught the fluorescent light—and both of them sucked in a breath.

It was the *Mona Lisa*.

Levi's chest tightened. Among all the masterpieces in the world, this was one of the most recognizable. He locked eyes with Alicia, noticing the incredulity that stiffened her posture. "How the hell did this get here?" he muttered under his breath. His pulse quickened; this couldn't be the real thing, or could it? His mind flashed back to the details of his conversation with the Don.

"...stuff the Nazis looted during the war..."

"It can't be real," Alicia said, but her voice sounded less assured than he would have expected. Her gloved hand hovered a few inches from the canvas, as though drawn to it.

"Probably not." Levi exhaled slowly, recalling the strange truths he had encountered in his line of work.

"Probably?" Alicia turned to him, her eyes wide. *"What do you mean probably? This has to be the most famous painting in the world, if it had been stolen, I suspect we'd all have heard something."*

"I've learned not to assume anything," he replied, arching an eyebrow. "I'm going to play Devil's advocate for a moment with you. Have you ever been to the Louvre?"

Alicia shook her head. *"No."*

He measured the painting's size—just a bit over two feet by just under two feet. "Then you wouldn't know that it's not exactly a huge painting. And it's roped off, behind bulletproof glass. A lot of people crowd around it, so who's to say the one there isn't just a copy?"

She shot him a sidelong look. "How is that even poss—"

"Alicia, whether this thing's authentic or not isn't our priority right now." He motioned back to the contents of the crate.

She blinked rapidly for a second and gave him a curt nod. *"Sorry, you're right."* Leaning in, Alicia brought her face inches from the surface, swabbing the frame with quick, practiced motions. *"This thing definitely has live brush strokes present,"* she noted. *"At school, they taught us how to spot fakes by examining paint layers, but since this is on a wooden panel, we can't check if the paint's seeped through the canvas fibers. That'd require a special kind of X-ray analysis."*

Levi watched her brow furrow as she prodded a tiny pit in the gilded frame with one of her swabs and sealed it into another clear plastic bag and labeled it. "This gilding... it looks too perfect," she murmured. "No flaws, no signs of hand-carving. Everything from the Renaissance era has at least some imperfection—here it's symmetrical, pristine. It could be real, but my gut says the frame isn't a period piece."

Before Levi could respond, his phone vibrated loudly in his pocket. He tapped the earbud he was wearing and said, "Yeah?"

Frankie's voice crackled through his earpiece. *"Autopsy results say both men died of asphyxiation. No bruises, no rope marks. They found internal bleeding in the lungs, eyes turned bloody red from some kind of pressure that stopped them from being able breathe. Levi, whatever was done to them blew out all the blood vessels in their eyes, so be careful. Those Russian bastards had to have a hand in what happened."*

Levi's jaw tightened. "I'm on it, Frankie. I'll get back to you when I know something more." He tapped the earbud, closing the connection and glanced at Alicia. She was looking over at him with a curious expression, having heard his side of the phone conversation. "This all smells rotten," he remarked, his gaze shifting to the pile of forensic samples lying nearby. "I just got confirmation that the two dead folks died from asphyxiation. And before you ask, no, there were no obvious signs of them being physically attacked."

Alicia's brows furrowed behind the clear face mask and she spoke with a determined voice. *"That sure as hell sounds like some kind of nerve agent or poison. Was anything in their bloodstream?"*

"Frankie made no mention of that, so let's assume not for now." He pointed at the collection of sealed plastic bags and asked, "You have anything else that you want to take a swab of?"

"No, I think I'm done here." Alicia began putting the bags into a larger plastic bag as she asked, *"Do you have a place that can process hazardous samples?"*

"Hold on a second." He walked over to where he'd left his phone and through the clear plastic punched in a number—Denny—and paced the claustrophobic safehouse as he waited for an answer.

"I'm here."

"Denny, I've got a bunch of swabs that I need analyzed for possible chemical and/or biohazards. Can you help a brother out?"

Static on the line, then Denny's voice: *"I've got a contact at a pharmaceutical lab who might help as a favor. They have a level-4 biosafety lab that should be capable of analyzing whatever you have. Bring me the samples, and I'll set it up."*

"Thanks, buddy. Alicia and I will be over in a bit."

Levi turned back to Alicia. She had arranged a neat row of Ziploc bags on the table, each labeled with the surfaces she had swabbed. He nodded toward them. "Pack it all up. We're taking these to Denny."

"Okay." Alicia glanced in the direction of the painting. *"What about the painting?"*

"What about it?" Levi asked, not sure what she was getting at.

"Well, I know we can't exactly ask anyone about whether this is authentic, but I know some folks at school over at Princeton that I could call and ask about verification techniques for a 500-year-old painting. I don't exactly need to say I'm staring at a copy of the Mona Lisa."

"One thing at a time." Levi grinned. "How about for now, let's just pack up our Italian girlfriend back into her box and leave her be. She's not going anywhere for now."

Levi gave a glance at the Mona Lisa—or whatever it was—carefully wrapped the painting in the bubble wrap just as Alicia gathered the last of the evidence bags into the larger plastic bag. He motioned for Alicia to follow. The small painting, re-wrapped and placed carefully on the table, looked ominous under the buzzing fluorescent light. Whether real or fake, that wasn't important, at least to him.

All he knew was that if any of those samples that Alicia had taken had anything to do with the deaths of two made men, there would be hell to pay. And this time, hell was located somewhere in Russia.

CHAPTER THREE

Alicia paused in the apartment's living room, glancing at her father's bedroom door, which was closed. She could have sworn she'd heard a woman's voice last night—almost certainly Lucy's, her father's on-and-off girlfriend. A woman who she liked quite a bit, even though she knew about some of the shady business she'd was involved in. She hadn't imagined the gentle murmurs, the soft laughter from the other side of her bedroom door. And now, with sunlight filtering in through the high windows of the penthouse, her father was uncharacteristically quiet, still cloistered in his room. Alicia decided against knocking, unwilling to risk walking in on anything intimate. Let him have his moment, she told herself.

She took the steps down to the basement gym two at a time. The building's basement corridor was a hushed space of painted concrete walls and gleaming tile floors. Faint notes of disinfectant mingled with the musky odor of stale sweat. A dull hum from overhead fluorescent lights reverberated in her ears, setting a low, mechanical backdrop to her thoughts. She passed a small lounge area—usually deserted at this hour—and then pushed open the reinforced door to the gym.

Inside, ambient techno music pulsated softly through hidden speakers. The air smelled of rubberized flooring and chalk dust. The entire space had been fitted with high-end workout machines, courtesy of Uncle Vinnie. Rows of treadmills and elliptical bikes lined one side, while free weights, benches, and a mirrored wall occupied another. But Alicia's destination lay at the far end: an open area of padded mats where her father had often run hand-to-hand combat drills for "the men," a group she privately knew to be part of the Bianchi family's entourage.

Tony Montelaro was already waiting for her near the mats. He was a lumbering wall of muscle—broad shoulders, thick neck, and hands the size of catcher's mitts. Salt-and-pepper hair framed a perpetual frown, though Alicia sensed amusement flickering in his deep-set eyes. She knew Tony well enough; they'd even traveled to Italy once together, searching for his missing uncle who had worked at the Vatican.

"You're on time, Princess," he drawled, a teasing edge in his voice.

"I'm glad you agreed to some sparring," Alicia replied, rolling her shoulders and feeling the tension she'd built up all night start to loosen. She dropped her gym bag on a nearby bench, brushed a stray strand of hair from her eyes, and stepped onto the mat. Her bare feet sank slightly into the padding, the rough surface a familiar texture beneath her soles.

"I would have thought your father would be a better choice,

but you knew I couldn't exactly say no to a lady in distress. I'm your humble punching bag for the morning."

Alicia snorted and shook her head. "Dad is preoccupied at the moment."

"Ready when you are." Tony cracked his knuckles and held a determined expression.

They squared off. A beat passed, measured by the faint whir of ventilation fans high in the ceiling. Then Tony lunged—he always made the first move, a bulldozer tactic that had served him well in street fights. But Alicia had been trained by her father from an early age, schooled in all variety of martial arts, and he'd always had her focus on speed and agility, emphasizing that she'd usually lose a contest when brute force was at play. She sidestepped, pivoting on her back leg and letting him rush past.

The air swirled with his sudden motion, bringing with it the faint scent of his cologne—something woody and peppery that clashed with the sweaty gym atmosphere. Alicia struck out in a snap kick, aiming for Tony's hip. He blocked it with a forearm, the impact reverberating through her shin. She winced but kept her balance, stepping back to draw him in again.

Tony wasted no time in responding. He swung a low kick at Alicia's calves, forcing her to jump back. His power was undeniable; even a glancing blow could rattle her bones if he connected. Alicia pressed forward, sending two quick jabs toward his midsection. He deflected the first with an open palm but missed the second, and her punch grazed his rib cage. She felt the thud against her knuckles, followed by his low grunt of approval.

Between exchanges, Alicia was keenly aware of the details

around her. The rhythmic hiss of the air-conditioning vents, the metallic clank of weights in the corner, the rubber mat's faint squeak under every pivot of her foot. She could taste the sharp tang of adrenaline in her mouth, could feel the heat building beneath her workout leggings.

They continued this dance, exchanging blows, dodges, and counters. Tony might have been a massive hulk, but his speed and reflexes were much better than anyone would expect from someone his size. Twice he nearly caught Alicia with a grab—his meaty hand grazing her shoulder, then her elbow. Each time, she twisted and slipped free, narrowly avoiding his crushing grip.

"You're like a slippery eel," Tony huffed at one point, stepping back to catch his breath. A bead of sweat rolled down the side of his face. "Just when I think I've got hold of you, you squirm out of it."

Alicia smirked, panting lightly. "I've had good teachers." She could almost see her father's face in her mind: stern, methodical, instructing her on how to shift her center of gravity, how to pivot smoothly. She brushed damp hair off her forehead, noticing the bruise forming on her forearm where she'd blocked one of Tony's hits.

Tony moved again, a quick jab-jab combination that Alicia managed to block, though the force rattled her arms. She responded with a roundhouse kick, catching him on the side of his thigh. Tony staggered slightly, then swung an elbow that Alicia ducked. Her chest burned with exertion, and she felt sweat dripping down the back of her neck.

Within another minute, they broke away, breathing hard, chests heaving in sync. The hush that followed was broken only by their labored breathing and the muted club beat coming from the speakers overhead. Alicia rested her hands on her hips, muscles alight with that familiar post-spar ache she secretly enjoyed.

Tony shot her a broad grin, wiping his brow with a towel. "Quicker than ever. You give me a year or two, I might catch up."

Alicia returned the smile, though her lips parted to let in more air. "Keep training. One day, you might land a clean hit." She said it teasingly, despite knowing Tony was a formidable fighter who'd bested bigger men than him in back-alley brawls.

He chuckled, the sound echoing in the mostly empty gym. "You want any more, or shall we call it here?"

"I'm good for now," she replied, rolling her shoulder to test for injury. The dull ache in her triceps told her she'd be feeling this session tomorrow.

Tony nodded, propping his hands on his knees as he caught his breath. "You're pretty good Princess but your old man would have kicked my ass in every imaginable way and probably invented a few new ones while he was at it."

"He's annoying that way." Alicia nodded. Even though her father didn't have the formidable mass that Tony had, he had a well-deserved reputation for being untouchable in hand-to-hand combat. She could only imagine what he was like when he was doing this stuff for real on the streets."

She grabbed her own towel from a bench, mopping the sweat from her face. A passing moment of dizziness flared and faded, replaced by the steady drum of her heartbeat. In the background, a treadmill hummed softly, though it remained empty. The mechanical swirl of the air conditioning returned to her awareness, as though the gym were reminding her that here, at least, she could seize a moment of normalcy—gritty, honest, and free of secrets.

It wasn't that long ago that she was in school studying neuroscience. In the last couple years she'd experienced cancer, a mysterious cure, an ancient puzzle, working for the Feds, and now helping her father. A thrill raced up and down her spine as she replayed last night's events, collecting samples, seeing a copy of the Mona Lisa, and it dawned on her that she *needed* to know if those samples held any hidden boogiemen. Could that painting be real? If there was some kind of Russian connection, would her father let her investigate with him?

It was then that she realized she needed those secrets in her life. She'd always loved puzzles, and these things were nothing more than high-stakes puzzles.

She wiped her face once again, waved to Tony and headed upstairs.

If he wasn't awake, she was about to wake his butt up. There was stuff to do. Puzzles to solve. Maybe even bad guys to hunt for.

∽

Alicia's pulse still thrummed with the rush of her workout as she stepped into her father's apartment. Her tank top clung to her back, the faint tang of dried sweat mingling with the cool, conditioned air. She paused in the marble-tiled foyer, trying not to breathe too loudly. From the living room, she caught a glimpse of

Lucy—a tall, slender Asian woman with a model's poise but a palpable, almost predatory edge. Alicia always thought of her as a dragon lady, but one who somehow let her father leash her wilder side. Lucy pressed a lingering kiss to Levi's cheek, then turned toward Alicia.

"Hey, Alicia," Lucy said softly, sweeping Alicia into a light hug. A teasing smile flickered on her crimson-painted lips. Perfume—floral with an undercurrent of jasmine—swirled around Alicia like a warm cloud.

Before Alicia could respond, Lucy slipped out the door with a graceful sway of her hips. The click of her heels on the polished floor faded until the apartment fell silent again. Alicia and her father stood there, the moment raw with unspoken questions.

"Dad..." She shifted her gym bag on her shoulder, eyes flicking to his robe. "We didn't get home until after midnight. When did she, uh, arrive?"

Levi tugged at the belt of his bathrobe. He looked almost sheepish, an unusual expression for a man who always seemed self-assured and confident. "Lucy tried to visit earlier, but the guys downstairs wouldn't let her in since we were out. She texted me five minutes after you went to bed."

Alicia's mouth twitched. "Ah. So basically, Lucy made a post-midnight booty call?"

"That, young lady, is none of your business," Levi returned, though the ghost of a smirk tugged at his lips.

"Which means yes," Alicia teased, forcing an air of nonchalance that only half disguised her embarrassment.

Levi cleared his throat and turned on his heel, padding into the kitchen. Morning light streamed through the floor-to-ceiling windows, illuminating a sleek cooking island outfitted with stainless-steel appliances. The smell of bacon and eggs soon enveloped the space as he set a pan on the burner, the sizzle snapping through the quiet. Alicia dropped her bag and joined him, leaning against the cool marble countertop.

"Why haven't you ever gotten remarried?" she asked gently, letting her gaze follow his movements: the eggs cracking cleanly against the bowl, the satisfying scrape of a spatula on nonstick metal.

The muscles of his jaw rippled with unspoken tension. "You and your questions," he muttered with forced levity. Yet the tension in his shoulders spoke volumes.

With the eggs nearly done, Levi slid an additional set of bacon strips onto a second pan. The fat popped and hissed, releasing more of the savory aroma that mingled with the musty smell of her own workout clothes. Alicia stepped back slightly, giving him room but staying close enough to sense his unease. She saw it in the tight line of his mouth, the haunted flicker in his eyes whenever he glanced toward her.

He finally set the spatula down and spoke in a measured tone. "Every time I look at guys my age—Vinnie or any of the older crowd—I'm reminded how they've changed over the decades. Meanwhile, here I am, barely different since…"

"Since Narmer's curse?" Alicia finished quietly. The sound of that words sounded strange in her ears as she recalled that bizarre twist in both of their lives. It wasn't a curse in the sense of it involving voodoo or other paranormal nonsense. This was more an affliction. A strange disease with unexpected side effects. This was a topic her father hated talking about, but she wasn't the one who'd brought the age thing up... what did marriage have to do with this?

Levi nodded, stirring the eggs again in a quick, restless motion. "I haven't aged a day since I first crossed paths with that cripple... that mysterious wanderer so many years ago. If there's one thing I've learned, it's that outliving the people you love is a heavier burden than it sounds. I already lost one wife, and it nearly broke me. I'm not eager to do it again." He piled the food onto two plates and they both walked into the dining room.

Alicia sat on the dining room chair opposite to him, pressing her palms into her thighs. His dead wife was a sensitive subject. Having been adopted after she'd died, this was something she wasn't comfortable bringing up, yet she'd started this conversation. "Dad, you'd said that Mary died in a car accident. It was an accident," she said softly. "Things happen on the road every day."

His mouth twisted, as though tasting something bitter. He filled his mouth with a spoonful of scrambled egg and chewed slowly. His gaze was focused on his plate and the longer he remained silent the more uncomfortable Alicia began to feel. "I hate talking about this."

"I'm sorry, let's drop the—"

"No," her father's eyes flashed with intensity as he stared at her. "It's about time you and I talked about this. It's something I've been dealing with—trying to learn to accept it, but you should also understand what that curse has done to us both."

She'd heard her father talk about Narmer on a few occasions, and he was always angry when the subject came up, often referring to Narmer as having cursed him. Alicia held a confused expression. "Dad, I don't see why you think what Narmer did was such a terrible thing. If he hadn't exposed us to this… this curse as you like to call it, we'd probably be dead."

"I know you see it that way, but I have trouble being so… understanding." Her father sighed and shook his head. "Shouldn't love mean sharing a lifetime together? I know you and I have shared the misfortune of encountering Narmer.

Alicia remembered vividly their encounter with the odd crippled man. He spoke like someone from another age. Like someone who'd live altogether too long and seen more than any human should see. Narmer kept talking about magic flowing in their blood.

In her mind's eye she saw herself with Narmer and her father.

The wizened old man old man spoke with a serious tone: "Coursing through your veins is a magic of sorts. I'm not one who can explain such things… The magic in your blood—"

Levi interrupted. "He means nanites. Not magic."

To her it didn't matter whether it was magic or a hyper-advanced inoculation. However she'd once looked up what nanites were and it didn't freak her out nearly as much as her father. The best analogy she could come up with was they were very tiny devices that could fix things at the molecular level. She imagined them as an uncountable number of microscopic robots floating through her blood, fixing whatever needed fixing.

And even though she only saw these nanites as a blessing of sorts, the look on her father's face spelled out a different opinion.

"Alicia, you need to understand what that means. I'm seeing people I grew up with get old. Sure, they probably all think I'm dyeing my hair and maybe have had a nip or tuck here and there, but I'm in my 50's now. What about ten or twenty years from now when I still look this way and hair dye and plastic surgery can no longer explain away what Narmer's done to me… to us. This is a problem that's only getting harder and harder to deal with, and Lucy doesn't know. She's even asked about what kind of skin treatments I use. If I got married, my lifetime would outlast hers—outlast just about anyone's. It's like being a vampire, minus the bloodsucking and the sunlight allergy." He pointed at Alicia's forearm, which had already developed a bruise. "That bruise will probably be gone tomorrow morning, but I'll be carrying the wound from Mary's death forever. I know Lucy wants more from me than I'm willing to give her. I've told her that I'm a lost cause, and that I wouldn't marry anyone—I don't think she believes me, but I wish things were different. I certainly can't advise you on your path with regard to love or whatever kids call it nowadays, but it's something to think about. For me, I've learned to keep people at arm's length. It's easier that way."

A cold ache settled in Alicia's chest. She understood the logic, but it still stung to hear him talk about love as a liability. The heartbreak at losing his wife had affected him more than she could probably ever know. She'd never really had that kind of love, at least not yet. It was a revelation to her how deeply trapped her father felt by the so-called curse. It was the same thing she had—he could never settle down, never grow old with someone—the idea twisted her stomach.

They ate in relative silence for a minute. The bacon was crisp, the eggs soft scrambled, just the way she liked it, and even though everything tasted great, she'd mostly lost her appetite.

She nibbled at a slice of bacon, cleared her throat and asked, "Any word from Denny yet? You know, about the swabs?"

Her father waved the question away. "He'll call as soon as he has results. Harassing him won't make the analysis come any faster."

Alicia drummed her fingers on the table. "Those samples… if there's something lethal in them—some weird chemical or nerve agent—do you think I can follow that up with you?"

Her father's otherwise somber expression brightened as he gave her a lopsided smile. "I'm sure we can figure something out." Having finished his breakfast, he gathered his plate and pointed at her half-eaten food. "Finish that up and shower up. We've got things to do."

Alicia set her fork down, curiosity piqued. "Such as?"

Her father stood taller, tightening the knot in his robe. "You said you want to set up your own private practice, right? Well, I've got some contacts you need to be introduced to. One of them you already know quite well."

"Oh? Who is it?"

"Hint, she's a zaftig Jewish lady who—"

"Esther!" Alicia practically squealed the woman's name. "I love her." She shoved a piece of bacon into her mouth and chewed quickly, the salty crunch giving her a jolt of energy.

Pushing her plate away, she said, "The food was yummy, but I can't eat any more."

Levi nodded, gathered their plates and loading them into the dishwasher. "I don't expect Denny to have any results until later in the day, but in the meantime, we've got a few errands to run. Go shower, get dressed, and we'll head over to Esther's."

With the mention of errands, she felt an electric thrill rush through her and hopped up from her chair.

"All right, Dad," she said, grabbing her gym bag. "I'll take a super quick shower. Be back out in a couple minutes."

She caught his faint smile as she jogged to her bedroom with the en-suite bathroom. Over her shoulder, she glimpsed the living room's panoramic windows—beyond them lay the city, roiling with hidden dangers. And somewhere out there, Lucy was weaving her own stories, Denny was testing swabs that might point to a deadly plot, and the puzzle of that Mona Lisa copy—and the Russians—lay in wait.

Her father's voice jolted her from her thoughts. "Stop staring out the windows and get ready."

Alicia smiled as a wave of déjà vu swept over her. The last time he'd chided her for daydreaming, she'd probably been a teenager. Back then, the same thought crossed her mind as it did now: that man had eyes in the back of his head.

CHAPTER FOUR

Levi felt a soft breeze at his back as he pushed open the glass door of Rosen's Sporting Goods. A small bell chimed overhead, and the crisp scent of freshly printed flyers and rubber matting filled his lungs. Five thousand square feet of sprawling merchandise greeted him: shelves loaded with archery sets, soccer balls, racks of athletic apparel, and stacks of dumbbells. Seasonal banners dangled from the ceiling—remaining summer gear marked down, additional winter gear waiting to be showcased.

He glanced over his shoulder to see Alicia stepping in with a bright expression. She was still flush from the car ride, seemingly brimming with anticipation. Outside, through the large windows, he could see Paulie, a giant of a man just a few inches shy of seven feet tall, leaning against the black sedan, ready to move at a moment's notice. With the uncertainties surrounding the recent deaths, the Don had ordered the entire Bianchi clan to be on alert. That heightened sense of security extended even to

Levi's travels, which resulted in Vinnie insisting he take one of the family cars and to have a backup with him. Paulie's size alone was enough to intimidate most people on the street, but as one of the head enforcers of the Bianchi family, Levi knew the man could be trusted if things went sideways.

Levi panned his gaze across the store and his lips curved into a smile when he spotted a round, gray-haired silhouette by the storefront window, partially obscured by some signage advertising ski trips to Aspen. The owner, Esther Rosen, stood there, heavy binoculars clutched to her face. Her broad figure filled the frame; her eyes gleamed with intense focus. She muttered something under her breath—something about bagels.

"Esther?" he called, approaching her from behind.

She didn't lower the binoculars. "Levi, hush," she snapped. "I'm doing something important right now!"

Levi exchanged a bemused glance with Alicia. Beyond the window, traffic hummed, and pedestrians scurried by, but nothing appeared out of the ordinary—just the usual Manhattan morning bustle. She seemed to be focused on the Meyer's Bagels across the street and about half a block away.

"There," Esther growled, her voice triumphant. "They've just brought out a steaming basket of fresh sesame! Moishe—go go go!"

A wiry college-aged kid with dark hair bolted from behind the counter area, weaving through displays of skis and snowboards. He burst through the door in a clatter of bells, almost colliding with a pair of startled customers on the sidewalk. Then he vanished across the street, presumably to hunt down the best of the morning's bagels.

Esther finally lowered the binoculars. Her plump cheeks shone with excitement, but she heaved a dramatic sigh. "Oy, I'm too old and too fat for these stakeouts. I've talked with the Meyers repeatedly and they refuse to call me when they're about to put out fresh sesame seed bagels. The old guy insists that it wouldn't be fair." She threw hands up in the air. "Fair! First come first serve, bah! Who cares about fair in these God-forsaken days? A neighbor deserves a call for fresh bagels, don't you agree Levi?"

Levi opened his mouth but before he could say anything the excitable woman shifted her attention to Alicia.

A split second passed before her face lit up in pure delight. *"Boobaleh!"* she squealed, enfolding the tall, lean girl in a fierce hug that nearly lifted Alicia off her feet. A swirl of floral perfume enveloped them both.

"Hey, Esther," Alicia managed, her voice muffled. Levi caught a smile flickering across his daughter's face—she clearly loved the older woman's over-the-top affection, which was very different than his style or that of his Amish mother's where she'd grown up.

Esther pulled back to eye Alicia from head to toe. "Are you *still* growing? You have a boy in your life yet?" She snorted and waved her hand as if the thought was ridiculous. "Who are we kidding, you're probably stringing along half a dozen suitors by now." The portly woman swiveled, pinning Levi with a scolding look. "What are you doing with my Alicia?"

"Your Alicia?" Levi asked, an amused expression blooming on his face.

"Don't you change the subject, Mister." She hitched her

thumb in Alicia's direction and glowered at him. "You're not putting this angel in harm's way, are you?"

Levi panned his gaze across the store, reassuring himself that it was empty. "Of course not, but maybe we should talk about these things in the back."

Alicia's face scrunched with curiosity as she looked back and forth between Levi and the large woman clucking disapprovingly at him.

Before either could say another word, the door jingled again, and Moishe reappeared—this time juggling two paper bags that issued faint wisps of steam. His cheeks glowed from the sprint, and when he locked eyes with Alicia, he turned beet red and mumbled something inaudible before darting off to the back.

Esther yelled after him, "Leave those sesame bagels on my desk and come back right away! I need you to man the front." She gave Alicia a long-suffering roll of the eyes. "His twin finally found a nice girl and settled down with her over in Canarsie, but Moishe is still a mess around pretty girls. One day he'll learn, but that day sure ain't today."

Levi slipped an arm across Alicia's shoulder, guiding her deeper into the store. He cast a quick glance at Esther. She stood around five-foot-four and, by his estimation, weighed well over two hundred pounds. But beneath her unassuming sweater and sensible skirt lurked a formidable force—she was sharp of mind, quick with wit, and few knew that she was a sharpshooter's sharpshooter.

"Moishe, keep an eye on things," Esther called to the gangly college-age kid exiting the back room. "And put away the hockey equipment in the big cardboard boxes before the customers start showing up." She glanced at her wrist and motioned at him impatiently. "It's getting late, hurry up or I'll whack you with one of the sticks—understood?"

Without waiting for a response, Esther beckoned them both. "Come on you two. I've got the goodies we talked about and a bit more."

Alicia gave him a quizzical look, which Levi ignored as he guided her through the aisles.

Levi took in every detail as they walked through the store. On his left, a row of hockey sticks glinted under fluorescent lights; on his right, brand-new dumbbells stacked in neat rows released a faint tang of metal. The store's hush was periodically broken by the rustle of plastic wrap as Moishe dug into a new shipment from a supplier. Above them, the dull buzz of fluorescent lights joined the distant street traffic in a low, humming symphony.

Near the rear of the store Esther led Levi and Alicia into a supply room. The space smelled of cardboard and dust motes, which danced in beams of overhead lighting. A simple metal table stood in one corner, stacked with papers, half-unfolded shipping receipts, and various sporting catalogs.

"Sit, both of you," Esther ordered, parking herself on a rolling stool. The stool creaked under her weight, but she wore the same beaming expression she always did when she had a surprise in store.

Levi complied, settling into the wooden chair and crossing his arms. He felt Alicia's curiosity practically vibrating off her. He shared her anticipation—coming to visit Esther was always like Christmas, her surprises were bound to be impressive... and likely unconventional.

Levi Yoder sat in the cramped back room of Esther's sporting goods store, watching the overhead light flicker across the battered metal table. He'd been here countless times before—though rarely with his daughter at his side. Alicia, in her twenties and determined to blaze her own trail, sat beside him, eyes bright with anticipation.

Levi cleared his throat. "We're here for the vest, but I want Alicia to have something better than just the normal stock stuff you have on hand," he said evenly. "Class 3A or better. She needs something that can handle .44 Magnum rounds. Plus, I want added protection against knives."

Esther did a poor job of suppressing her amused expression and shifted her gaze to Alicia. "Under regular clothes, I assume?"

Alicia glanced at her father, and he nodded. "Yes. Something thin, flexible, and easy to conceal."

Levi leaned forward, resting his elbows on the table. "What do you have?"

Esther retrieved a slim binder from beneath the counter and flipped to a page featuring a schematic of a sleek vest. "Titanium-gold mesh, woven with Kevlar. It's the same new alloy you're wearing now—four times as tough as steel mesh but lighter. There's a calfskin backing that makes it comfortable to wear, even for extended periods."

Levi eyed the diagram. It looked familiar—the same stuff she'd handed him just a few months ago, and exactly what he wanted Alicia to be wearing.

"Dad, I've got vests from... well, you know. They're—"

"Total crap," Levi cut her off and shook his head. "They're using the same stuff the feds use and it's okay in a pinch, but Esther's got wizards at her beck and call that can do us one better." He shifted his attention back to Esther. "Give me the price," he said, already steeling himself for whatever number she would throw at him.

With a theatrical sigh, Esther wrote a figure on a small slip of paper and slid it across the table. Levi glanced at it and suppressed a grimace. *She never misses a chance to maximize her profit*, he thought, but kept his face impassive.

Alicia looked at him questioningly, and Levi tossed her a wink. "All right, Esther," he said, "I know you're giving me the friend rate, but how about something a bit better than that. I'm trying to get Alicia started, and... well." He paused briefly. "Maybe, for now, the off-the-shelf stuff will do."

"I forbid it!" Esther exclaimed, dramatically placing her hand over her heart. "Levi, please. When it's your daughter's safety at stake—"

He cut her off with a good-natured scowl. "I'm not saying it's not worth it, but half of that number seems more reasonable. We both know you'll still make a profit."

Esther pursed her lips, then glanced at Alicia. After a moment, she scribbled a new figure on the paper and handed it back.

Levi studied the revised price. It was significantly lower—still expensive, but roughly what he'd haggled her down to for his own vest. He turned to Alicia, softening his tone. "I'll cover this as part of your startup cost."

Alicia opened her mouth in protest, but he silenced her with a raised hand. "It's done," he murmured. "Consider it my investment in your future."

Esther exhaled loudly, as though she'd been holding her breath. "*Mazal?*" she asked.

"*Mazal*," he repeated, and they shook hands.

Mazal was the Hebrew term used in some circles—especially in the diamond district—to confirm a deal had been reached. There would be no paperwork. No backing out. A mazal was tantamount to a blood oath on both sides.

Esther turned to Alicia and said, "Now, let's get the measurements. I'll need a perfect fit for the vest to do its job."

Alicia stood, and Esther circled her with a measuring tape, scribbling dimensions onto a small notepad. Levi's throat tightened with emotion as he watched. After Mary had died he never imagined parenthood for himself, but here was his little girl getting measured for a customer vest. In his mind he still saw the rambunctious pre-teen herding her new younger sisters like a mother hen.

Once Esther was done, she carefully set the pad aside. "That's the vest," she said, turning to Levi. "Now, what about these throwing knives you mentioned on the phone?"

Levi's eyes flicked to Alicia. He gestured for her to show Esther the sketch she'd drawn. Alicia removed a folded paper from her jacket pocket and placed it on the table.

"Dad and I talked about this, and I'll need something I can hide under regular street clothes, but also if I'm wearing a dress or something formal."

Esther looked over the drawing and pursed her lips. "You'll

need something we can sheathe and keep hidden under even a mini-skirt. I know where I can get some garters that will work for that." She glanced up at Alicia and asked, "What do you need them to do?"

Alicia made a quick throwing motion with her empty hand and said, "They need to be balanced for throwing. But I also need them for close combat—slashing and stabbing. The handle should be wrapped in paracord for grip, just in case it gets…" she hesitated. "… well, if it gets wet."

Esther gave Alicia a nod and shifted her gaze to Levi, her expression suddenly turning into one of disapproval. "She's just a baby and shouldn't be involved in wet operations."

"Esther," Alicia huffed. "I'm twenty-three and have been blown up at least once, shot at, stabbed, you name it, I think a little blood is well within my operating theater."

Esther's eyes widened and she sat back as she stared at Alicia.

Levi held the same surprised expression at the normally quiet girl's outburst of frustration. Inside he wanted to laugh and cheer her on, but he remained frozen, watching as the two women stared at each other.

Without warning, Esther burst out with raucous laughter and patted Alicia on the knee. "Well, young lady, I guess you told me, didn't you?"

"I didn't mean to—"

"No," Esther cut her off with a whip-crack of authority. "You're a woman in a man's world. You have to be tough, especially in the kind of world your father inhabits. There's not many of us, but…" the large woman's voice took on a steely edge, "we must do everything better than they do to even be treated as equals. Is this really going to be your new life?"

Alicia replied without a second's hesitation. "Absolutely."

The tone of her voice was no longer that of his little girl. He heard the Dragon Lady inside of her for the first time. And hearing that tone in her voice gave him a warm feeling in his chest.

"Okay." Esther grinned. "You and I will have to talk a bit more about some things. But for now, let's get what you came for taken care of. What metal composition were you looking for in your blades?"

"I'm not really sure," Alicia replied. "Something that can hold an edge and is strong enough to pierce through whatever it needs to. You have any suggestions?"

Esther tapped the sketch with a manicured nail. "For general purpose knives, 420 steel isn't terrible, but it can chip if you strike something hard. I'd suggest 1055—properly tempered, it's almost indestructible. Or we can go with the Japanese YXR7 matrix steel. Less chipping, very durable if you maintain it."

Levi listened as Esther rattled off metallurgical details and forging processes. Alicia's eyes widened with surprise as a new aspect of Esther unfolded before her eyes.

He'd known the grandmotherly storekeeper for years and she was a fountain of information when it came to weapons and how they're manufactured. In fact, she was a sniper's sniper—likely a better shot than anyone in the city, if not the entire East Coast.

"Dad, do you have any suggestions?" Alicia asked.

"Esther, the ones I'm carrying now are made with the YXR7, right?"

The woman nodded. "The stuff makes the best blade money can buy."

Levi reached down to his ankle, unsheathed a paracord-wrapped throwing knife, and handed it to Alicia. "Here, try the feel of this and see what you think." His phone vibrated in his pocket. Rising from his chair, he said, "Excuse me ladies. I need to step out for a second."

"Dad, do I—"

He motioned dismissively and, as he walked out of the supply room, called over his shoulder, "Go through the list you and I talked about with Esther. I'll be right back."

As Levi walked past a few customers toward the front of the store, he tapped his earbud, heard a series of clicks, and then the low hum of a live phone connection.

Paulie was still standing in front of the car as Levi stepped out of the store and onto the sidewalk. "Yes?"

"Hey, I've got some new news for you." It was Frankie, Vinnie's head of security. *"I'm letting you know that we've reached out and arranged for a sit-down with our shipment contact."*

"You mean the Russians? Oleg has men in the States?"

"He does, and the Don asked that you represent us. Just so you know, this guy fronting for Zharkov is some French dude I've never talked to before."

Levi leaned against the store's front wall as tires screeched with a driver stomping on his brakes, just barely missing a kid who'd raced across the street.

"Where's the sit-down happening?"

"It's an eight o'clock reservation under the name Pierre Laroche at Le Bernardin."

"Fancy." Levi's brow furrowed.

"I'm not sure what to tell you, Levi. When I told him that you'll represent our interests he asked that you bring a date to keep things cordial. I'm guessing you have a reputation with Zharkov's people."

"Who knows, maybe Oleg remembers what I did to his boss." Levi saw in his mind's eye the image of a man lying in a pool of his own blood. Vladimir. The man had indirectly been responsible for the death of his wife. "Frankie, how exactly are we supposed to have a sit-down with the wives and girlfriends in the mix?"

"I don't know, but I'm sure you'll figure it out. The Don told me about how you and Alicia are working on getting some answers about the shipment, but Zharkov must answer for what happened."

"I'll see what Frenchie has to say." Levi glanced at his watch, did a mental calculation and said, "I need to get a couple things taken care ahead of this meeting and I'll let you know when I get something. Anything else?"

"Nah, just be careful. Word is out that the family got hit—the street is tense, they're waiting for our response."

"I hear you. Talk at you later." Levi tapped the earbud and frowned.

His mind raced with what he'd just learned and knew that something was up.

A sit-down in the world of *La Cosa Nostra* was usually when there was a format meeting between two made men with a high-ranking family member sitting as mediator. It was done only to settle some dispute or renegotiate some terms between the made men, with the decision being finalized by the high-ranking family member or even the boss in some cases.

This wasn't that.

Whoever this Pierre Laroche guy was, he was associated with the Russian mob in some way. The same mob that was currently suspected of having shipped something to the Bianchi family that caused the death of two of the family's soldiers.

Levi turned and the bell above Rosen's Sporting Goods chimed as he walked back into the store. As he walked past a customer, he nodded at Moishe and patted at the side of his chest. The Glock rested comfortably in its shoulder holster.

A sit-down was normally an unarmed affair between both parties—tonight was not going to be normal.

Levi stepped into the back room of the store; the acrid scent of gun oil hung in the air. Fluorescent lights buzzed softly overhead, casting sharp-edged shadows across the workbenches.

Alicia stood next to a table, holding a sleek, compact handgun in her hands, her gaze focused down the barrel. The rose-gold finish caught the light, giving it an almost delicate appearance—deceptive for something designed to kill.

Next to the table, Esther, the zaftig, sharp-eyed arms dealer, glanced up from a disassembled rifle. She studied Levi for a moment, then flicked her attention back to Alicia. "She's found something that fits in her hand nicely," she said, her voice even, confident. "SIG Sauer P238. Rose Gold. Damn near perfect for a young woman in her situation."

Levi stepped closer, hands in his pockets. "That so?"

Esther wiped her hands on a rag, then nodded toward the gun in Alicia's grip. "Alicia, it's small enough to hide, big enough to stop a threat. Single-action, .380 ACP, which carries minimal recoil—you won't be fighting the gun. Seven in the mag, one in the pipe." She tapped a finger on the countertop. "And when you need it? It's there. No fumbling. No second chances."

Alicia turned the pistol over, weighing it in her palm. "I like the balance."

"You should." Esther nodded. "It's the perfect concealed weapon for any occasion. Now, sweetheart, before we go any further, tell me—you got a permit?"

Alicia hesitated.

Esther snorted. "*Bubbaleh*, you know this is New York City, right? You can't just waltz around with a piece unless you're an ex-cop, a billionaire, or the mayor's cousin." She glanced at Levi and arched an eyebrow. "Of course, if you know people, I'm sure something could be arranged."

Levi exhaled through his nose. He knew exactly what she meant. The Bianchi crime family had long-standing relationships with the right officials—permits, favors, discreet paperwork. Money moved; problems disappeared. "Alicia's already got all the permits she'll need. Right, Alicia?"

Alicia's eyes widened and she nodded. "Oh you mean… yes, I guess so."

Alicia still held the permits she'd gotten from being a member of the Outfit, the covert intelligence ring he'd also been associated with. And if Levi had any influence with Mason, a Director at the Outfit, that status wouldn't be changing any time soon.

Esther held up a thigh holster. "You're not going to carry that thing in a purse, not if you need quick access. If it's just you and a cocktail dress, you need a thigh rig. Left leg for your blade, right for the gun."

Alicia took the holster, running her fingers over the reinforced elastic straps. She threaded her right leg through it and it rested comfortably on her thigh, over her jeans.

"I've never drawn from under a dress." She pantomimed drawing the gun from it and asked, "What draw time should I expect?"

Esther grinned. "Well under two seconds, if you practice."

Levi's voice was quiet, thoughtful. "And you'll be practicing tonight."

"Tonight?" Alicia blinked and stared at her father. "What do you mean?"

"We've got a dinner to attend tonight, and it'll be good for you to practice playing dress up with me. You're my date."

"Ew, Dad." Alicia feigned disgust. "Are you serious? We're dressing up tonight?"

"Yes, we are." Levi shifted his attention back to Esther. "Are you two almost done here?"

"Yes, but hold on a minute before you go." Esther caught Alicia's attention and pointed at the center of her own chest. "Alicia, just remember that this isn't a heavy caliber. If you shoot once, I want you to shoot four times. Two to the chest, two to the groin." She tapped her chest, then shifted her aim downward. "Center mass is standard, but if they've got body armor, you might not stop them. Always aim lower, too. Shatter the pelvis, rupture the femoral. They're down for good."

Alicia considered that for a moment, then slid the P238 from the holster and dropped it into her purse. "I appreciate the advice."

Esther handed Alicia another reinforced elastic band with a sheathed knife inside. "This will tide you over until the knife order arrives."

Alicia gave the big woman a warm hug. "It was so much fun talking with you."

Esther returned the embrace and said, "*Bubbaleh*, you can always stop by for some girl talk." She turned to Levi, but before she could speak, he interrupted.

"Just put everything on my tab, and I'll settle it at the end of the week." Levi kissed Esther on the cheek. "Alicia and I have some errands to run."

As they headed toward the exit, Alicia unsheathed the knife and offered it back to her father.

"Keep it until the new knives arrive," Levi said. The bell chimed as he opened the shop's front door. "Do you still have that black dress in the guest room closet?"

"I'm not sure," Alicia replied, pursing her lips. "It's been ages since I wore that, I'm not sure that it still fits. Is it that kind of place we're going to?"

"It is." Levi gestured to Paulie, who opened the rear passenger door for Alicia. "Paulie, Alicia needs a dress for Le Bernardin."

"Bergdorf Goodman?" Paulie suggested.

Levi slid into the back seat beside Alicia and said, "That'll work."

As the car pulled away from the curb, Levi's thoughts shifted to Pierre Laroche. He pulled out his phone and dialed a number.

Almost immediately, Denny's voice came through. *"No results yet for—"*

"That's fine. Can you email me everything you can dig up on a guy named Pierre Laroche, L-a-r-o-c-h-e?"

"Okay, does he have any aliases or associations that could help me narrow down the search?"

"I know almost nothing about him, other than he might be linked to Oleg Zharkov, a mobster based out of Russia."

Alicia shot him a sidelong glance.

"Got it. I'll see what I can find."

"Thanks, buddy." Levi hung up, and Alicia cleared her throat.

"Anything you can share?"

Levi met her gaze with a grin. "You're my plus-one for a meeting with this guy named Pierre."

"Okay." Alicia nodded. "Do you have any .380 ACP ammo at home? Esther only had some cheap training rounds she could spare. I was hoping for something with better expansion and penetration for tonight, just in case."

"Hey, Levi," Paulie called from the front seat. "If you don't have any, I know a place just outside the city where we can pick up some good stuff."

Levi chuckled and patted Alicia's leg. "Easy there, tiger. Nah, we're good Paulie, thanks. I've got some Hornady Critical Defense loads that should work in Alicia's new toy." He met Alicia's gaze and his tone took on a steely edge. "Let's chill on shooting anyone; this is just a meal. I'm pretty sure you won't need to pop a cap in anyone tonight."

CHAPTER FIVE

Levi stepped into Le Bernardin, Alicia at his side. The entrance was crowded—half a dozen patrons loitered near the host stand, checking their watches, murmuring in hushed tones. But their attention shifted the moment Levi walked in. He felt their gazes latch onto him, then slide to Alicia. She moved with effortless confidence, her tall frame accentuated by the sleek black dress that clung to her like a second skin.

He adjusted his suit, scanning the room. Chandeliers cast a muted glow over crisp white linens, the air humming with the low murmur of Manhattan's elite. Years of instinct kicked in. He noted the exits, the staff, the subtle shifts in body language from the diners. Nothing unusual. Not yet.

To an outsider, they made an unusual pair. A man whose sharp features and precise movements suggested a mind that never rested. A young Asian woman, poised, calculating, taking in every detail without a flicker of expression. They didn't look like family. They looked like a couple—striking, enigmatic, impossible to ignore. But reality was rarely that simple.

The maître d' glanced down at the open reservation book, running a practiced finger along the names. "One moment, sir."

Levi turned slightly, murmuring to Alicia. "You ready?"

She gave a small nod and, without hesitation, laced her fingers into his. A calculated move. To anyone watching, they weren't father and daughter, they weren't associates. They were a couple.

Denny's research had turned up almost nothing on Laroche. A French passport, yet much of his youth had been spent in Moscow. A single police report in Ukraine—briefly detained under suspicion of being a Russian spy. The charges had evaporated, the records buried. A ghost. The kind of man who was almost certainly more dangerous than he appeared.

The maître d' straightened. "Monsieur Yoder and madame." A polite nod. "Monsieur Laroche and his wife, Margaux, was just seated. I'll lead you to the table."

He guided them through the restaurant, past hushed conversations and the occasional clink of glassware. The back table was already occupied. As they neared, a distinguished figure stood—Pierre Laroche. He was in his fifties as well, but where Levi's features remained sharp, Laroche wore his years differently. Silver streaked his dark hair, fine lines traced the corners of his eyes. His suit spoke of quiet wealth, tailored to perfection, the kind worn by men who never rushed, never worried—at least, not outwardly. But Levi's instincts flared. The Frenchman's smile was too precise, his eyes too sharp. He was assessing Levi, measuring him the way a predator sizes up potential prey. Beneath the polished charm, something coiled, waiting.

Levi recognized the man for what he was because he was doing the exact same thing to Pierre. Studying. Calculating. Weighing strengths and weaknesses. Predators recognized their own.

Beside him stood a woman, striking in her own right. Late forties, perhaps. Voluptuous. Poised. Her auburn hair was swept into an elegant twist, her posture immaculate.

They exchanged greetings—cheek kisses, pleasantries layered with unspoken calculations—and sat.

A waiter appeared, menus in hand, but Pierre barely acknowledged him. With a flick of his wrist, he dismissed the gesture entirely. "The chef's tasting, for all of us. I've talked with Eric ahead of time and made the necessary arrangements."

The man's accent was muddled. Not a Frenchman's accent, but one that hinted at a more mixed background.

Levi caught the waiter's attention and asked, "What does that involve?"

The waiter, a wiry man with a pencil-thin mustache, brightened. "A journey of the senses, sir," he said, voice carrying the rehearsed enthusiasm of a man who had delivered the same speech a hundred times before. "We begin with yellowfin tuna, pounded so thin it's almost translucent, layered with foie gras and chives. It's accompanied by a Grüner Veltliner to sharpen the flavors. Then, steamed lobster—tender, bathed in kumquat and a spiced broth that lingers just long enough. Paired with a Savennières from the Loire, crisp and dry.

And for the finale—poached rhubarb, tart and delicate,

crowned with vanilla Chantilly. A Tokaji to accompany, sweet but not cloying, the last note in a perfect symphony."

He finished with a practiced smile, hands clasped, waiting for a reaction.

With a slight shake of his head, Levi said, "I do not care for alcohol, I'll take a sparkling water instead."

"The same for me," Alicia chimed in.

"Of course, monsieur and madame." The waiter panned his gaze across the table. "Anything else?"

Pierre made a dismissive motion, and the waiter pivoted smoothly, vanishing into the hum of the dining room.

Silence descended, taut and heavy. Levi glanced at Alicia. She was still, unreadable, her fingers resting lightly on her water glass.

Pierre leaned in, resting his elbows on the table, his gaze locking onto Levi. "Have you been to this restaurant before?" His voice was smooth, effortless.

Levi allowed a small smile. "A time or two. I make it a point to visit any three Michelin-starred restaurant in whatever city I find myself in."

Pierre chuckled, nodding slightly. "I've heard you're a bit of a gourmand." His eyes shifted to Alicia. "And you?"

She shook her head. "Not to the same extent as Levi, but I appreciate fine dining when I encounter it."

Pierre's smile widened as he glanced between her and his wife. "That's good. Because I've arranged something special after dinner for you two."

Alicia's eyes flickered with a moment of surprise. Across the table, Pierre's wife mirrored the expression—but Levi saw through it. Feigned. Too deliberate. She knew. Which meant something was in play.

Something was off.

Before he could press further, a set of waiters approached, trays balanced on their palms. Levi let the moment pass.

As one of the waiters set drinks on the table, the mustachioed waiter set his tray down with practiced grace. He lifted the silver cloche, revealing the first course—tuna, pounded thin, layered with foie gras, and finished with a scattering of chives. A dish that spoke of precision, of careful artistry. He described it in a measured cadence, detailing the interplay of flavors, the balance of texture. His voice carried the same certainty as a surgeon explaining a delicate procedure.

He stepped back, hands folded in front of him. "Enjoy."

Then, as seamlessly as he had arrived, he turned and vanished into the sea of motion that was the restaurant.

Pierre took a sip of wine, swirling it absently before launching into a story about the last time he'd hooked a tuna.

Levi barely heard him. He stabbed a piece of the appetizer with his fork, the flavors dissolving on his tongue—exceptional, no doubt—but he wasn't here for the food.

"… we managed to haul it in, weighed nearly seven hundred pounds."

Levi made a noncommittal sound. "That's a lot of tuna."

"Took four hours to bring it in, damn near capsized the boat," Pierre said.

Alicia leaned in. "What do you even do with a fish that size? Seems like a nightmare to filet."

Pierre grinned. "Quick-frozen. Flown to Tokyo by morning.

Fetched a damn good price." He took another bite of his tuna, chewing with satisfied expression. "For all we know, we could be eating some of my catch right now."

The conversation drifted—travel, real estate, an art exhibit in Paris. Casual. Superficial. Noise. Levi let it play out, but he was waiting.

Dinner unfolded course by course, each dish an exercise in precision—the tender lobster steeped in spiced broth, the rhubarb tart capped with velvety Chantilly. He barely tasted any of it. His mind churned, fixed on the reason he was here.

Then Pierre shifted. A slight change in posture. A flicker of something in his eyes. A tell.

"Ah," Pierre murmured, glancing past Levi. "There he is."

Levi turned.

A figure moved through the room with quiet assurance—Eric Ripert. The celebrity chef himself, all lean elegance and controlled precision.

Ripert reached the table, offering a warm nod. Disarming. "A pleasure to meet you all," he said smoothly. "I thought the ladies might enjoy a glimpse behind the curtain—some tricks of the trade, yes?" His smile was easy. It seemed genuine, oblivious to the undercurrents of why they were there.

Alicia hesitated, her gaze flicking to Levi.

He gave the smallest of nods. Go. Play along.

She stood, took Margaux's hand, and followed Ripert toward the kitchen.

Levi watched them walk across the dining area, a set of silhouettes vanishing through a swinging door.

Now it was just him and Pierre.

The restaurant's hum faded into the background. The easy warmth of moments ago dissolved, replaced by something else.

Pierre leaned back, swirling the last of his Tokaji. The polished veneer cracked, just enough to reveal the steel beneath.

"I trust you don't mind the subterfuge," he said, his tone almost amused. "I've neglected my wife for years—pleasant enough woman, but hardly a priority. Your girlfriend, however, seems a delight. Regardless, tonight provided a convenient excuse for an evening out."

He set his glass down with deliberate precision.

"But now, I believe, we have business to discuss." He gestured subtly. "The waiters won't interrupt. We can speak freely."

The air between them shifted. The pleasantries were over.

Now came the real conversation.

Levi's jaw tightened. "I need you to tell me everything you know about the shipment that my associates received from Oleg."

"Received?" Pierre adopted a puzzled expression, and he leaned in and spoke softly. "I'm not sure I understand. I know of a shipment due to arrive *tomorrow*, but that shipment is intended for the Bianchi Trust, LLC. Is that what you mean?"

"Tomorrow?" A chill raced down Levi's spine as he shook his head. "We received something a couple of days ago—"

"That's not possible. One second." Pierre pulled out his phone and put it to his ear. After a moment he began speaking in rapid-fire Russian.

"The Bianchi shipment—where is it?"

Levi heard the muffled sound of a reply.

"Tomorrow, 6 a.m.? Are you sure? Have you confirmed this with the live tracking device?"

More muffled replies.

"Okay." Pierre put his phone away and shook his head once more. "I'm not sure what to tell you, but the shipment Oleg sent is due to arrive in the morning, as scheduled. What makes you think you received a shipment from us already?"

In his mind's eye, Levi saw the unopened crate in the basement as if it were directly in front of him. He read aloud from the Cyrillic lettering that marked the outside of the crate, "*Красный Горизонт Транспорт.*"

Pierre frowned. "Red Horizon Transport? That was on the shipping container?"

"It was." Levi confirmed. "One of my associates was sent an email with the arrival time and location, and that's the container they found. Why, is there a problem?"

"There is." Pierre began texting on his phone as he talked. "Something isn't right. That transport company is one of Oleg's ventures, but they wouldn't have been the shipping carrier for your associates. We use that for different things. May I ask what was in the container that caused the concern?"

Levi sensed uncertainty coming off the Frenchman. He wasn't feigning surprise. "Let's just say we ran into some serious issues that caused us some damage."

Pierre stared for a moment at his phone and looked directly at Levi. "It's 5 a.m. right now in Moscow and Oleg doesn't have his phone turned on now. To be honest, I didn't know why your organization demanded this meeting, so I presumed it was about the pending shipment or maybe an additional arrangement you wanted to talk about. I really have no idea what you might have received, much less anything that would..." his frown deepened "have caused your associates any damage. Can you elaborate? What kind of damage?"

"No, I'm not going to talk about that." Levi shook his head. "I'd rather you explain what was supposed to be in that crate. Also, what is in the shipment we're receiving tomorrow? Also, I don't think we've been told about another shipment. Has a notification been sent to us?"

"One second. I can check that." Pierre tapped a few times on his phone and put it to his ear. After a moment, he again spoke in fluent Russian. "Pavel. Pavel! I need you to look something up for me, right now."

Levi leaned closer as he heard the faint rustling sound coming from the phone.

"Okay. What do you need?" The barely audible voice sounded groggy, like he'd just been woken up.

"Look up the Bianchi account. Tell me what you see."

"A container is en-route to the US, arriving tomorrow around dawn."

"Okay, has the customer been notified of its arrival?"

"They should have been. One second... oh crap! Um, Mister Laroche, there's some kind of mix-up. Hold on, I'm checking something else..."

Pierre's jaw tightened, his expression hardening, as if he were gritting his teeth.

"Mister Laroche, I don't know how this happened, but it looks like two shipment notifications were switched. The Bianchi

Trust, LLC was notified about another customer's shipment, and that customer was notified about the Bianchi shipment."

The Frenchman pulled in a deep breath, held it for a moment and let it out slowly as he shook his head. "We will talk about this later." He put the phone down on the table and held a frustrated expression. "It seems like there's been a mix-up. It seems you received another customer's shipment notification, and they received yours. I'll have to talk with Oleg about this, but I presume you have the other customer's container?"

Levi's gaze narrowed and he felt a rising sense of anger. "I need to know everything about this other customer. If I don't get some information on them right away, we're going to have a serious problem."

Pierre sat back for a moment, pressing his lips into a thin line as he studied Levi for a long few seconds. "I don't actually know who the other customer is, nor could I tell you anything without Oleg's permission. I also don't know what the problem is with what you received. Can you tell me anything about that?"

Levi shook his head. "No. We need Oleg involved ASAP. My superior isn't going to be very patient about this, and we need to resolve things."

"I understand. Let me at least do this as a sign of good faith." Pierre picked up his phone, swiped a few times, and showed the screen to Levi. "This is the address of where tomorrow morning's shipment is arriving and how to find it. I'll try to have one of my associates reach the other customer to avoid any conflicts, but your container is arriving in the Red Hook Terminal in Brooklyn. Not far from here." He pulled a pen and notepad from inside his suit jacket and offered it with a scrap of paper to Levi. "Here you go."

Levi studied the information on Pierre's screen, committing it to memory. He tapped the side of his head. "No, I've got it."

"I apologize for this mix-up," Pierre said with a note of sincerity. "It's never happened before, and if I have anything to do about it, it'll never happen again. Oleg tends to be a late riser, but I'll keep on him and let you know what I hear. It might be late at night, is that okay?"

"Any time is fine." Levi motioned dismissively as he spotted the ladies weaving their way across the dining room. "It looks like the kitchen tour is complete."

Alicia was smiling as she arrived, an unusual thing for her, and she held up two dark-colored take-out boxes with "Le Bernardin" stenciled on them. "We got dessert lessons from Eric!"

"Oh?" Levi and Pierre both said at the same time.

"Hope you guys like banana sticky toffee pudding. We were shown how to make it, and Margaux and I made some for when we get home."

Levi returned Alicia's smile and asked, "Did you guys have fun?"

Alicia and Margaux exchanged glances, giggled, and both nodded.

"Pierre, are you two done with your business talk?" Margaux asked.

Pierre patted Levi on the shoulder and they both nodded at each other. "I think so." The Frenchman leaned closer and spoke under his breath, "I'll call you tonight with a follow-up."

They both stood, exchanged goodbyes and Levi walked out of the restaurant with Alicia on his arm.

Levi tapped on his phone, put it to his ear and said, "We're ready." He looked over at Alicia and said, "Job well done."

She gave him a smirk and shook her head. "That wasn't exactly a challenging assignment. Have a three-star dinner and then get flirted on by some of the kitchen staff."

"Is that what the giggling was about between you and Pierre's wife?"

"Pretty much. That and Margaux was an out-of-control flirt with Eric. The poor man's face was so red, with his white hair he reminded me of a candy cane."

Levi chuckled as he panned his gaze, looking for their ride. "Well, part of this kind of gig is to be able to socialize. Fit into groups. Gather intelligence."

"Dad, I did get trained by the Outfit. I'm not exactly a total novice."

Levi gave her a withering stare.

Alicia rolled her eyes. "Okay, fine. Maybe I'm a total novice to you, but I at least have some clue."

He leaned over and gave her a one-armed side hug. "You'll be fine. Nobody died, you didn't have to pop anyone's cap or anything."

She gave him a horrified look, "Pop anyone's cap? You *do* realize how stupid that sounds, right? It's pop a cap—"

"I know that, Alicia." Levi chuckled and pointed at the approaching sedan. "I've been on the streets longer than you've been alive, baby girl. I'm just teasing."

Paulie hopped out of the car and opened the rear passenger's door.

As Alicia piled into the car, Levi's phone buzzed.

"Oh crap," Alicia's tone was tense as she showed Levi her phone. "Look who's calling."

The car pulled away from the curb as Levi glanced at his phone and shook his head.

Somehow, they were both getting called by the same number.

He put his phone to his ear and said, "Hey, Mason."

It was the Outfit calling.

CHAPTER SIX

"Levi, long time no talk." Mason's voice sounded unusually upbeat.

"Hey, Doug, you never call without a reason." Levi glanced at Alicia and she shrugged. Her phone had stopped ringing the moment he picked up. "What's up?"

"I need a favor, and I think this is one you're probably already looking into in some ways."

Levi sat up straight as the car headed east on West 51st Street. "I'll need to hear a bit more before I can commit to anything."

"This is sensitive. I don't want to be chatting about national security issues while you're sitting in an Uber. I know you just finished dinner at a swanky French restaurant with Alicia, but this can't wait."

Levi frowned. The Outfit regularly tapped into video cameras to watch over persons or places of interest, so it wasn't a surprise

Mason knew exactly what he'd been up to, at least to a first approximation.

"I need you two at the Harlem SCIF. I'll have a few things waiting there for you, but your skills are needed on this."

"And what skills are those?"

A SCIF was US Intelligence Community talk for a Sensitive Compartmented Information Facility. Basically a place where it was safe to access and talk about classified material.

The car pulled in front of the Helmsley Arms. Paulie parked, hopped out, and opened the passenger-side door.

Levi climbed out of the car with the phone still to his ear.

"Listen, I can't explain it to while you're standing on the street. I've sent an Uber to get you, and I swear to you, you won't regret coming to the call."

He glanced at Alicia as she stepped out of the car. "How far is the car? We're not exactly dressed for a trip to Harlem."

"It's less than a minute away, and I'd send you south to the FBI Field Office, but I can't exactly drop-ship things to you over there. Don't worry, our guys will be waiting for you."

"Doug, you had better not be wasting my time." Levi grumbled into the phone as a black Ford Escalade pulled up to the curb.

"Hey Levi," Paulie patted him on the shoulder. "You need a ride to Harlem. I can take you, no problem."

"Levi, the Uber is a black Escalade. From the app, it says it's there. Do you see it?"

Levi patted the big man's arm and shook his head. "I've got this, Paulie. If anyone from the top floor asks, tell him Alicia and I are working on family business."

"Um, Dad?" Alicia glanced back and forth between her father and the large SUV waiting on them. "What's going on? Harlem?"

Doug Mason didn't make calls like this unless the sky was already falling.

Levi gave a barely perceptible shake of his head, then walked to the back of the SUV, opened it, and said, "Let's go. Tonight's not yet over."

⁓

Levi watched as the large SUV drove northbound along the eastern side of Central Park, Mason buzzing in his ear the entire way.

"Of course it's not a surprise to me what you're saying. Alicia might not be your blood daughter, but she's stubborn as a mule, just like you. I know being full time with the Outfit isn't your style, and you've got familial distractions, but if Alicia changes her mind, I still think she'd be better off as a full-time employee with us."

He glanced at Alicia, who shook her head vigorously with a frown, making it obvious what she thought of the idea of going back to the Outfit.

"That's her choice to make." He switched the phone to his other ear, hopefully making it harder for her to hear. "We're almost there. I have no idea where the SCIF is in that place, so—"

"Don't worry, Watkins will show you the way."

Levi's phone buzzed. "Okay, I've got another call. Talk to

you in a bit." He glanced at his phone, smiled, and put the phone back to his ear. "Denny, you got something for me?"

"I do, but I don't think you're going to like it. Have you ever heard of Novichok?"

"Nope. That's a name I've not encountered. Is it a person, place, or thing?"

"It's a bioweapon, Levi. A nasty piece of work that first came out of Soviet Russia. Those swabs had remnants of the components all over them. In fact, so much so that my guy figured whoever took the swabs is probably dead."

Levi glanced at Alicia. "How you feeling?"

"Fine." She gave him a puzzled look. "Why?"

The Uber pulled up to the corner of Lenox Avenue and West 127th Street in Harlem.

"Denny, I need to call you back, I'm in the middle of something."

Levi put the phone back into his pocket, thanked the driver and hopped out.

It was just about eleven at night, the streets were relatively quiet, and even though the neighborhood was mostly residential, there was a mix of businesses in the area.

"Dad, what are we doing here?" Alicia panned her gaze across the street. The streets weren't empty, but she stuck out like a sore thumb.

They both did. Very much overdressed for the area they were in.

"Come on." He motioned for her to follow as he walked down the block.

As Levi approached the unmarked nightclub, Alicia whispered, "This is one of the Outfit's safehouses, isn't it?"

He looked over at her, his eyes wide. "Have you been here before?"

"Not here in the city," she smiled, "but this feels like one of those places I've been to."

Techno music hummed through a door surrounded by purple neon lights, and the two bouncers outside stared at them as they approached.

The men were huge, probably three hundred pounds each, with a powerlifter's build and no hint of a sense of humor on either of them. It was as if these guys were drawn from central casting and the description sought someone that looked like Clubber Lang on steroids.

He walked up to them and before he could say a word, the nearest one spoke with a mild Jamaican accent. "I'll need to see some ID, Mister Yoder, you too Miss Yoder."

They were obviously expected.

Levi dug for the coin in his pocket as Alicia presented hers.

The coin had a silver sheen, one side emblazoned with a pyramid with an eye in it, surrounded by some Latin, on its reverse side, the familiar image of a wolf stared back at him.

He smiled as the bouncer grabbed the other side of her coin, and when the coin's eye lit up, both men looked to him and he also presented his coin, repeating the identification process.

He bumped shoulders with her and whispered, "You *have* been to one of these places before."

Both men stepped aside and motioned for the two of them to enter.

Even though he knew that the front of the building was a façade, Levi braced himself as he opened the door, expecting an auditory onslaught.

But the moment the door opened, the sound of techno music ceased and he found himself stepping inside the building. It was utterly silent.

Just like last time.

When the door closed behind him, the muted sound of the music started again—from the *outside*.

The music was a decoy of sorts, something coming from within the door itself.

It was one of the many ruses that the Outfit had setup, and he'd encountered others that were similarly cloaked in trickery in other parts of the world.

Levi and Alicia both stood inside a wood-paneled lobby, fresh with the scent of wood polish and pipe tobacco. The reception desk stood across the room, manned by a tall, thin, white-haired gentleman.

"This is so cool," Alicia gushed. "Of all the things the Outfit is, this always struck me as the coolest thing ever. Does this place also have rooms that vanish?"

"I'm sorry to say, this place is probably a maze of shifting rooms. I've only been here a couple times. Let's get this over with." Levi walked to the desk and grinned at the familiar face.

"Hello, Watkins."

"Mr. Yoder, it's good to see you again. You are expected. As are you, Miss Yoder." The man spoke with a very posh British accent, reminding Levi of the butler from *Downton Abbey*. "ID, please."

They both held out their coins, and when the attendant grabbed the other side of each coin, the eyes began glowing. "It's good to see you again, Watkins. Are you going to do another disappearing trick on me?"

"Sir?" The elderly man tilted his head, and the slightest hint of amusement appeared on his otherwise stoic face.

"Never mind, I suppose you know why we're here better than I do."

"Ah, yes." Watkins nodded. "There's a SCIF for you both to gain access to. That is not a problem, but Director Mason has asked me to handle a few things on his behalf that will involve both of you. Please follow me."

Levi followed Watkins down a hallway that was lit by old-fashioned sconces with lightbulbs that flickered as if they were aflame. With his senses on high alert for anything and everything, Levi focused on every little detail.

The last time he was here, Watkins had vanished seemingly as if by magic, and the hallways in this place didn't always return to the same place they started. This entire building had a weird, haunted house vibe, what with shifting hallways and disappearing proprietors, but this time Levi was paying careful attention. He leaned over to Alicia and whispered, "Keep your eyes peeled. This place gives me the willies."

Alicia smiled. "I think it's awesome."

At the end of the hall a door stood slightly ajar. Watkins paused at its entrance. "Sir, madam, this is our quartermaster's domain." With a grand sweeping gesture, the proprietor motioned toward the door. "After you."

Levi pushed the door open, noticing that it was nearly half a foot thick. It must have weighed hundreds of pounds, but it moved noiselessly on well-oiled hinges.

As he stepped through the doorway, a loud meow erupted from the darkness as lights flickered on, revealing a room filled with individual lockers.

Alicia yelled, "Bagel!" She rushed to the other side of the room where a cat carrier was sitting on top of a table.

Seconds later a black ball of fur darted out of the carrier and hissed in Watkins' direction.

"I'm sorry, Mister Bagel. I was only doing as I was told."

Alicia scooped up the cat and turned to Watkins. "How did Mason know to get him? He was staying at my neighbor's apartment."

Watkins shrugged his thin shoulders. "It was arranged for him to be brought here. I don't know the specifics beyond that, I'm afraid."

Bagel began purring as he rubbed his head under Alicia's chin.

Levi frowned. "Mason's clearly up to something, and that's not making me all that happy." He turned to Watkins. "Can we get to the SCIF?"

Watkins shrugged. "I'm simply following instructions, Mister Yoder." He motioned toward a pole in the center of the room. Affixed at about eye level was a visor, like one might see on a submarine's periscope. "If you will, please peer into the biometric scanner."

Levi shook his head as he approached the scanner. This was the exact same routine he'd played through before, and it felt a bit odd this time around. All he needed to do was get into a room.

Putting his eyes against the visor, Levi saw a green light flicker, followed by a series of clicks. And then nothing.

Levi stepped back and noticed that a locker popped open.

Watkins motioned to Alicia. "Madam, can you please do the same?"

Alicia approached the scanner, peered into it, and a moment later another locker popped open.

"Sir," said Watkins, gesturing at the nearest locker, "Please examine your items." He shifted his gaze to Alicia and gestured at the other locker. "Madam, you as well."

Levi walked over to the locker and peered inside.

He withdrew a long, flat wooden box and laid it on a nearby table.

The seemingly hollow, lacquered box didn't have any obvious latch or means of opening it.

Alicia also laid a similar-looking box next to his and they both glanced at Watkins.

"Is there a trick to opening this?" Levi asked.

"I must say, you two are in for a treat." Watkins approached the table, a sly expression blooming on his face as he ran his finger along the edge of Alicia's box. "Director Mason felt that your usual body armor, albeit effective, needed to be upgraded, and this is a proper leap forward."

The elderly man pressed both of his thumbs on the corners of the box and it smoothly yawned open, revealing neatly folded sportswear and what looked like a woman's suit.

Watkins removed a stack of black hoodies from the case, set them aside, and removed a sheet of typewritten paper from within the box. He adjusted his spectacles and read aloud, "Meet the G7 Phantom. Graphene-infused, ballistic-resistant, lightweight, and, crucially, unassuming. Unlike the vests the two of you are used to, you'll find that these are more comfortable and will allow you to blend in more naturally."

Bagel squirmed out of Alicia's arms and plopped onto the table, sniffing at the box and its contents, all the while glaring with its golden eyes at the safe house's proprietor.

Levi mimicked Watkins' motion on his box, and it too yawned open. His box contained the same hoodies and a men's suit jacket.

He reached in, lifting the hoodie by the shoulders, letting it drape naturally. It looked soft, flexible—completely normal, albeit a bit heavier than he'd have expected. He tugged at the fabric and noticed that it barely stretched at all.

"It looks completely ordinary, doesn't it?" Watkins remarked. "The outer shell is a triple-layer weave—graphene-composite fabric, aramid fibers, and a shear-thickening fluid membrane. It's soft, breathable, and the testing has been quite promising. Take a bullet to the chest in this, and the impact disperses across the entire panel, reducing penetration to nearly zero. It's almost as if you're wearing armor plate, but for only a fraction of a second."

"You said the penetration is nearly zero?" Alicia asked. "How nearly?"

Watkins smiled. "Yes, there are, of course, limits. It'll stop standard 9mm, .45 ACP, .357 Magnum, and is good for maybe one shot from a high-powered rifle round such as a .308 at point-blank range. What's nice about the shear-thickening technology is that under high-speed impact, the molecules in that layer lock up, turning the material momentarily rigid, very much like you're wearing armor plate for a split-second. That also means that stabbings, slashes, and blunt force trauma are almost all entirely neutralized."

"That sounds good on paper." Levi said as he removed his jacket and tried on the Outfit's new one. Unbeknownst to Alicia and Watkins, the idea of having an STF layer in his suit jacket was something Esther had come up with a couple years back, and it had saved his bacon at least on one occasion.

This suit felt lighter than the one he'd been wearing, which might be a good thing, or bad. He gave Watkins a sidelong glance and asked, "Do you mind if I give this a quick test?"

"A test?" Watkins shrugged. "I suppose so, this is yours now."

Levi drew a gleaming blade from his shoulder harness.

Alicia scooped up Bagel in her arms and backed away, kissing the top of his head.

Without warning, Levi plunged the dagger into the pile of hoodies with all of his strength. The table rattled from the impact and Bagel made a growling sound.

Levi's fingers and wrist ached from the impact.

The moment the blade had contacted the thick pile of material, he felt like he'd plunged the knife into a chunk of hardwood.

"So, how'd it go?" Alicia asked as Bagel hopped back onto the table and sniffed at the hoodies Levi had stabbed.

Confirming that the knife hadn't taken any damage, Levi quickly sheathed it and picked up the topmost hoodie.

Running his fingers over the point of impact, he let out a low whistle. He glanced at Watkins. "You said the outer shell of this is made of graphene?"

Watkins nodded.

Levi stuck his hand on the inside of the hoodie, looking for any damage. "Well, whatever that is, it didn't seem to care much about a razor-sharp blade trying to pierce it."

Levi put the hoodie up against him and looked over at Alicia. "Looks like it'll fit?"

Alicia nodded as Watkins said, "The Outfit has both of your measurements and everything should fit properly."

Levi swapped back into his old suit jacket and put everything back into the box. "Is this everything, Watkins?"

"I believe so, Mister Yoder. And if everything seems to be in order, I'll ask you to gather your things. Director Mason has just arrived at this site, and I'll lead you to him."

"He's here?" Alicia's eyes widened as she picked up her new clothes.

Levi shrugged. He hadn't expected this to be a face-to-face meeting.

The white-haired man smiled and motioned for them both to follow him.

Levi grabbed the box and they all went back down the same hall through which they'd entered. But like last time, the lobby was no longer there.

"Huh…" Alicia panned her gaze up and down the hallways with a puzzled expression. "I didn't hear a thing. No gears turning or walls sliding around or anything."

With a yowl, Bagel walked next to Alicia's feet, his tail fluffed up and pointing arrow-like up at the ceiling.

He too had been paying attention and somehow, despite his focus on the details, the hallways had been switched.

They continued walking down the hall, past where the lobby should have been, and found themselves entering a small room.

A room that Levi recognized. It was empty except for the presence of a set of stairs going down.

Levi looked back at Watkins and froze.

The hallway behind them was empty.

"God damn it, how the hell does he disappear like that every time? It's like he's a damned ghost."

"What now?" Alicia asked. She pointed at the stairs, which Bagel was sniffing at. "I guess we go down?"

Levi looked down at the cat, "Bagel, let me take the lead here. We don't need anyone else vanishing."

The cat looked up at him with his large gold-colored eyes and meowed in what he had to assume was an affirmative response as he backed away from the stairs, bumping into Alicia before he stopped.

Levi walked down the steps.

In the small subterranean chamber, Levi spied a sleek railway car, its doors were open. Fluorescent lighting bathed the entirety of the chamber.

A disembodied voice announced, *"The train will be leaving in thirty seconds. For safety, please hold on to a rail. This is your only warning."*

"Wait a minute," Alicia yelled as she scooped up Bagel and hurried to the train. "I thought Watkins said he was here."

"You and I are on the same level of cluelessness right now." Levi rushed forward and boarded the train. "This is why I don't like to work with Mason."

This wasn't the first time he'd been on this thing, and that warning was no joke. It was going to take off on time, regardless of anything else.

Levi sat on one of the bench seats in the train, next to Alicia and warned her, "This thing will take off like a Formula One car, hold on tight."

"I know, Dad. I've been on one of these before, but over in China."

Bagel meowed nervously.

Levi glanced at the cat and wondered how he'd managed to convey a sense that the fuzzball was nervous.

"Ten seconds."

Levi tightened his grip on the pole in front of him.

"Five seconds. Four. Three. Two. One."

The train surged forward—then inexplicably the acceleration stopped as the car coasted on the tracks at a leisurely pace.

Levi exchanged a puzzled look with Alicia. Confusion etched identical creases into their foreheads.

Every other journey on this thing had been an adrenaline

rush, thrusting him violently backward under ferocious acceleration.

This was different.

Suddenly, darkness swallowed the cabin as it left the chamber.

"Dad?" Alicia's voice, thin and uncertain, cut through the silence.

Something was wrong. Levi could feel it—they weren't going faster than a slow crawl, maybe ten miles an hour.

Abruptly, the train jerked to a halt, pitching Levi forward slightly. Fluorescent lights crackled to life, outside the train as the doors yawned open.

The same cold, mechanical voice returned. *"You have arrived at the Lenox Avenue Conference Room. Please disembark."*

Levi stood cautiously, scanning the platform. Across from them lay a shadowed corridor that stretched into the darkness, terminating at an open doorway bathed in sterile white light. Framed in the doorway was a familiar silhouette. He motioned for them to approach and stepped through a doorway.

It was Doug Mason.

CHAPTER SEVEN

Levi exchanged a glance with Alicia. Bagel let out a soft, disinterested meow, but Levi wasn't fooled. The cat didn't like this place either.

They stepped onto the platform as more lights flickered to life, revealing a long corridor of polished black concrete heading straight into the bedrock. As he panned his gaze across the worn and mildly stained concrete floor, it was obvious that the Outfit had constructed this place long ago. It was a hidden alcove he'd never been aware of—likely one of thousands of secrets he didn't know about the organization that both he and Alicia had become associated with.

Walking away from the train, he stepped into the corridor and noted the smooth texture of the walls. There were no seams, cracks, or signs of wear, almost as if this part had been more recently installed. He sensed no smells, no sounds whatsoever other than his and Alicia's footfalls, and the whole approach had a feeling of sterility, almost like walking down the corridor of a hospital.

Alicia walked beside him, gaze sweeping the space. "Ever get the feeling you've stepped into a Bond villain's lair?"

Levi smirked. "All the time."

At the end of the corridor, a metal door noiselessly yawned open as they approached. Beyond it, the conference room was reminiscent of the ones he'd seen at the Outfit's headquarters.

It was large—easily capable of hosting twenty people around a dark-hued conference table.

The air had the crisp, sterile bite of industrial-grade HEPA filtration, again reminding him of the highly-filtered air of a hospital.

The door sealed behind them with a quiet thud.

Doug Mason stood at the head of the table. Five foot seven, light brown hair receding at the temples. Wrinkles creased his forehead, settling into permanent frown lines. His pale, almost silver eyes studied them with cold efficiency. He gave them both a silent nod and motioned toward the leather chairs lined up against the conference room table.

Bagel walked next to Alicia, his tail high in the air, twitching. The cat glanced up at Mason, sniffed in his direction, hopped onto one of the leather chairs, curled into a furry ball, and hid his face.

As Levi and Alicia sat, he spotted two others at the table. Both were typing furiously on their laptops as a soft hum echoed through the room.

The overhead projector flickered to life.

The image that filled the far wall was gruesome.

A dead man, slumped over a desk.

His face was bloated, discolored—veins blackened beneath the skin. His eyes were frozen wide open, lips twisted in a rictus snarl. The skin around his mouth and nose was a sickly shade of purple, almost necrotic.

The home office around him was disheveled—papers scattered, a lamp overturned. Behind him, a wooden bookshelf lined with first editions. A bottle of scotch sat untouched beside an expensive-looking pen set.

Alicia's breath hitched. Her mind raced, trying to connect the symptoms to anything she'd studied.

Levi exhaled slowly. What in the world were they looking at?

Mason gestured to the first of the men. "You both know Brice."

Levi nodded, recognizing him immediately. The Outfit's quartermaster. Q-style. The man who built the gear that gave many of the Outfit's agents a leg up against their adversaries. Brice was pudgy, dressed in a charcoal suit that somehow looked both expensive and utilitarian. Levi had normally seen the man in a lab coat hunched over a workbench. A smart guy, reliable, one of the Outfit's good people.

"Brice is leading the intelligence acquisition on the case being projected on the screen." Mason motioned to the second person. "I pulled in one of our specialists to attend this meeting. This is Dr. Patrick Wilkins out of Fort Detrick. His specialty is bioweapons."

Levi reached across and shook hands with the older gentleman.

The Outfit often had specialists on retainer, not unlike Brice, whose forte was electronics and computers. They weren't field agents but typically supported them when necessary.

Dr. Wilkins had neatly combed gray hair. As expected, he didn't have the swagger of a field operative, but there was something about the way he sat: his posture was rigid, his hands resting lightly on the table, and his eyes were bright and probing.

As Alicia greeted both men, Levi turned to Mason and grumbled, "Bioweapons? How the hell did you know?"

Denny's last words to him replayed in his mind.

"Have you ever heard of Novichok? It's a bioweapon, Levi. A nasty piece of work that first came out of Soviet Russia. Those swabs had remnants of the components all over them."

Mason waved the question away and gestured to the screen. "That man was Senator William Calloway."

"I know that name." Alicia's eyebrows lifted. "Isn't he on the Intelligence Committee?"

"Yes, it's the same guy." Brice nodded. "Died three nights ago. Cause of death was listed as undetermined." He tapped something on his laptop. The screen flickered, shifting to a toxicology report.

. . .

Office of the Chief Medical Examiner
District of Columbia
Toxicology Summary Report

Case No.: ME-2025-0329
Decedent: William Jesse Calloway
Date of Examination: March 29, 2025
Medical Examiner: Dr. Francisco J. Diaz, M.D., Chief Medical Examiner

Levi scanned the image, his gaze falling onto the toxicological findings.

Toxicological Findings:

- Acetylcholinesterase Activity: Profoundly suppressed, measured at approximately 4% of standard reference levels, consistent with acute exposure to a potent cholinesterase inhibitor.
- Blood/Tissue Analysis: Positive detection of metabolites indicative of a high-potency organophosphorus compound.

The data scrolled in real time—columns of biomarkers, enzyme inhibitors, neurotoxic signatures.

"The Outfit normally doesn't pay too much attention when

some politician has a heart attack in his home office." Brice cleared his throat and pointed up at the screen. "We have systems plugged into major forensic labs—watching for a litany of things that could be indicators of a national security issue. It turns out that Calloway's toxicology report fit a disturbing profile. That triggered an alert at NSA's Utah Data Center."

Alicia tilted her head in the direction of the screen. "And what's the toxicology telling us?"

Brice's fingers drummed the table. "That has all hallmarks of a bioweapon."

Silence.

Mason turned to Dr. Wilkins. "Pat, explain to our agents what you told us earlier."

Wilkins folded his hands. His voice was measured, precise. "Novichok."

Levi frowned. His mind raced as he contemplated how the death of some mobsters in New York could be related to the death of this senator he'd never heard of.

Alicia's expression darkened, matching her father's frown.

Wilkins continued. "Novichok is one of the most lethal nerve agents ever created. Soviet era. Cold War legacy. Designed to be more potent than VX, undetectable, and incredibly persistent in the environment."

Wilkins motioned to Brice and the image on the screen advanced—a molecular breakdown of the compound.

Levi studied it. Not exactly sure what he was looking at.

"It's a binary agent," Wilkins continued. "That means it exists in two harmless forms until mixed. Once combined, it becomes a weaponized neurotoxin—shuts down the nervous system at an enzymatic level. Full paralysis. Organ failure. Death in under three minutes."

Alicia shifted. "And that's what killed Calloway?"

Wilkins nodded. "The toxicology showed an acute poisoning by a powerful organophosphate cholinesterase inhibitor. There would only be two possible sources that I'm aware of for such a thing to happen: either exposure industrial-strength agricultural pesticides or a nerve agent. When traces of the binary components were found on two objects in his study, the answer was definitive."

Brice tapped a key, and the screen changed again.

Two Renaissance paintings. Small. Framed.

Wilkins continued. "The poison was embedded in the paint. One remained intact. The other had been disturbed—likely releasing a fine aerosol mist when the frame was moved. Calloway must have triggered the nerve agent and inhaled it."

Levi narrowed his eyes. "So he was assassinated by a goddamn painting?"

Wilkins shrugged. "I'm not one to speculate on motivations."

Levi shifted his gaze back and forth between Brice and Mason. "It seems like the FBI or some other law enforcement agent has a pretty clear thread to follow, why are Alicia and I called into this?"

Brice looked over at Mason, who was staring at the screen, ignoring everyone in the room.

Levi's voice took on an edge. "Mason, you said this was something—"

Mason gestured to Brice. "Go ahead."

Brice tapped another key. New images appeared on the screen.

Levi immediately recognized the names on the autopsy reports.

His chest tightened.

He was staring at the toxicology reports for Vito Maniscalco and Carmine Ricci.

The words were a little different, but the conclusion written up by the New York City Medical Examiner said, "Findings indicate death resulted from acute poisoning by a powerful organophosphate cholinesterase inhibitor."

"You may not realize this," Mason drummed his fingers on the table and said, "but I know Vincenzo Bianchi very well. I know him well enough to say that Vinnie has almost certainly asked you to investigate this. This is what *you* do, Levi." He looked over at Alicia and smiled. "And you're trained to—"

"Doug," Levi cut him off and asked, "what's going on?"

Mason rolled his shoulders and let out a small sigh. "Levi, I know you met with someone at Le Bernardin who's connected to some unsavory types overseas. You're already on this case, you just didn't know it. We know these paintings came from overseas, and I am hoping we can work something out. Brice can help with some intelligence and maybe some supplies as needed, and I can pull a few strings to make some things a bit easier.

The silence in the room thickened.

"What do you need from us?" Levi asked.

Mason shook his head. "Nothing much. Just share what you learn about the origin of this attack. I have no idea what the possible relationship would be between a US senator in the DC area and two of your associates in this city, but something doesn't add up. And as always, depending on where this leads you, I may or may not be in a position to rally the troops for an evac, so be careful." He glanced over at Alicia. "Both of you."

Bagel's head popped up from the chair he'd commandeered and let out a multi-syllabic meow.

Mason looked at the black cat and pointed at the Yoders. "Keep those two out of trouble, you hear me?"

Alicia reached over and scooped up the cat, plopping him in her lap as he purred. "Director Mason, do you guys have any intelligence on the package the senator received? Where it came from, who the shipper was, all that stuff."

Mason motioned in Brice's direction. "He'll send both of you a mission packet with all the intel we have." He looked over at the older gentleman. "Wilkins, I need you to gather everything you know about this bioweapon, its precursors, detection methods, possible cures, everything and share it with Brice."

"There is no simple cure or vaccine for Novichok exposure," Dr. Wilkins responded with a serious tone. "I'll give Brice information on the pre-exposure protocols we've used for military personnel in the past." He looked in Levi and Alicia's direction. "That can buy some critical time for treatment to be administered."

Levi glanced at his watch. "Doug, Alicia and I have a couple things we need to take care of before we commit to any travel. It'll probably be a day or two before that's taken care of. Is there any other intel we need to know about before we part ways?"

Mason shifted his attention to Brice as he hitched his thumb in Levi's direction. "I need you and the doctor to get that pre-exposure protocol squared away before these two start on their mission."

Brice began typing on his laptop and nodded. "Roger that."

"Okay, and before the Yoders travel anywhere, you both need to sync with Brice on whatever treatment protocol exists." Mason got up from his chair, crouched between Levi and Alicia and spoke in a whisper, "Brice is taking point on this from HQ. If either of you need anything, you know how to reach me. I'll be tracking some things down in DC, but I need you two to keep us informed of what you learn. There's no way that it's a coincidence that two members of the mob got taken out by the same thing a that took out a retired high-ranking senator, turned lobbyist. Something isn't adding up and I need your help on this."

Levi rolled back from the table, stood, and stared at Mason. "You're agreeing to pay the normal fees?"

A grin registered on Mason's expression as he gave Levi a nod. "Standard fees apply."

Levi pointed back and forth between himself and Alicia. "We're both getting fees, not just one of us, agreed?"

Mason's grin faltered for a moment, and he sighed. "Agreed."

Alicia's eyes widened.

Levi panned his gaze across the room and landed it back on Mason. "Anything else we need to cover?"

"This was all last minute." Mason shook his head. "Brice will put together the packets and get them to you."

Levi motioned for Alicia. "Okay, then we need to get going." He hitched his thumb in the direction of the train. "How do we get back aboveground, the train?"

Mason looked over at Brice and Dr. Wilkins, "Gather your things, I'll program up the train to get these two back to the Harlem safe house and then we'll run it back to DC."

Bagel let out a yowl as he squirmed out Alicia's grip and plopped onto the floor.

As the two men packed up their laptops, Alicia walked over to Levi and whispered, "Dad, what's next?"

His mind was racing with all the things happening at once. There was a shipment arriving in the morning that needed to be intercepted, he owed Denny a call back, and he knew that he was probably going to be contacted at any moment either by Oleg's French representative or Oleg himself.

He gave Alicia a wink and said, "You'll see."

∼

Levi leaned against the rusted metal doorframe of an old warehouse, tucked just far enough into the shadows to be invisible from the dock. The musty smell of old fish crates and rotting wood mixed with the sharp tang of saltwater. From his vantage point, he could see most of the dock, the faint glow from scattered lampposts highlighting patches of cracked concrete and flickering reflections on the water.

His phone buzzed in his pocket. He pulled it out and glanced at the screen—Paulie. He hit the call button, keeping his voice low. "Yeah?"

Paulie's gravelly voice rumbled through the line. *"I just want to confirm the arrival time of the ship. You said it's supposed to be 6:00 a.m., right?"*

"That's what my contact said," Levi affirmed, hoping that Pierre's information was reliable. "Check with the dockmaster and see if the ship's called in with a change of time or something."

"I'll do that. Also, just so we're clear: the package arrives, we take it to the safe house. Don't open it. Don't mess with it. Treat it like it's wired to blow."

"Right, and remember, the last package we received from this shipper ended up with Vito and Carmine on a slab. Make sure the guys are extra careful."

There was a grunt of acknowledgment from Paulie. *"Got it. We'll be careful. Anything else I need to know?"*

Levi's eyes scanned the dark expanse of the dock. "No, but I'm thin on assurances right now. I can't vouch for anything. Just don't take any chances. You're the only one I trust not to screw this up."

"Understood," Paulie said, and the line clicked dead.

Levi glanced at his phone and shook his head. No call from Oleg yet.

He slid the phone back into his pocket and shifted his stance, staying close to the early morning shadows. There was a thick blanket of fog lying on the water, and even though he couldn't see it, he heard the rumble of a large ship's engine growing louder, competing with the lapping of the water against the dock. At the far edge of the dock, the Bianchi crew had gathered—six of them, smoking and talking in low voices. Paulie's silhouette stood out among them, even from a distance, his sheer height towering over the others.

Levi stared intently across the dock into the fog when he

heard a car's engine. He turned, spotting a cargo van rolling into view, headlights bouncing over the uneven ground. It drove past him and pulled up near the docks.

Pulling out his phone, Levi activated Denny's remote video app and aimed the camera at the dock.

The smartphone began transmitting and an image flickered in into view through his contact lenses. Spreading his fingers on the touchscreen, the image of the docks zoomed in with crystal-clear clarity.

Several men climbed out, tough-looking guys—short hair, bulky jackets, hands flexing at their sides. They moved with a comfortable swagger across the dock. From his vantage point, they looked like longshoremen.

Pierre's words replayed in his mind: *I'll try to have one of my associates reach the other customer to avoid any conflicts...*

Had Pierre's associate been able to reach the other customer in time? If not, were these the delivery men for that customer? A chill raced up Levi's spine as he realized, maybe the Mona Lisa shipment had been meant for this other customer, and if so, he was now very curious to learn who these people were.

He tapped at his earbud and whispered, "Denny."

The phone began ringing as he pulled a cigarette-sized box from inside his suit jacket.

"Yes?" Denny's voice broadcast through the connection.

"Denny, I've got a vehicle I need to have tracked. I've got it on visual right now."

"Hold on a second, let me bring it up."

Levi heard typing through the connection as he withdrew

from the plastic container a miniaturized drone and set it on the floor.

A tiny blue LED came to life on the drone as it unfolded itself into a helicopter-like form.

"Okay, is the target the panel van you're staring at?"

"Yes, the one with Virginia plates."

The drone's rotor came to life, and within seconds hovered two feet off the ground and drifted toward the van, which was about one hundred feet away.

"Okay, it looks like nobody is looking our way, I'm putting it down onto the roof of the van and will turn on the magnetic clamps to hold on."

Levi watched as the fist-sized drone flew low toward the cargo van, quickly flitted up, and onto the roof where Levi lost sight of it.

"I'm on the target, going into surveillance mode and activating the GPS tracking."

"Did you catch the license plate? Anything you can tell me?"

"I have it, and it looks like it's registered to some courier service I've never heard of. Certainly not DHL or FedEx or one of the majors."

Levi nodded. "I want to know who hired these guys to come here today. You think you can dig that up?"

For the next handful of seconds the only sound on the line was the occasional click of a mouse. *"I'll see what I can find. I have some stuff that arrived for you, so if you come later today, I'll hopefully have some data if any is available."*

"That works, I'll be over today, just not exactly sure when,

I'm sort of in the middle of something right now. Keep track of this thing if you can."

"I'll do the best I can. See you whenever you come by."

Levi tapped his earbud, disconnecting, as a tall, wiry guy with a jagged scar cutting through his left eyebrow—strode up to Nico, one of the Bianchi crew members. Levi couldn't make out the conversation, but the body language was clear. Scarred Eyebrow was agitated, pointing repeatedly at the ship as it emerged from the fog, aimed directly at the dock. Nico shook his head, gesturing back toward the cargo van, his voice rising in pitch.

Levi strained to hear, but the ship's motor drowned out the words, just low, angry murmurs carried on the wind. Scarred Eyebrow pushed closer, his hand briefly touching Nico's chest. That was enough—Nico shoved him back, and the rest of the mobsters tensed, hands inching toward their waistbands.

Scarred Eyebrow wasn't backing down, though. He jabbed a finger in Nico's face, barking something that made the younger mobster's shoulders tense. Levi felt himself getting tense, his instincts screaming for him to get involved, but these guys were pros. It wasn't the first time some muscle stood in the way of something.

If only he knew when Oleg was going to call...

Just then, the door of the dockmaster's cabin swung open. Paulie stepped out, his stride deliberate. He didn't rush—just moved with a steady, unhurried pace. The Bianchi crew stepped back to let him through.

Paulie walked right up to Scarred Eyebrow, not saying a word. His face was a mask—calm, almost bored. Then, without warning, he pulled a gun from his coat and pressed it against the man's forehead.

Scarred Eyebrow froze, eyes wide, hands spreading out slowly in a gesture of surrender. His buddies from the cargo van hesitated, caught by surprise at the deadly escalation. Paulie didn't move, his gaze fixed on Scarred Eyebrow, not a hint of emotion on his face.

Scarred Eyebrow finally took a step back, giving a slow, exaggerated nod. The rest of his crew backed off, cautious at first, then faster as Paulie advanced slowly, his gun still aimed at the group's leader. After a dozen strides backward, the group turned, piled into the van and peeled out, tires screeching as they vanished into the early morning.

Paulie holstered the gun and turned to his crew. A curt nod was all it took. They didn't waste time—Nico and the others moved to the edge of the dock as the ship finally settled into position. Less than fifteen minutes later, a wooden crate was lowered onto the concrete—large, roughly three feet square, covered in Russian writing. The Bianchi crew wrapped it in a thick tarp and carefully lifted it onto a flatbed truck in one smooth motion.

Levi watched from the shadows, his senses on high alert. He didn't move, didn't make a sound as the truck rumbled off into the night, the crate safely tucked away in the back. Only after the sound of the engine faded did he step out of the doorway, his mind racing.

With a swipe on his phone, Levi put it to his ear and listened as he heard it ring once… twice…

A connection was made and it sounded like someone on the

other end had dropped his receiver before Frankie's voice finally echoed through the receiver. *"What's up?"*

"Frankie, the package is en-route. Alicia's in place, waiting for it, but I need a favor."

"What can I do you for?"

"Alicia's more than capable of safely examining the crate, but I want someone in there with her just in case something unexpected happens. Carmine and Vito both got taken out by whatever was on that crate last time, and I don't want her in there solo. She'll be in charge, but having some muscle as backup is—"

"I hear you, Levi. Consider it done. Is she at your apartment now?"

"She is, I'll call her and let her know things are rolling. Just make sure that whoever you send isn't some *mameluke, capisce?* Oh, and he needs to be able to fit in a hazmat suit."

"I got it covered. Let me make a call or two. I'll have him meet up with Alicia in the lobby."

"Thanks, Frankie." Levi hung up and dialed up Alicia.

The phone rang once, and Alicia's voice broadcast loudly through the receiver. *"Did it arrive?"*

"It's on the way. Also, I have Frankie rounding someone up to go with you into the room."

"Dad, I don't—"

"Don't start with me. There's a saying, two is one, one is none. This task isn't something to mess around with, and you need backup just in case something goes sideways."

He heard the rustle of sheets as Alicia probably was scrambling out of her bed. *"Okay, I'm getting dressed."*

"You didn't lose the security card for the room, right?"

"Dad, I'm not a complete moron. Of course I have it."

Levi's phone vibrated. "Okay, I have to go. Good luck and stay safe."

He tapped the phone, switching lines, and heard a rash of static on the line. "Yes?"

There was only static for a second and then a familiar voice yelled across the noisy connection. *"Levi, my friend! It has been a while."*

It was Oleg.

CHAPTER EIGHT

"Levi, my friend. It has been ages." Oleg's thick Russian accent echoed loudly in Levi's earbud.

"It's good to hear your voice again," Levi responded in fluent Russian. "I assume Pierre told you why I reached out."

The Uber Levi was in turned right onto Hamilton Avenue.

"He did." Oleg's voice took on a serious tone. *"I must apologize for the confusion about the package. It seems like your organization was given the wrong arrival information. I hope that you now have possession of the correct delivery."*

Oleg was being careful with his language, as was wise on any open line.

Levi clenched his jaw and shook his head. "Oleg, I assume Pierre also told you about the unfortunate incident with the first package? I need to understand why that happened."

"Levi, this would be much easier to discuss face-to-face. Is there a chance we can meet?"

Levi took in a deep breath, held it, and let it out slowly. "I need to know why we had that incident. We both know how serious this is."

"I understand perfectly, but I'm afraid I'm not yet sure how or why that incident occurred. I cannot make up for your loss in that way, but I will try to make it up in other ways."

"Oleg, did your people send that package?"

"Well, to be perfectly honest, no. But it's complicated. I have an arrangement with people in the former Eastern Bloc who help me create some of what we ship."

Create? Likely some high-end art forgers.

"But understand that your company was not supposed to have received that package. Today's shipment was shipped directly from my shipping department, but the other originated from another location I don't have direct control over."

The tires of the sedan rumbled as it crossed the Brooklyn Bridge.

"Oleg, I'm having today's shipment tested—"

"I guarantee you will not have any problems with what we sent you. Trust me when I say that I value our business relationship as well our personal friendship."

Levi felt himself getting angrier at the Russian. "Then you intended the outcome we received earlier to happen to your other customer?"

There was silence on the line for a few seconds before Oleg responded. *"No, I never have such intentions, and I'm deeply concerned with what happened. I would like to better understand what and how it happened."*

"Who is this intermediary that shipped the first package?"

Oleg sighed. "Unfortunately, I only have an address in Ukraine, but I know the work isn't being done there. I have a phone number and an address to ship things to. Everything else is done electronically."

Levi closed his eyes as the car veered onto the FDR Drive heading north. His mind was racing about what to do with what Oleg had just told him. "I need to get answers. Oleg, I'm asking this as a personal favor, send me the addresses and phone number you have. I'll investigate further on my own."

"I'll send you what I have. I wish I had more solid information to give you, but I also want to get to the bottom of this. I can't have my customers having issues like your people ran into. Please forward my apologies to Vincenzo."

Levi pressed his lips together into a thin line and clenched his fists. He hated not having the answers to his questions. "Okay Oleg, send me the data, and I'll follow up."

"I'll have Pierre send it directly to you. Again, thanks for your patience, and if you need anything when you get here, let me know."

The phone line went dead and Levi opened his eyes as the car turned onto Park Avenue.

Vinnie wasn't going to be thrilled with the lack of answers.

∼

Alicia paused at the steel door, her eyes sweeping the narrow alleyway. The faint yellow glow from the single overhead lamp barely penetrated the lingering fog. Her pulse quickened slightly as she withdrew the white plastic keycard and swiped it over the recessed panel. A soft beep, a click, and the heavy door opened.

Tony Montelaro stood silently behind her, patiently waiting but clearly uncomfortable. She'd spent quite a bit of time with Tony in Italy, looking for a missing relative of his, and Alicia was happy that he was the one sent to act as her teammate. He was reliable enough, but it wasn't the same as having her father standing by—Tony was just muscle, sent here in case things went sideways. Other than that, she couldn't exactly lean on him for advice.

They moved through the dimly lit corridor. Fluorescent lights snapped on as they approached, then flickered off behind them, making Alicia's skin crawl beneath her clothes. The place felt alive, watching their every move. At the end of the hallway stood another heavy steel door, vault-like and forbidding. Alicia entered the keycode and swiped the card again, and a louder click echoed as the lock released.

Inside, the hidden safe house smelled stale, musty. Alicia took a cautious breath, her eyes instantly locating the worktable at the center of the room. On it sat two wooden crates—the first was familiar, battered, and previously opened, the one that held the Mona Lisa clone she'd taken swabs from earlier. Alicia instinctively avoided that crate, her stomach tightening at the knowledge of what had happened to two of her father's associates.

The second crate was new, waiting untouched, the Russian lettering—Red Horizon Transport—stenciled across its front. Alicia eyed the crate warily, nerves twisting inside her. Tony cleared his throat behind her, already unpacking the hazmat suits from a large duffel.

"Let's get suited up," she said quietly. She didn't want to even approach that table without every possible protection she could muster.

Alicia methodically donned her protective gear, double-checking the seals on her gloves and boots. Tony mirrored her movements, though less confidently, fumbling with his helmet until she motioned impatiently toward it.

"Here, let me check," she said, turning him around and inspecting his seals. "You're good."

"Thanks," Tony replied, his voice tinny through the suit's speaker. He sounded anxious. She didn't blame him—she felt it too.

They moved together toward the second crate. Tony positioned himself nearby, mostly silent, his presence reassuring but somehow irritating at the same time. Alicia reached for the crowbar, cautiously prying the wooden lid. It came loose with a loud creak, revealing bubble wrap inside.

"Careful," Tony said unnecessarily. Alicia shot him a quick glance through the faceplate.

"I know," she said, more sharply than she'd intended.

She peeled back the wrapping slowly, methodically swabbing every exposed layer, placing each swab meticulously into labeled Ziploc bags. Her movements were precise, focused, yet beneath the controlled motions, her hands trembled slightly. Tony must have noticed.

"You feeling okay?" he asked through his suit's built-in microphone.

"I'm fine," she answered, barely keeping irritation from her voice.

She peeled back another layer, revealing not one painting, but several—six small Renaissance-era pieces carefully stacked. Alicia drew in a breath. Even to her minimally trained eye, they looked authentic, museum-worthy masterpieces. They were beautiful, though she wasn't sure if they were authentic or who the artists might have been.

"Are you okay, Alicia?" Tony asked again. "Feeling faint or anything?"

"I'm good, Tony," she snapped lightly. "Just let me concentrate."

"Sorry, I'm just doing what your pops made me promise to do." Tony mumbled. He shifted awkwardly from one foot to the other, and Alicia sighed inwardly. He was just doing his job, but the constant interruptions weren't helping her nerves.

Alicia resumed her careful inspection, swabbing each painting's frame and surface, methodically searching for signs of contamination. She wasn't worried about authenticity anymore, frankly, she couldn't care less if they were the real thing or not. She just wanted to know whether these beautiful, potentially priceless objects had been slathered with any toxic materials. She carefully sealed each swab, placing them into double-bagged containment envelopes.

"It's been another minute," Tony said again. "You sure you're okay?"

"For God's sake, Tony, yes. I'm okay." Alicia felt herself flush slightly from the frustration. "Let me finish this."

"Right. Sorry."

Ignoring Tony now, Alicia studied the paintings closely. They seemed flawless, the frames beautifully gilded, the colors vibrant, the brushstrokes lively and precise. Her heart sped up a bit as she considered their significance. Could these be real?

She shook her head sharply. Irrelevant, she reminded herself. Stay focused.

Once the final swab was secured, Alicia carefully rewrapped the paintings in their bubble wrap and replaced the wooden lid. She exhaled slowly, tension draining from her shoulders.

"All done?" Tony asked again.

"Yeah. We're good."

They carefully retraced their steps through the corridor. Alicia carried the bag of double-sealed samples in a larger double-sealed bag, her grip tight, praying she'd been meticulous enough. Behind her, Tony's heavy footsteps echoed in the silence.

As they emerged outside into the cool, misty air, Alicia took another deep breath. Tony began removing his helmet, glancing at her nervously.

"How do you feel? Everything okay?"

"I'm fine, Tony," Alicia said, managing a weak smile. "You can relax now."

He nodded, visibly relieved. "I've never done that kind of thing before. You know, worn a blue monkey suit like that." He looked at his hands as he flexed his thick sausage-like fingers. "Not sure how you do it—deal with that kind of stuff. I'd rather beat on someone than have something I can't even see try to take me out."

Alicia let out a laugh and shook her head. "Trust me, Tony. I don't like it any more than you do."

She tightened her grip on the sealed bags and motioned to her companion. "Let's go. I've got what I need, and I have to check in with my dad to see if he's done with his own meeting."

∼

It was nearly closing time when Alicia walked into Gerard's, the familiar bar just off Delancey Street, deep in New York City's Little Italy.

The place was almost deserted. Rosie, the feisty Puerto Rican bartender, was busy ushering out a tipsy young woman whose laughter echoed awkwardly through the empty room. Rosie glanced up at Alicia, her face registering mild surprise before returning her focus to her unsteady customer. "Honey, you sure you don't want me to call you an Uber?"

"No, Rosie, it's literally around the corner," the girl insisted, giggling as she stumbled through the doorway that Alicia held open for her. Rosie rolled her eyes, sighed heavily, and turned to Alicia.

"Denny's expecting you. He's in the back already with your dad," Rosie said quickly. "Do me a favor and tell folks I'll be back in a second. I'm just gonna make sure this girl doesn't fall flat on her face on the way to her apartment."

"Sure," Alicia said, nodding. She watched Rosie steady the young woman, gently gripping her elbow as they headed down toward Delancey Street. Usually, Rosie greeted her with sharp wit or friendly sass—seeing this gentler side of her was a reminder of how complex people could be.

After closing the front door, Alicia announced to the few remaining patrons that Rosie would be right back and walked toward the back, past the bathrooms, then turned left down the dimly lit corridor.

She glanced at the gaudy tile mural of a tropical beach scene that decorated the wall, recognizing it immediately. Her father had shown her once the precise combination of tiles Denny pressed to open the hidden door, but before she could even lift her hand, there was a quiet click, and the outline of a hidden door became visible.

It swung inward to reveal Denny, his hair longer and messier than usual, his eyes slightly bloodshot from hours spent staring at screens. He beckoned her quickly. "Come on in, Alicia. Close the door behind you."

Denny vanished back into his lair and Alicia stepped into the hidden room.

"…industrial district in Dnipro," Denny said as he sat at his desk, her father looking up at the workstation's monitor. "I pulled up the address you gave me and this is what we've got. As you can see, Ukraine's still a mess. Anyway, that place is next to—Kryvyi Rih Highway, Block 14. It's a warehouse strip. From the security feeds I tapped into, there's no reception area, no signage. Just trucks pulling up, crates getting moved inside. Pure logistics. No foot traffic. No office lights. It's not a front for anything—it *is* the thing." He looked over at Levi and asked, "Is this what you were looking for?"

"To be honest, I'm not sure what I was looking for." Levi shrugged. "Can you get that AI of yours to monitor who is coming and going and keep me posted on anything interesting that you see?"

"Sure." Denny turned to Alicia and asked, "You've got the swabs?"

She nodded, holding the collection of double-bagged swabs carefully as she walked deeper into Denny's lair. "Yes. They're here."

Her gaze flickered across the large, brightly-lit workspace, cluttered floor-to-ceiling with shelves packed with electronic devices, computers, gadgets, and various pieces of dissected technology. It never ceased to amaze her how chaotic yet precisely organized the room appeared—like a high-tech laboratory disguised as a garage sale.

It sort of reminded her of Brice's lab at the Outfit's headquarters.

Her father sat in one of the swivel chairs at the main workstation, leaning forward intently. Levi glanced up as she approached, his eyes softening briefly in acknowledgment. "Everything go okay?"

She nodded again. "No issues, Dad. Tony was there to bug the snot out of me like you asked him to."

Levi smiled and nodded with approval.

Denny approached carefully, extending his hands toward her. "Let me take those samples off your hands before anything unpleasant happens."

Alicia carefully passed the sealed bag over to Denny,

watching closely as he gently placed it in a cooler with biohazard stickers and closed the lid. He moved quickly, already prepping a nearby machine, his fingers dancing swiftly over the keyboard. He shot her a sideways glance. "How're you feeling? No dizziness, headache, anything?"

"I'm fine," Alicia replied firmly, shifting her weight from one foot to the other. She hated the nervousness in her voice and steadied herself. "I triple-checked everything."

Denny nodded and said, "I'll send it to the lab first thing in the morning and I'll try to get a rush on it."

Levi leaned back in his chair, observing silently. She glanced toward him, waiting expectantly.

"So, Dad," Alicia finally asked, breaking the tense silence. "What's our next move?"

Her father turned to Denny and asked, "Didn't you have something she needed to try on?"

"Try on?" Alicia asked, not having a clue what he was talking about.

Denny opened a small drawer, rummaging briefly before producing a small plastic container. He held it toward Alicia, a subtle smile playing at his lips. "Here, I almost forgot. I have an upgrade to your contact lens. Your old one can serve as a backup for now, but this one has a new feature that should be useful."

Alicia tilted her head, taking the small container from his hands. "Another lens? What's different about this one?"

He pointed toward her pocket. "Let me have your phone—I need to install an app that'll pair with the new lens."

"My phone?" She gave him a curious look as she handed it over. She unscrewed the lid of the container and saw a familiar-looking lens submerged in clear contact solution, tiny silver filaments shimmering through the curved surface. She looked closer into the container. "More nanotubes?"

"Yup," Denny said, already swiping quickly on her phone screen. "The design is mostly the same, I've just added a bit of special sauce, if you will. This lens has the AR functions the previous one had—automatic translations, overlays, all that. But now, when the app's activated on your phone, it'll be able to stream exactly what you see. It records or broadcasts your visual feed directly to your phone or a remote location. Pretty handy, especially if things get complicated."

"Don't forget to tell her about the zoom capability." Dad flicked his fingers in the direction of her phone. "That was one of the prime features I was looking for when we were first talking about the new contact."

"Wait a minute…" Alicia's eyebrows shot up as she considered the possibilities. "So it's almost like… livestreaming whatever I'm seeing?"

"Live what?" Dad interjected, turning from where he'd been quietly examining a piece of electronics on the cluttered bench. His face showed genuine puzzlement, the kind that Alicia often teased him about.

Alicia laughed softly, shaking her head. "Dad, it always amazes me how out of touch you can be with some things. Livestreaming—it's a social media thing, where people broadcast live video feeds of whatever they're doing. Kids do it all the time now with their phones. It's very popular."

Levi frowned slightly, a bemused look crossing his face. "And people watch this stuff?"

"Millions of people do," Alicia answered with exaggerated patience, rolling her eyes playfully. "Welcome to the twenty-first century."

Denny handed back her phone. "The app's installed. Same one your dad's been using."

Alicia dabbed contact solution onto her fingertips, carefully removing the lens from its case. "How do you know it'll fit?"

"I used the same measurements from the last lens I gave you," Denny said. "This one should be a perfect match. Just pop it in—same as before."

Alicia hesitated for a moment, then gently placed the lens onto her eye. After blinking away the blur of the solution, her vision cleared instantly, feeling as natural as her own sight. She looked around Denny's cluttered workshop, waiting for something unusual to happen.

"Try the app now," Denny prompted. "You have several modes it can work from. One is the translation, the other is query, and the other is the simulcast feature. You can select any of them or all of them, but when you turn on the simulcast feature, the app will launch a new window where you'll get a view of what's being transmitted."

"And that's when you can zoom things in," her father added.

She activated the app on her phone and immediately saw a tiny, discreet red dot flashing in the corner of her vision. It wasn't distracting, just enough to know the system was active. She selected the simulcast feature and her phone's screen began displaying the exact perspective of her vision.

"Holy crap," she murmured, moving her head and seeing the screen reflect precisely what she saw. "That's impressive."

Her father made pinching and then spreading motions with his fingers. "You can pinch and zoom and it's like you have a set of binoculars."

Alicia touched the screen and spread her fingers. She frowned as the image of her phone in the window got larger.

"Alicia," her father held up his own phone and held it out in the direction he was looking. "Don't look directly at your phone, but have it in your line of sight so what you're looking at does zoom in. It takes some getting used to but you'll get it."

With one hand, Alicia held up her phone and looked past it at Denny's monitor, and with the other hand zoomed in.

The screen came closer and she could just make out some of the text, where previously it had been too small.

"Obviously it's not an optical zoom but a digital one that you're seeing." Denny added. "However, I have some pretty good AI filters doing lots of cleanup so you should be able to get a pretty good 8x digital zoom without too much fuzziness or artifacts."

Alicia panned her arm and gaze as one and played around with zooming in and out of things. It was immediately obvious to her how useful this could be.

"I'm not sure if you noticed it," Denny held up his own phone and showed the app. "There is a radio button on the simulcast that allows you to automatically save to video locally or reach out to me and transmit the feed remotely, obviously with secure end-to-end encryption."

Her father cleared his throat and pointed at the monitor. "Let's finish up with what you found out about the delivery service."

Alicia looked over at her father and he quickly explained, "There was a bit of a misunderstanding with this morning's delivery and another set of couriers showed up."

"What'd you do?" Alicia asked.

Her father shook his head. "I didn't do anything, but let's just say we placed a tracking device on the van and convinced them to go away."

Alicia grinned, knowing full well that it was a bit more than simple convincing that had occurred, but that wasn't important.

Denny's fingers became a blur across his keyboard. Data flashed across the monitor screens, maps zooming in, coordinates scrolling by.

"Okay, here's the thing," Denny began, leaning back slightly in his chair and swiveling to face her father. "I tracked the cargo van from New York straight back down to the DC area. It took I-95 most of the way, exited onto the Beltway, then down New York Avenue before cutting over to a warehouse district near Ivy City."

Alicia folded her arms across her chest, listening carefully. Her father stood silently, arms crossed, clearly deep in thought as Denny continued.

"The GPS coordinates were crystal clear—they ended up at a warehouse off of Okie Street. The exact address wasn't too hard to pinpoint." Denny paused dramatically, holding Alicia's attention. "But here's where it got interesting: as soon as the van parked, I tapped into the Utah Data Center and requested an override priority surveillance of that location's landline and cellular traffic."

"Did you find anything?" Alicia asked impatiently.

"Within five minutes, there was an outgoing call made from the warehouse. The call was placed to a DC-based number, but nobody answered. I checked for any follow-up communications or activity, but there was none. At least none as of yet. The warehouse went quiet immediately after that one unanswered call."

Alicia's eyebrows knitted together, tension tightening her shoulders. "Who were they calling?"

Denny swiveled back to his keyboard and quickly typed something, pulling up a profile on the monitor. "The number belongs to the direct line into a senior member of the House of Representatives."

Alicia shot a sharp look at her father, who mirrored her surprise, the silence heavy as they processed what Denny had just revealed.

"I didn't dig any further than that yet," Denny said, glancing over his shoulder. "Figured I'd better fill you in before going any deeper."

Her father's frown said it all.

This was something the Outfit needed to know about.

Alicia looked up at her father and asked, "Do we need to reach out to you know who?"

Her father turned to Denny and pointed at the cooler with Alicia's swabs. "I want to know what you find in that. I need it as soon as possible."

Denny glanced up at the wall clock and nodded. "If it's an emergency, I know somebody I can call. If I can swing it, maybe I can reach someone who can tell me what we've got sometime early tomorrow." He shrugged. "That's probably as good as it gets, Levi. I'd do it myself if I knew how, but I'm not qualified to handle this stuff."

Levi patted the bar owner on the shoulder. "Just get it to me as soon as you can." He looked over at Alicia and said, "You and I have a few phone calls to make."

Alicia got up, gave Denny a quick hug, and rushed after her father, who was already on his way out.

CHAPTER NINE

Levi felt the heat radiating from the crackling fire in the fireplace. He and Frankie were sitting in two of the three leather wingback chairs, both watching as Vinnie paced back and forth.

"Let me get this straight." The mob boss glanced at Levi and asked, "You're telling me that the new shipment checked out fine, but the first shipment from the Russians—the one that killed Vito and Carmine—was meant for someone else?"

"Pretty much." Levi nodded. "My guy Denny just got the lab results on the fresh shipment; the half-dozen paintings are all good to go. And yes, Oleg's guy told me that one of their clerks screwed up and accidentally swapped who was getting the two delivery notifications."

Frankie leaned forward, his elbows on the arms of the chair. "I get that the Russians sent us something that was meant for someone else. And frankly, I don't give two damns about the other guys they were obviously trying to take out, but it was us who paid for their screw-up."

"Like I said, Frankie, that shipment didn't come straight from Oleg but from some middleman. I've got an address out in Ukraine that I need to follow up on, but it's no sure thing that I'll be able to pin down who's responsible—"

"Bullshit," Vinnie interjected. "I don't believe in mistakes. We got that package for a reason."

"Actually, I got a little more dirt on that package."

Vinnie froze mid-pace and turned to him, his eyes narrow like a hawk's, waiting for him to continue.

The mob boss shifted his gaze to Frankie, who was the family's head of security but also ran the streets with the mafia soldiers. "Did Paulie tell you about having to scare off some delivery goons at the docks yesterday?"

Frankie nodded.

"Well, I managed to track where that delivery crew came from, and I'll have you know they weren't any kind of FedEx-type chumps. They slunk back to a warehouse near DC. I'm having that place watched, and from what my guys have figured out, it looks like a few made guys are hanging out in that warehouse."

"DC? That's Don Marino's territory." Vinnie frowned. "Why the hell would any of his boys be getting a delivery all the way up here? I should know about that."

Frankie's troubled expression matched Vinnie's.

"Well," Levi continued, "I was hoping that while I'm tracking down whoever sent the first package from overseas, you could maybe reach out and see what's up with those guys. To be honest, Paulie pulled out his piece and was about to blow one of those guys' heads off when the pickup crew decided to back off."

"They'd be idiots to start friction with us up here." Frankie said, his voice dripping with menace. "Sounds like we might have some bad blood with the Marino family."

"Calm down, Frankie." Vinnie waved away his comment. "I'll talk to Giancarlo and figure things out." He looked up at the ceiling and said, "If what Levi's saying is true, then the Marino family might have been the real mark for that first package."

"Seems so." Frankie nodded.

Vinnie smiled and locked eyes with Levi. "That's perfect. And you're tight with one of Giancarlo's capos, right?"

Levi nodded. "Yeah, I've worked some with Dino Minelli. He's solid." Levi locked eyes with Vinnie, wondering what he was thinking.

The mob boss turned to Frankie and made a shooing motion. "Frankie, go get some breakfast with your family, I'll call you in a bit and we can work out what to do with next month's jobs."

Without another word, Frankie sprang up from his seat, gave Levi a nod, kissed Vinnie on both cheeks, and slipped out of the parlor.

The moment the doors closed, Vinnie took a seat and said, "I smell the Outfit's grubby paws all over this. What aren't you telling me?"

Levi looked over at Vinnie with a blank expression. "What do you mean?"

"Levi, I wasn't born yesterday." He began counting on his fingers. "Let's see—we got our boys iced by some poison last used when the Soviet Union was around. We have punks messing with our crew who came up from the DC area. And we got old Don Marino involved, whose people are deep into DC politics and pulling favors—that geezer wouldn't know art if it was painted on his face by da Vinci himself. This all smells like something the Outfit would be neck-deep in, and somehow, we got dragged in." Vinnie nodded in his direction. "Have they reached out to you?"

A scene replayed in Levi's mind from a handful of years ago in this very room. It was a moment that shocked Levi to the core. He repeated what Vinnie had done by digging into his pocket for one of the large silver coins the Outfit had assigned him and extended it toward the mob boss.

Vinnie smiled, leaned forward, and grasped the other half.

It took no more than a second or so before a small LED flashed green from the coin, verifying that both were members of the Outfit.

Levi cleared his throat and shook his head. "Vinnie, it still feels like a fever dream that you were ever a part of that group. So, you don't know? They didn't tell you?"

Vinnie waved the question away. "I have no need to talk to them, and they have little need to talk to me, after all, they have you to handle their dirty work—and I know where your loyalties lie. So, are they in on this?"

Levi nodded as he put the coin away. "Some retired senator got clipped by a poison that matched what Vito and Carmine were killed with and that got them crawling out of the shadows to figure out why, so they reached out." He shrugged. "I was already looking into Vito and Carmine's deaths anyway, so they just wanted a sit-down to share some intel about what I've found so far, which was mostly nothing they didn't already know."

"What about the Ukraine angle?" Vinnie asked. "Do they know about that yet?"

Levi shook his head. "No, but I didn't really see that as crossing any lines if I did share it. What are you thinking?"

"I need you to handle the DC angle of this thing, whatever it is. My gut's scream something's going on with the Marino family that'll probably raise eyebrows with our friends at the Outfit. I'd rather the Outfit stay out of our family business, same as the other families. But with a dead senator and some loose ends with these shipments, one thing's going to lead to another, and I need you to help keep that from happening."

"But what about Don Marino? He might—"

"I'll talk to Giancarlo and see if there are any feathers that have been ruffled and smooth them over." Vinnie pursed his lips. "This isn't something for Alicia."

"Agreed." Levi knew exactly who he'd reach out to to get the ball rolling, but not with Alicia present… this was a *Cosa Nostra* thing and not something he'd ever drag her into.

"That Ukraine lead you got, it also needs to be handled right away, otherwise, the rats tend to scatter quickly, if you know what I mean."

"You want Alicia to go to Ukraine while I'm digging into the DC thing?"

"Yes, but I was thinking about Alicia's safety." The mob boss leaned forward and locked eyes with Levi. "She's a good kid, tough as nails, but she's not you. I know the Outfit's trained her, so do you think she's got the chops to do this… to nail who's responsible for this?"

A twinge of uncertainty surged through Levi. "To be honest, and this might be me talking as her old man, I'm a bit nervous about her going out solo."

Vinnie nodded. "I totally agree. Since it's me asking for this favor, I was thinking of sending some muscle with her. What do you think?"

Levi took in a deep breath and let it out slowly. He was nervous about her going on a dangerous job, with or without backup. "Well, I won't say no, but ultimately, it's her call. Who did you have in mind?"

The mob boss stood and shot Levi a sly grin. "I know just the guy."

∽

The mirror in Alicia's en-suite was fogged, obscuring her reflection like a ghost behind glass. She lifted her hand, tracing lazy circles through the condensation, watching as clarity briefly appeared before dissolving back into opacity. Steam swirled around her, infused with the subtle fragrance of lavender from her shampoo.

She tightened the thick terry-cloth robe around her, savoring its comforting weight as she vigorously toweled her damp hair. Droplets of water tapped softly onto the polished marble countertop below, blending with the mechanical hum of the building's ventilation system—a steady, low-frequency reminder of the luxury apartment's hidden features.

Suddenly, the metallic scrape of the front door latch echoed from the apartment entrance, followed by muted, authoritative voices. Her pulse quickened slightly. Alicia stepped swiftly into her bedroom, cooler air prickling her damp skin, goosebumps rising along her arms. The deep aroma of freshly brewed coffee penetrated her room. She breathed it in deeply and caught a whiff of her father's cologne—a familiar blend of spice and worn leather that always made her feel secure.

She emerged from her bedroom just as her father, Levi, and Uncle Vinnie walked into view, locked in serious conversation. The click of their heels resonated against polished hardwood, sending subtle vibrations through the floor. Alicia felt momentarily exposed, standing there in her robe, hair still damp and tousled.

"Morning, Dad," she said, her voice casual but masking a flicker of embarrassment.

Levi glanced at her, his eyes warm but tinged with amusement. "Morning, Alicia."

Uncle Vinnie averted his gaze politely, a faint smirk on his lips. "Hey, young lady. Didn't mean to catch you unprepared."

Alicia rolled her eyes, folding her arms across her chest. The robe was large enough to cover her entirely, making the mob boss's exaggerated politeness unnecessary. "Good morning, Uncle Vinnie."

Levi lifted an eyebrow slightly. "Maybe get dressed? The three of us have some business to discuss."

The three of them? She'd never discussed anything serious in the mob boss's presence.

"Sure thing. Give me five." Alicia spun around, robe swirling gently around her ankles, and hurried back to her room. Quickly shedding the robe, she changed into jeans and a soft cream sweater, the fabric comfortable against her cooling skin. She ran her fingers hastily through her hair, leaving it casually tousled.

Returning to the main living area, Alicia found the scent of coffee intensified—rich and inviting, with hints of roasted chocolate beans drifting through the room. Uncle Vinnie stood near the entrance to the kitchen, sipping from a steaming mug, his expression thoughtful. Levi poured orange juice into two tall glasses on the dining room table, its bright citrus fragrance sharp and refreshing.

"Thanks, Dad." She took a sip, the juice sweetly acidic, cutting through the last traces of sleep. Her senses sharpened, fully awake now, acutely aware of the unusual weight behind the mob boss's morning visit.

"So," she said, voice even, "what's going on?"

Her father motioned toward the dining table. "Grab a seat. There's been a slight change in plans."

Alicia swallowed nervously, feeling the tang of orange juice turn slightly bitter in her throat. Her father and Vinnie exchanged serious looks. Alicia forced herself to speak, hoping her voice sounded steadier than she felt. "So, you're going to handle something for Uncle Vinnie in D.C., and I'm heading to Ukraine. Can't I help you in D.C.? Maybe speed things up?"

The moment the words left her lips, she winced, knowing how pathetic they sounded.

Her father smiled warmly but shook his head. "I'm afraid not. This is something I have to do myself."

Which meant that whatever he was doing, it was almost certainly mob business.

"Alicia," Uncle Vinnie said, reaching across the dining room table to pat her hand. "I know this isn't what you expected, but your father's told me you can handle almost anything. Since I'm the one throwing a monkey wrench into the works, I'll try to make it up to you." He pointed to the nearby living room and said, "Do you remember when you and I were talking last, and I was sitting in that seat over there?"

Alicia remembered the conversation as if it had just happened and the annoyance she'd felt back then suddenly rushed to the forefront. "You told me that a girl needs a chaperone when visiting Italy."

Her father chuckled, and Vinnie reacted with a good-natured shrug. "I suppose it was something like that. I seem to recall your father was indisposed, and I felt responsible for your safety. Well, I'm in a similar position where I'm intruding on the natural order of things and feel obligated—"

"But Uncle Vinnie, you're really not," Alicia managed to interject even though she didn't like the idea of talking back to her father's boss. "I'm an adult and—"

"Listen, I know that. But this is different. I don't know what dangers I'm sending you into…" Vinnie's expression turned dark and foreboding. "To be honest, the more I think about this, the less I like it, but I'll trust your father's confidence in your abilities. Nonetheless, you need backup. I cannot in good conscience let this go forward without making whatever assurances I can for your safety. I won't take 'no' for an answer on this. Give me a second." Uncle Vinnie dug his phone out from inside his suit jacket and put it to his ear.

Alicia looked at her father, who surreptitiously made a hand gesture for her to calm down. The idea that Uncle Vinnie thought he could interfere with what she did or didn't do felt terribly wrong, but she choked down the urge to protest, took a deep breath, and let it out slowly.

Uncle Vinnie put the phone away and stood, turning toward the front door.

At the same moment, Bagel popped his head up and yowled just as someone knocked on the door.

Uncle Vinnie walked over, opened the door, and Tony stood in the doorway, wide-eyed with a nervous expression.

The mob boss motioned to Alicia and gave her a kiss on both cheeks. "Tony will accompany you. I've arranged the flights for tomorrow at three-thirty in the afternoon." He walked over to the mob enforcer and hitched his thumb in Alicia's direction. "Get yourself packed for the trip, listen to her, and watch her back, *capisce*?"

Tony nodded, a look of utter confusion on his face.

"Good." He patted Tony on the cheek and hitched his thumb in Alicia's direction. "She'll fill you in on the details."

Vinnie walked out the door, and Tony gave Alicia a weak smile. "Uh, I guess I should cancel my poker night tomorrow—um, where are we going?"

Alicia stared at the poor, confused man and, for a moment, was stunned into inaction.

Bagel walked up to Tony, stretched his paws upward, and the big man lifted the cat up as it purred in his arms.

Her father cleared his throat and motioned from her to Tony, as if to say, "Answer the man."

The stunned and confused expression on the big man's face made Alicia burst out laughing. "Well, I guess you and I are going to Ukraine."

CHAPTER TEN

As Levi stepped through the battered wooden door of Ma Kelly's Bistro, the smell hit him like a slap—stale beer, greasy meat, and something sour he preferred not to identify. No self-respecting New York wiseguy would be caught dead in a dive like this. The place reeked of desperation; dim lighting filtered through dusty fixtures, and the floor was sticky beneath his shoes.

The pub was a relic, Irish in name only, lit dimly by flickering bulbs that barely cut through the dingy interior. The linoleum underfoot was sticky, tugging slightly at his shoes as he made his way inside. He scanned the near-empty room, spotting Dino Minelli instantly.

Dino rose from a battered booth near the back, a smile spreading easily across his rugged features. Barrel-chested, his dark hair peppered with gray, Dino moved with the confidence of a made guy. As a capo for the Marino family, he carried himself with the easy authority of someone who'd earned his place. The swagger was there—but subdued. Like Levi, he could just as easily blend in at a boardroom negotiating a deal as he could hand out street justice.

"Levi," Dino said warmly, gripping Levi's hand firmly, a gesture more fraternal than formal. "Been too long, my friend."

Levi returned the handshake, matching Dino's strength. "Good to see you, Dino. You look good."

Dino smirked, glancing around the squalid interior of Ma Kelly's. "You too. Gotta say—you really class up the joint." He chuckled, waving dismissively at the empty tables.

Levi raised an eyebrow, suppressing a smile. "Yeah, real classy spot you picked. What's with you and this place? Same joint I first met you in a couple years back."

"You've got a good memory, my friend." Dino laughed, loud and hearty. "Come on, Levi." He gestured to the door with a nod. "This place is strictly for meetings where nobody else shows up. Let's take a walk."

They stepped out of the pub, emerging into the late afternoon sunlight of D.C. Traffic hummed past them, cars gleaming in reflected sunlight. Dino led the way casually down the crowded sidewalk, weaving through tourists and businesspeople who paid them no attention.

Once they turned onto a quieter side street—away from the prying eyes of traffic cameras and oblivious pedestrians—Dino's voice dropped into a lower, more serious register. "When you called me out of the blue, I figured I'd probably get some answers about a couple things Don Marino's been asking me to look into."

"Oh yeah? What did the Don been saying?"

"Don't play coy with me, Levi. You know damn well." Dino snorted and shook his head. "There was some excitement up at the docks near your territory. Your big man, Paulie, was running a crew, and one of our crews was in the area. They had a little dust-up."

"That's exactly what I wanted to talk about." Levi nodded, slipping his hands into his pockets, his eyes casually scanning the street for any tails or cameras. "I did a little digging into what happened, and it looks like there was some confusion about a particular shipment. Paulie tells me your boys were there for the same package. You want to tell me what your crew was doing in our backyard?"

"I asked the same thing." Dino grimaced, shaking his head. "Didn't get a straight answer—just a lot of sidestepping. Those boys at the docks were freelancers—connected guys, yeah, but maybe not the sharpest tools in the shed if you know what I mean. They might've screwed up." He shrugged, eyes narrowing. "If we want to get to the bottom of this, I think you and I need to take a little trip to the warehouse. Talk to a few of these *momos* face-to-face."

Dino pressed a button on a key fob and a black Lincoln Navigator parked half a block down gave off a double beep, its glossy paint and chrome accents at odds with the beat-up neighborhood. The SUV was spotless—detailed, waxed, the kind of ride that screamed money without tipping into flash.

Levi opened the passenger door and slid into the seat. Inside, the leather seats still smelled new, the dashboard clean except for a small St. Christopher medal dangling from the rearview. "Nice ride."

"It gets me from point A to point B without being too flashy," Dino replied, tapping the ignition. The engine purred to life, quiet as a whisper despite the size of the vehicle. "Besides, the cops barely glance twice at a family-guy ride like this."

Dino pulled away from the curb, easing the Navigator into the flow of D.C. traffic.

Levi pulled down the visor as the sun glared in his face. They rolled south down New Jersey Avenue, the Capitol dome just visible between the buildings in the visor's tiny mirror. He kept his gaze moving—habitual, scanning mirrors, side streets, faces in passing cars. Old reflexes.

"So, these connected guys," Levi said, his voice casual but edged, "how well do you know them?"

Dino grunted, one hand draped over the top of the wheel, the other resting on the gear selector. "I'm not exactly sure who all was in that crew, but if it's the guys I'm thinking of—the ones who mostly handle the warehouse area—they're decent earners. One or two might be candidates for our thing. Levi, to be honest with you, I just heard about what went down less than twelve hours ago, so you've caught me a bit unprepared."

"I guess we'll know soon enough," Levi said, eyes still tracking the streets outside.

"Don't worry." Dino's jaw worked tight, chewing on the thought. "We'll get to the bottom of this, there's no reason for these kinds of misunderstandings. Just let me handle the intros and you can take care of the rest. Just try not to break any bones, then we gotta get doctors involved, I have to explain to the Don what happened, and it just—"

"Forget about it." Levi grinned. "There's no need for any of that... unless they get stupid."

The Navigator cruised past M Street, weaving through the late-day traffic near Buzzard Point. Down near the Anacostia waterfront, the streets grew quieter, lined with old warehouses and industrial lots, some abandoned, some still clinging to business. A stack of shipping containers loomed behind rusted fencing. The smell of the river drifted in—brackish water mixed with diesel fumes and the faint metallic tang of old dock lines.

Dino made a slow turn onto Water Street, easing into a side lot halfway down the block. A long, low brick warehouse squatted near the end of the pier, its metal roll-up door half-open, the shadows inside revealing nothing about what might be tucked away in the building.

Two men stood out front, smoking, trying to look like they weren't paying attention. Both wore cheap jackets and the kind of jeans that didn't quite fit right—street thugs, by the look of them.

Dino killed the engine but didn't move right away. His eyes narrowed as he watched the pair outside the warehouse.

"See those two?" he muttered. "The one on the left I don't recognize. The one on the right's a guy named Manny. Manny's sort of a retard, not literally, but he's a well-meaning idiot and that doesn't speak well for the other guy."

Levi smirked faintly.

Dino pulled the keys from the ignition, slipping them into his jacket pocket. "Let's go see how much these *momos* really know."

They stepped out of the Navigator, the heavy doors closing

with a solid thunk behind them. The air outside was thick with humidity and the low drone of tugboats out on the river. Overhead, a pair of seagulls circled, crying out against the darkening sky as the sun slipped lower toward the horizon.

The two men straightened when they saw Dino approaching, nervous energy radiating off them like heat from asphalt. One dropped his cigarette, grinding it out under his boot.

Levi gave the guy a slow once-over, his gaze cool. "Gentlemen," he said softly—the threat in his tone as subtle as it was unmistakable.

Dino didn't bother with introductions. He jerked his chin toward the warehouse door. "Open it up. We're gonna have a little talk."

～

The office inside the warehouse was barely more than a broom closet with aspirations—cinderblock walls painted a sickly off-white, the corners scuffed from years of abuse. A battered metal desk sat under a flickering overhead light, and the air smelled faintly of motor oil, cheap aftershave, and stale cigarettes.

Manny stood near the door, leaning awkwardly against the frame like he wasn't sure whether to stay or make a run for it. Four other men were crammed into the room, their postures stiff, eyes wary, all of them seated on metal folding chairs. None of them spoke as Dino stepped inside, holding the door open for Levi with the kind of deference that didn't go unnoticed by the room.

All four men stood; their gazes focused on Dino.

"Relax guys, grab your seats." Dino gave the crew a nod then focused on a thin man sitting behind the metal desk, his voice calm but edged. "Franco, this here's Levi, a friend of ours." He paused, choosing his words carefully, eyes drifting briefly toward the ceiling—as if reminding the room that bugs were always a possibility. "Levi's closely associated with some friends of ours from New York."

Despite the innocuous phrasing, the use of the term *"friend of ours"* coming from Dino clearly signaled to all in the room that Levi was a member of *la Cosa Nostra*. And by Dino addressing Franco specifically, it implied to Levi that the man behind the desk was a member of the Mafia as well, while the others were likely associates.

The weight of Dino's words settled heavily in the cramped space. Four sets of eyes shifted to Levi, reading the cues. They didn't know exactly who he was, but they sure as hell knew to be respectful.

Levi stayed silent for a beat, giving them time to stew, then offered a small nod.

Dino gestured to the group. "Manny, you met out front. The rest of you—this is Franco, Pete, Joey, and Richie."

Franco—a wiry, sharp-faced guy who looked like he hadn't slept in a week—nodded once, hands shoved deep into the pockets of his threadbare jacket. Levi clocked him immediately as the brains of the operation.

Levi took a few steps back toward a corner of the room so he could see everyone at once. His tone stayed level, conversational, but there was a weight behind the words. "So, a couple days ago there was a situation at the Red Hook Terminal in Brooklyn. Which of you were on that crew?"

Franco, Pete, and Joey raised their hands.

Levi pointed at Manny and Richie. "You two don't need to be here."

Without hesitation, the two men left the room, leaving a bit more breathing space in the otherwise cramped office.

Levi turned to Franco and asked, "Were you leading the crew?"

Franco gave a hesitant nod, his Adam's apple bobbing as he swallowed.

Pete and Joey both kept their eyes focused on the floor in front of them.

Levi smelled the fear coming from them. Both had a sheen of sweat on their faces. He turned to Franco, who looked less nervous than the other two, but still held a concerned expression. "What the hell were you doing up in Brooklyn?"

Franco cleared his throat and looked over at Dino, who was leaning against the doorframe. He gave the man a slight nod, as if to give him permission to speak to Levi. "We got an email from the shipper. Said the package we were expecting got rerouted up north. Different dock. Said we needed to pick it up there instead."

Levi raised an eyebrow. "Who from the shipper?"

Franco shrugged. "Some logistics guy over in Russia. We don't talk direct, just emails through the company rep. Said there was a mix-up on their end."

So far, everything matched what Levi already believed to be true.

Levi nodded slowly, letting the silence stretch just long enough to make Franco shift behind the desk.

"Okay," Levi said. "Who were you supposed to deliver the package to once you had it?"

Franco's lips pressed into a thin line, his eyes flicking back to Dino like he was again asking permission to speak. Dino gave the faintest nod.

"Name I got was Kendra Holstrom," Franco said finally. "Never met her. Don't know much about her—just what the order said. Supposedly the package was a gift for her father. She was real particular about the artwork—made a point about her old man's taste. She'd written down all sorts of specifics and I'd just forwarded it on to the supplier."

Levi's eyes narrowed. "You got an address for this Kendra?"

Franco nodded again, stepping toward one of the dented filing cabinets shoved against the wall. He tugged open the top drawer and flipped through a stack of folders, finally pulling one out. Thumbing through a few pages, he turned the file toward Levi, jabbing a finger at the delivery sheet.

"Here. The Hay-Adams Hotel. Downtown D.C."

There was a contact number scrawled next to the address—a 323 area code, which, if Levi recalled correctly, was a West Hollywood number.

Levi took a moment to study the sheet, committing the details to memory. The Hay-Adams—classy joint. Not the kind of place he'd expect a low-life to be hanging their hat.

Franco cleared his throat, tentative, and looked over at Dino. "So... uh... Dino, what do we do about the delivery? The lady paid the deposit already. We never got the package, but she's probably still expecting it."

Dino leaned back against the door; arms folded across his chest. His eyes slid toward Levi. "What do you think?"

Levi gave a slight shrug, his expression unreadable. "Shred the folder. Tell her the shipment was lost in transit. Your end of the deal's covered by the deposit. No sense chasing ghosts."

Franco winced.

"Listen to me." Levi gave the guy a steely stare. "You know how to ignore phone calls and e-mails?"

Franco nodded. "Sure… do it all the time."

"Well, do it one more time for this chick." Levi waved dismissively at the manila folder containing her order information. "I'm going to meet up with this Kendra person and take care of things. Don't worry about the delivery. It's done."

Franco nodded, not looking thrilled about it, but clearly relieved to have the decision made for him. He yanked the folder apart at the binding and fed the pages into a small shredder buzzing away on the desk.

Levi stood, giving the crew a final glance. "That's all I needed."

Dino pushed off the doorframe, opening it wide for Levi. The two men stepped out into the warehouse's echoing main floor, the smell of salt air and rust seeping in from the docks.

Once they were clear, Dino shot Levi a sidelong glance. "You got what you need?"

Levi nodded, eyes already distant, focused on the next step. "Yeah. Time to meet this so-called art buyer."

CHAPTER ELEVEN

The business-class cabin of the Lufthansa Airbus A350 was hushed, except for the occasional clink of glassware and the soft hum of the engines. Alicia sat by the window, fingers lightly tapping the armrest, watching as the ground crew outside moved like ants beneath the bright lights of Frankfurt Airport. In the seat next to her, Tony was already half-dozing, his bulk stuffed into the wide leather seat, arms crossed, chin dipping toward his chest. Stowed under the seat directly in front of her, Bagel had curled himself into a black furry ball inside his airline-approved carrier.

"Two more hours until we hit Kyiv," Tony murmured without opening his eyes.

Alicia drained the rest of the mimosa that she'd been drinking and frowned as her head throbbed with a dull ache.

She needed to stop drinking alcohol. Ever since she'd turned twenty-one, she'd had an occasional drink and had enjoyed the very slight buzz it sometimes gave her, but those days had vanished. Now, any time she drank alcohol, it gave her a mild headache. No buzz, no enjoyment, just a dull ache.

She looked down at Bagel and his head popped up, his gold-hued eyes flashed at her, and he settled back into the doughnut shape that he favored. In fact, ever since her bout with cancer and Bagel coming into her life, she'd had this strange reaction to the alcohol.

She remembered what Bagel had done—even though she'd been asleep—or maybe she remembered it as part of a fever dream. In her mind's eye, the cat, who was only a kitten at the time, had puked something onto her stomach. Had she been awake, she would have instantly run to the shower, but instead, all she could recall from that moment was a burning sensation from the golden-hued saliva or whatever it was—that had covered her. It was only later that she'd been told some hard-to-believe tales about tiny, gold-flecked nanites coursing through her system. At the time, she firmly believed Bagel—and those microscopic little fixers he'd puked up on her—had helped her overcome the cancer.

Now, she didn't know what to believe.

Her headache worsened as it registered the most recent gulp of alcohol and Alicia's eyes widened. What if the nanites were treating the alcohol like a poison? Having a strong science background didn't mean she knew how these impossible things worked, but it suddenly made a bit of sense. Instead of letting the alcohol affect her, like a normal person, those so-called little helpers might be breaking down the alcohol with the side-effect being the headache. A literal buzzkill.

Her father had admitted to also being infested with these things, though she had no idea how that had happened. Was that why he never consumed alcohol? She stowed that question away for later, surprised it hadn't dawned on her to put two and two together.

Alicia leaned back, adjusted the seat to recline, and nodded. "At least this leg is direct."

Their route had been straightforward enough: Newark to Frankfurt, quick layover, now on to *Kyiv Boryspil International Airport (KBP)*. Lufthansa's first-class upgrade made the long haul bearable—lie-flat seats, hot towels, the works. But even luxury couldn't strip the edge from the mission ahead.

She'd gotten a meager intelligence briefing from Denny about the location, studied the satellite images of the area as well as a road map of that part of the capital city.

The flight attendant stopped by, smiling politely. "Would you like a top-up on your drink, ma'am?"

Alicia waved it off with a soft smile. "No, thank you." She slid her headphones back on and scrolled through the flight tracker. The map displayed their progress: skirting Polish airspace, soon descending into Ukraine. ETA just under two hours.

As the engines throttled up for takeoff, Alicia felt that familiar moment of pressure—gravity pinning her to the seat as the aircraft clawed its way into the sky. She glanced down at the carrier. Bagel barely stirred, eyes closed, his fat body sprawled comfortably across the plush liner, oblivious to the physics at play.

The announcement came overhead in clipped German-accented English: "Cabin crew, prepare for landing." Followed immediately by the same in Ukrainian, the consonants sharp and unfamiliar. Alicia tapped the small earpiece in her right ear—a sleek little device Denny had supplied for her previous trip to the Vatican. The Ukrainian phrase buzzed softly into translated English against her eardrum.

"Please remain seated. We will be on the ground shortly in Kyiv."

The descent was smooth. The wheels kissed the runway with a low rumble as the A350 rolled to a gradual stop. Overhead compartments clicked open almost before the seatbelt sign was off, the rush of passengers eager to deplane, conversations in Ukrainian, Russian, and German blending into a dissonant backdrop.

The air that greeted them as they stepped off the jet bridge was heavy, tinged with jet fuel and the faint metallic tang of snow-dampened air outside. Frost clung to the edges of the windows, and somewhere in the distance, the orange glow of sodium lamps washed over the tarmac.

Bagel stretched within the confines of his carrier and let out a massive yawn.

Alicia crouched down, unlatched the carrier door. The cat

gave a dismissive flick of his tail before maneuvering out of the cramped box. She adjusted the baby sling—black canvas, adjustable straps, purchased for her last international trip with the cat.

Bagel wasn't an ordinary cat by any stretch of the imagination. He was smarter, by far, than any animal she knew. So much so that he'd learned to communicate through a series of large plastic buttons he'd pounce on, each broadcasting a copy of her voice saying a particular word. Alicia's apartment back in D.C. had nearly 100 of those stupid things scattered on the floor, and Bagel had taken full advantage. He knew what each one said and made his desires known throughout the apartment.

That was only the beginning…

Bagel stretched once more as Tony grabbed their bag from the overhead compartment. He patted at Alicia's knee alternating between rapid-fire swats and longer presses with his paw, spelling out letters in Morse code.

"Food."

Just because those buttons weren't around, that didn't mean Bagel couldn't tell her what he was thinking. His vocabulary was limited, but the idea that he could do any of this made him a super-genius of the animal world.

Alicia smiled at the cat as he stared at her, his large golden eyes unblinking. "As soon as we get to the hotel and settled, I'll make you get something. I promise."

The cat sniffed loudly as his gaze shifted to the pouch.

Alicia loosened the straps enough to give him space.

Hopping up onto her lap, he slid into the sling, settling his bulk across her torso, head poking out just above the rim like a furry sentinel. His tail swished once, then he gave a resigned sigh and rested his chin on the fabric.

"Looking good, Bagel," Tony smirked as he hauled a large duffel onto his shoulder.

∼

The airport's interior was sterile, lit by harsh fluorescent lighting, the ceiling a grid of black acoustic tiles. Overhead, an announcement echoed through the hall in Ukrainian:

"Шановні пасажири, багаж рейсу з Франкфурта зараз доставляється на стрічку номер три."

Alicia's earpiece quietly translated:

"Attention passengers: Baggage from the Frankfurt flight is now arriving at carousel number three."

The smell of over-brewed coffee mixed with the faint sting of cleaning chemicals. Travelers clustered at baggage claim, some shouting into phones, others tugging at stubborn suitcases.

They retrieved their bags without incident—one hard-shell Pelican case marked discreetly with standard travel stickers, nothing that would catch the wrong kind of eye.

Outside, the cold snapped at their faces the moment the sliding doors hissed open. It was only November, but this place was at least ten if not twenty degrees cooler than back home.

Suddenly Alicia felt a surge of nervous energy flush through her. This was no joke. They were in post-war Ukraine and she didn't really know what they were facing.

To make things even worse, she currently had no weapons on her whatsoever.

Bagel squirmed, rearranging himself so his back faced the cool breeze instead of his face.

Taxi drivers clustered at the curb, smoking under the yellow glow of streetlights, holding placards scrawled with names in Cyrillic. Beyond them, the dark outlines of transport vans and black sedans idled along the curb.

Tony flagged a cab—an aging black Mercedes sedan, the interior smelling faintly of wet leather and clove cigarettes.

The driver, a wiry man with deep-set eyes and a wool cap pulled low over his forehead, gave them a nod and tried to help with the bags Tony was carrying, but with a simple look the man backed off and opened the trunk and held the rear passenger door open.

Tony closed the trunk and entered through the driver's side.

Alicia slid into the back seat beside Tony, Bagel adjusting in her sling with a soft grunt.

As the man slid behind the wheel, Alicia leaned forward slightly and spoke in Russian. "Do you speak Russian?"

The driver's eyes met hers in the rearview mirror. He gave a small, tired smile. *"Yes, a little. Russian is fine."*

Alicia nodded, relieved that the Russian language training

she'd gotten with the Outfit would come in handy since she had practically zero knowledge of Ukrainian. She still had her phone ready on her lap, its translation app open and waiting, but it looked like she wouldn't need it—at least not yet.

As they pulled away from Boryspil Airport and merged onto the main highway toward the city center, the driver spoke again in Russian, his voice calm, enunciating the words carefully, which made it easier for her as well as her earbud to keep up.

"This road here, it used to be lined with trees—old linden trees, before the expansion project."

She glanced at Tony, who almost certainly had no clue what was being said, and she gave him an ongoing abbreviated summary of what the driver was saying.

"Back when I worked at the Kyiv History Museum, I gave tours about this area. Then... things changed."

He didn't have to say what "things" meant. The war was a constant ghost in the conversation.

"They turned my museum into a supply depot in 2022. Some of

the exhibits were saved, many weren't. So, I started driving a cab."

He shrugged, not bitter, just resigned. *"You adapt. Ukrainians are good at that."*

The city gradually unfolded outside the windows—post-Soviet apartment blocks, brutalist architecture softened by cold streetlamps, the occasional glint of gold onion domes peeking between buildings. Streets were quiet, wet from earlier snowmelt, the air heavy with diesel and chimney smoke.

"We are entering the cultural district," the driver noted as they turned down a narrow cobblestone street. *"Old Kyiv. This area survived the worst of the shelling. Many buildings here are pre-revolution. It has character."*

The conversation continued for another ten minutes until they turned onto a quieter street lined with worn cobblestones and wrought-iron balconies, the driver gestured ahead with a gloved hand.

"There it is," he said. "Готель 'Прем'єр Палац', Київ."

He glanced at them in the mirror, then repeated in English, "Premier Palace Hotel." He switched back to Russian. *"Very famous. Used to be where ministers and artists stayed—even before the war."*

Alicia nodded, recognizing the cadence of the local pronunciation. Bagel shifted in her sling, his ears twitching as the cab rolled to a gentle stop under the glow of the hotel's entry lights.

The Premier Palace Hotel Kyiv, an ornate holdover from the days of czars and oligarchs, stood like a wedding cake at the edge of the city's cultural district. Marble floors, heavy drapes, the faint smell of polish and expensive cologne. The concierge gave the briefest glance at their passports before handing over two keycards.

"We have adjoining rooms," Alicia reminded Tony as she slipped her card into the reader. Room 514 for her, 516 for him.

Bagel stirred in the sling, eyes blinking slowly as Alicia palmed the door open, stepping into the room. Warm air, thick carpeting, neutral tones. She dropped the Pelican cases near the wall and gently lifted Bagel out of the sling, setting him onto the bed. He yawned, stretched languidly, then immediately began grooming his tail, not particularly curious about his new surroundings.

Alicia looked over at Bagel and said, "I'll be back in a second."

She walked over to Tony's room, gave the thick wooden door a knock and almost immediately the door opened.

"What's up?" Tony asked as he removed his leather jacket.

Alicia leaned in from the hallway and spoke barely above a whisper. "Our target in the morning is only about four blocks from here. It should be about a ten-minute walk, max. My guy says that there's someone entering the warehouse at 8:00 a.m. every morning, so be ready."

"Is 7:00 a.m. good?"

She nodded. "That works, see you then."

"Have a good night."

Alicia turned away from Tony's door and checked her watch.

Her night wasn't over yet.

She needed to fix their weapons problem.

∼

Alicia turned down a narrow side street just past Taras Shevchenko Boulevard, her breath misting in the cold night air. The wet pavement gleamed beneath amber streetlamps. She pulled up her collar and kept walking, passing shuttered cafes and a bar playing muffled pop music through double-paned glass.

The address Brice had given her didn't look like much—a faded building facade with Cyrillic graffiti spray-painted across the lower bricks, a heavy green door set into an arched stone entryway. Having memorized Brice's rather extensive set of instructions, she grinned, knowing that the door wasn't the entrance.

The real entrance was across the alley, set behind a wrought iron gate that looked sealed shut from the outside. Rusted, overgrown with ivy—but near the base, hidden in the shadow of a drainpipe, was a small brass bust of Tsar Nicholas II mounted on a pedestal no taller than a footstool. She knelt and did what Brice had instructed: tapped the crown twice, then twisted the bust's head to the left.

A faint *click* sounded.

A section of the iron fence disengaged with a hydraulic hiss and swung open silently.

She stepped through.

A second steel door waited just beyond, tucked behind the

façade of a bricked-over storefront that hadn't sold anything since the Cold War.

Fluorescent lights flickered to life above her as the front door sealed itself from the outside world. Alicia couldn't help but wonder how her life had turned into a James Bond film.

The hallway had a décor that reminded Alicia of some old-time movie sets. She panned her gaze across the walls and spotted what she was looking for. It was a hand scanner disguised inside the frame of an old Soviet-era payphone bolted to the wall. Alicia walked up to it and pressed her palm flat against the rusted keypad. A second *click* echoed, deeper, like the tumblers of a safe unlocking.

The inner door swung open into another world.

Warmth washed over her, dry and heavy with pipe tobacco, old wood polish, and dust baked into velvet drapes. The Kyiv safehouse was modeled not after post-Soviet utilitarianism, but after pre-revolution opulence. A grand chandelier, though missing a few crystals, hung above a parquet floor. Heavy red curtains framed the tall windows, which were blacked out from the inside with matte panels. The wallpaper was floral, faded, and authentic—probably hadn't changed since 1912.

Alicia stepped in and paused just inside the threshold, boots clicking against the wood.

From behind a curtain, a man appeared—thin, pale, in his late sixties, wearing a dark Cossack-style coat over pressed slacks, his silver hair combed straight back. His posture was erect, his gaze sharp behind wire-framed glasses.

He said nothing at first. Then: "Good Evening" he said in Russian.

Alicia gave a nod and replied in semi-fluent Russian. "I think I'm expected."

Instead of moving aside, the man stepped closer. In one hand, he held a small-caliber Makarov pistol, already drawn but kept low and steady—not aimed with obvious hostility, but seemingly out of ritual. His other hand extended palm-up.

Alicia reached into her pocket, retrieved the Outfit identification coin, and held it out, as if for inspection.

The older man gripped the other half of the coin and almost immediately a green LED flashed brightly, confirming their membership in the clandestine organization.

He let go of the coin and holstered the pistol in one fluid, polite motion—like a maître d' putting away a wine opener. Then, silently, he gestured her forward.

Just like Harlem, the layout was more labyrinthine than it appeared—false walls, corridors hidden behind sliding panels, cameras set into antique frames. The Outfit had retrofitted the past into a secure present.

They entered a large room and on the far side, a false wall swung open, revealing a small arched vault lit by a chandelier no bigger than a dinner plate. The locker inside bore no lock—just a metal chessboard mounted to the door, with what she presumed were magnetized game pieces placed on various squares.

When she'd read Brice's instructions, she'd thought the man had gone bonkers, but this puzzle meshed inside of an enigma was unfolding just like he'd described. Alicia scanned the game board, found the knight and with some force moved it to the position Brice had described. She did the same for the rook and as soon as she set the pawn into position there was another mechanical *click*. The locker opened.

She peered inside and spotted plastic cases. Clean and matte black.

The first held her Ruger LCP II, nestled inside a foam cutout, a spare mag, in-waistband holster, and a suppressor the size of a Sharpie marker.

The second case was marked with a thin red stripe—Tony's. Inside, a Sig P229 with two fifteen-round mags, and an IWB holster fit for the 9mm.

She packed the gear into her satchel, the weight settling against her hip with a sense of comfort.

The idea of being unarmed on any mission was beyond comprehension, and unfortunately some of Esther's goodies hadn't yet arrived, so leaning on the Outfit for some help seemed like the sensible route.

The old man stood in the doorway, arms folded behind his back. Silent. Watching.

She turned away from the locker and gave him a small nod. "Thank you."

He replied with only a slight incline of the head.

As she turned to leave, the chandelier overhead flickered once—and almost certainly that meant something had just happened. A hallway moved or something else happened to disorient her, just like in Harlem.

But to her surprise, the old man escorted her back the way they came and in no time the steel door sealed behind her with a hydraulic hiss as she exited the safe house. Outside, the iron gate clanked shut, and the bust of the last tsar returned to his eternal vigil.

CHAPTER TWELVE

Levi stood in the shadows of the hotel ballroom as it pulsed with the low hum of conversation, punctuated by bursts of applause as hopeful contestants filtered on and off the stage. Stage lights flared against deep-red velvet curtains, and a panel of judges perched at a table draped in black linen, sipping bottled water and murmuring into microphones. Overhead, a giant banner declared in bold serif font:

The Diva: National Tour Auditions.

He stood just behind the velvet rope, overdressed in a dark-gray pinstriped suit, sipping bad hotel coffee from a plastic cup, pretending he was only half-interested. In truth, he'd worked the angles to be here. A quick call to Dino scored him a connection with a local union member who was working the show. That got him a badge to slip past the ropes, the throngs of people outside, and into the event, but it was the blonde near the judges' table he was watching.

Kendra Holstrom was in her mid-forties—luminous skin, piercing gray eyes, and a posture that radiated old-Hollywood confidence. She wore a black sheath dress with subtle gold threading, her honey-blonde hair swept into a glossy twist. She was talking to someone from the production crew, but every now and then her gaze skimmed the room—and eventually landed on Levi.

He wasn't dressed like one of the crew, nor did he look like one of the contestants or their family. He looked more like a business executive in a fitted suit, red tie, and not a hair out of place.

Her gaze lingered on him for a moment. Their eyes met, and she turned away—just as a faint smile flickered across her otherwise stoic expression.

Levi navigated his way toward her, passing through a throng of crew members and contestants, easing in beside her just as the next contestant took the stage. He had spent much of last night learning more about this woman—her job history, and even spent a few hours learning about the technical aspects of music appreciation. The domain had an entire set of vocabulary that was unique to itself, and he listened to the contestant on stage.

The girl was pretty, and she launched into a pop ballad with operatic flourishes—ambitious, but dangerous territory. The studying from last night and into the early morning helped him hear things that he'd previously not even been conscious of. The girl was leading with her chest voice but trying to float through the high notes like a soprano. He heard strain creeping in. Her passaggio wasn't clean—there was no breath anchor under the transitions. Then came the run. Sloppy articulation.

"She's scooping notes instead of placing them. Pretty tone, but what's with the vocal fry all of a sudden?" Levi muttered under his breath, just loud enough for her to hear.

Kendra glanced in his direction and then shifted fully toward him as she raked her gaze from head to toe, assessing the stranger standing within arm's length of her.

As the next contestant walked up to the microphone, she shifted her attention back to the stage.

"I thought she had a pretty tone as well, good natural resonance in the mask. But I agree, some of her choices were less than ideal." The talent scout glanced at Levi. "Are you one of the contestants' music coaches?"

"No," he said with a hearty chuckle. "Just a longtime fan of the genre."

"Which genre of music is that?" Kendra shifted her gaze back to Levi, ignoring the warbling contestant on the stage.

"Opera mostly. But I've been following this show for a while, and I like the idea of it. Finding a diamond in the rough is always a draw for the audience."

She tilted her head, eyes focused on his green visitor's badge. "So, what exactly are you doing here? This is a closed set. If you're not a coach or a contestant or working the show—"

"To be honest, I know a couple people from the production company." He didn't, but at least he'd done enough research to be able to name-drop a couple of them, to avoid having to say how he got the visitor's badge. "I pulled a couple strings just to get a bit of a backstage view of what's going on. I'm just curious, and like I said, *The Diva* has had some fantastic opera in the past, which is really my thing."

Levi pointed at the stage as a new contestant launched into a stripped-down cover of a Rihanna ballad. "Do you hear that? She's fusing the ballad with coloratura phrasing. Pop phrasing layered over bel canto breath control. That's gutsy."

Kendra closed her eyes, listening to the singing and nodded. "You've got a good ear. Do you sing at all?"

"No, that's not one of the things I have in my toolbox of skills. My singing is only good for attracting buzzards and scaring away anyone who isn't deaf."

Kendra laughed, low and genuine. "That's just like my dad. He's obsessed with opera, but I've never heard him even sing a single note."

Another singer began—a male baritone putting a pop twist on Puccini.

Levi's eyes narrowed. "He's got breath control, but his placement's shallow. Beautiful tone, but he's pulling from the throat. He's going to burn out by the bridge."

And just as he'd predicted, the singer's voice practically fell apart a minute later.

Kendra looked at him again, eyes narrowing in appraisal. "Who are you?"

He offered a lazy smile. "Just a fan of opera with a decent ear. A friend told me about the open auditions today and I wanted to see how the sausage is made. You know, get a peek at the stuff that I don't see on TV."

She gave him a long, appraising look. "Well, I'm Kendra."

"Levi," he replied, extending a hand.

They shook. Her grip was firm.

She stared unblinking at him and said, "There's another hour or so of auditions, and then I must talk with the judges a bit. Are you going to be around?"

Levi felt his face getting a bit warm as he nodded. "I can be. Were you interested in grabbing a bite to eat?"

"Are you sure your wife would be okay with that?" she asked, a sly expression blooming on her face.

"Not married. No girlfriend. Not gay."

Kendra laughed heartily and smiled ear-to-ear. "That's very good to hear." She pointed toward the judge's table. "I have to get back to work, but let's meet back here at 7, okay?"

Levi nodded. "I'll be here."

～

They went to *Le Diplomate* on 14th Street, a classic French bistro with white-tiled floors, red leather banquettes, and soft golden lighting. Waiters in crisp shirts and aprons moved gracefully between tables.

"You've been here before," Kendra said, glancing over the menu.

"A few times," Levi replied, unfolding his napkin. "The steak frites are excellent. And the escargots are a guilty pleasure if you're into that kind of thing."

"Oh, I'm pretty adventurous when it comes to a lot of things, food especially." The blonde smiled flirtatiously at Levi and then buried her nose in the menu.

Their waiter arrived—a young man named Henri, whose Parisian accent was too perfect to be faked.

"*Bonsoir, mademoiselle, monsieur.* Are you ready to order?"

Levi let Kendra go first. She skimmed the menu with the ease of someone who dined out often, pausing briefly before tapping a manicured nail next to the *trout almondine.*

"I'll have this," she said, handing the menu to the waiter. "And can we go a bit light on the brown butter sauce?"

"Of course, *mademoiselle.* Light on the brown butter." He turned to Levi, "And you, *monsieur*?"

Levi closed the leather-bound menu with a soft snap.

"The duck à l'orange," he said. "And I'll take it medium rare, please. Whatever root vegetable medley comes with that is fine. And a seltzer to start."

Kendra glanced at him. "Old-school," she said, smiling approvingly. "I like that."

The waiter asked with a polite smile, "Have you had a chance to look over the wine list?"

Levi glanced at Kendra. "You're having the trout, I'm having duck. Might need a little help."

"Of course," the waiter said, nodding. "Let me send over our sommelier."

A moment later, a tall man in a charcoal suit with a silver tastevin around his neck approached their table. He greeted them warmly. "I hear we need a pairing challenge?"

Kendra smirked. "Trout almondine and duck à l'orange."

"A classic contrast," the sommelier said. "But not a problem."

He leaned in slightly. "May I suggest the 2019 Meursault Premier Cru from Domaine Comtes Lafon? It's a white Burgundy—rich, structured, creamy. Has the finesse for the trout and enough backbone to hold its own against the duck's citrus glaze."

Levi nodded. "That sounds like a winner."

He turned to Kendra. "You okay with that?"

She smiled. "More than okay. Let's do it."

∼

Over entrees, they talked—not just music, but childhood memories, travel stories, and their mutual hatred of hotel pillows.

Levi had long ago become a pro at constructing a mundane background for himself to suit whatever purpose he had.

Her trout arrived delicately pan-seared, topped with toasted almonds and a glaze of butter-lemon sauce that shimmered under the ambient lighting. Levi noticed the chef had laid it over a bed of haricots verts tossed with roasted hazelnuts and just the faintest glaze of citrus. His own duck came sliced in medallions, glistening under an orange reduction, plated beside heirloom carrots and a smear of truffle-infused parsnip purée.

"I've had a lot of trout in a lot of cities," Kendra said, taking her first bite, "but this is shockingly well-balanced. Not greasy. That crunch on the almonds? Chef's got a good hand. Thanks for bringing me here, I'd never have treated myself to such a place."

Levi chuckled. "I'm just glad to have an excuse to eat a nice meal versus grabbing generic hotel fare. This is a pleasant surprise for me as well."

She dabbed her lips with her napkin and leaned slightly forward. "So, tell me—what does Levi do when he's not dissecting the singing skills of contestants?"

He smiled and set his fork down with purpose. "I own a private security firm," he said. "We specialize in executive protection. Sometimes VIPs, wealthy clients, sometimes… politicians."

At that, Kendra paused—her wineglass halfway to her lips. A flicker crossed her eyes, the briefest tightening at the corners. Not fear exactly. But interest.

"Politicians, huh?" she said, voice lilting. "That must be a hell of a clientele. Anyone I'd recognize?"

He offered a mild, noncommittal shrug and took a sip of some sparkling water, his wine mostly untouched. "We try to stay behind the curtain, so to speak. Discretion's part of the job."

Kendra tilted her head and studied him a moment, her lips curling. "That's sexy as hell," she said. "I mean, I meet a lot of guys in my line of work, but I don't think I've ever had dinner with a real-life bodyguard type."

He chuckled. "Technically, I'm just the guy with the clipboard these days."

"Uh-huh," she said, clearly unconvinced.

Then it was her turn. "I'm a talent scout," she said. "For *The Diva*. I head up the callback vetting team for the national auditions. That's what brought me to D.C."

"I figured you were someone important," Levi said. "You command a room."

She laughed softly. "That's kind of you. Honestly, though, I'm mostly herding cats—filtering out the delusional, keeping the hopefuls from melting down, and fighting off the occasional stage mom with a vengeance complex."

"I imagine you see the whole spectrum of humanity in a single day."

"Oh, honey," she said, lifting her glass for a toast, "you don't even know."

They clinked glasses. And just like that, the night deepened, rich as the sauce on the duck.

∽

After dinner, they walked along the Tidal Basin, the path lit by low lamps and the shimmer of the water. The Jefferson Memorial loomed white and solemn across the way, and cherry trees rustled faintly in the breeze.

Kendra paused near the railing, gazing out at the reflection of the monument. "That dome almost looks like something out of Florence," Levi said, nodding toward it.

She gave a soft laugh. "Florence. God, my dad would love you."

Levi arched a brow.

"I never really got into art," Kendra admitted, folding her arms as she leaned on the railing. "But my dad—he'd drag me to museums all the time growing up. At least that before he moved to D.C."

"Moved to D.C.? What for?" Levi already knew.

"My dad's Senator Holstrom—from Wisconsin," she said

with a small shrug. "But I don't really connect with that side of him. I was out of the house by the time he turned to politics. My childhood memories with him were cheese curds and Raphael."

Levi turned to her, eyebrows raised. "That's probably what I'd expect from a Midwestern girl, at least the cheese curd part."

She laughed, swatted his arm. "Dad's still obsessed. Sends me on these impossible errands. You have no idea how hard it is to find original Renaissance pieces. Anything remotely authentic gets snapped up before it hits the market."

"Sounds like he's got expensive taste."

"Oh, you have no idea. Last month I was in Lisbon trying to close a deal on a minor Florentine portrait. Turned out to be a forgery."

"You're in the art business now?"

She shook her head. "No, just trying to find something meaningful for him. Something real."

Levi nodded, absorbing that. A collector senator with a thing for Renaissance art.

"Are you ever on the West Coast?" she asked, shifting the mood.

"From time to time," he said. "Especially if I have a reason to go."

She reached into her purse and handed him a sleek black business card. "If you're ever in L.A., call me."

"I will." Levi glanced at the card and pocketed it.

"I'm serious," Kendra said, bumping her shoulder into his. "My feelings will be hurt if you don't call."

Levi smiled. "You have my word. You'll be the first person I call."

They walked back toward civilization and using a phone app, called up an Uber.

"Levi, I really had a good time. I'm not just saying that—you're different than anything I expected."

Levi looked down at her upturned pixie-like face and her eyes glowed under the amber streetlamps. "What exactly were you expecting?"

"I don't know." She shrugged. "Disappointment, I suppose. But you're a mystery wrapped up in this rugged package. It's very sexy."

She leaned in, arms sliding around his neck.

Their lips met in a soft, lingering kiss

Levi was acutely aware of her body against his, the streetlamp overhead casting them in a quiet, golden spotlight.

Her fingers brushed against Levi's chest—and paused.

"Is that a gun?" she whispered, breath catching.

"Yes."

She didn't pull away. One arm still draped around his neck, the other slipping around his waist as she pressed in closer. "So you weren't kidding about the security gig."

"I rarely kid."

She shivered as she pressed against him. "That's so ridiculously hot."

He chuckled.

A car approached, slowing to a stop right next to them.

It was her Uber.

"Want to come up for a drink? My suite's at the Hay-Adams, not too far away."

"I'm on meds," he said with a crooked smile. "I shouldn't be drinking."

She bit her lower lip, voice husky. "You don't have to drink if you don't want to."

He brushed a curl from her cheek. "I'm tempted. Believe me. But I've got work in a few hours. Rain check?"

Kendra studied his face for a couple seconds and sighed. "You promise?"

He kissed her once more, slow and soft. "When I'm on the West Coast, you'll be the first call I make."

She gave his upper arm a gentle squeeze, then turned and climbed into the waiting Uber.

As the Uber pulled away, Levi watched her disappear into the night. He pulled out his phone and dialed.

Brice answered on the second ring, groggy.

"You in the office?"

"It's eleven at night, Levi. No. I'm in bed like most sensible people."

"Fine. I'll see you in the lab first thing in the morning. We've got some old-fashioned legwork to do."

He ended the call and replayed snippets of the evening in his mind.

Dad's still obsessed. Sends me on these impossible errands. You have no idea how hard it is to find original Renaissance pieces.

It had been a productive night.

CHAPTER THIRTEEN

The light outside had barely brightened into morning when Alicia cracked open the window of her hotel room. The air in Kyiv was brittle and cold, sharp with chimney smoke and frost. Inside, the room was quiet save for the faint clink of ceramic as Bagel crunched down on a small bowl of dried sardines she'd picked up at a 24-hour market just around the corner. The cat's ears twitched in rhythm with the noise, clearly enjoying his salty breakfast.

Her phone vibrated.

She grabbed it from the nightstand and put it to her ear. "Yes?"

"Hey, Alicia. Catch you at a good time?"

It was Denny.

"You're calling just in the nick of time. If you've got any good stuff for me about the warehouse, now is really the time I need it."

"Yeah, I figure since your GPS popped up in that part of the world I'd give you a dump of what I know. I'm sending you a couple of MMS messages over Signal, each with some surveillance photos I think you'll find interesting."

Her phone vibrated as her encrypted communication app received the first of Denny's texts.

Alicia thumbed open the encrypted message. Tapping the first attachment, her phone's screen was engulfed with grainy, timestamped stills taken from security camera footage.

"It looks like you tapped into the city's street-level feeds."

"Yup, pretty much all of Europe, especially the Eastern Bloc is surveillance crazy, so that's not too hard to get remote access to."

Alicia flipped through the various images. The warehouse stood in dull gray silhouette against a concrete horizon. One of the messages had video showing men going in and out with routine regularity.

"What am I seeing here, Denny. Anything I should focus on?"

"Yeah, there are two guys that I included in the stills. One's a particularly beefy guy but first let's talk about the other one."

Alicia flipped through the images, focusing on the average-looking Ukrainian dressed in layers, a large nose and jutting chin were the key facial features that stood out to her.

"The first figure is Maksym Petrenko, a Ukrainian national and known Zarkov courier. It took some doing for me to figure out who this guy was, but I was able to track him as he was often running all over Kyiv to buy art ingredients. His purchase history was a bit eclectic—pigment powders, hide glue, calcium carbonate, even rabbit-skin glue."

"Almost sounds like a science project in the making." Alicia said.

"I know, right? Well, you and your father didn't exactly tell me what was going on, but I can kind of figure out from that ingredient list and a bit of research on my part, he's definitely doing something with art using traditional Renaissance-style ingredients that would have been available back then. On one of the purchases, he ended up having to use a credit card and that's all I needed to unwind that mystery. He's traveled back and forth between Ukraine and Moscow at least half a dozen times in the last year. Based on surveillance in the Russian state, which has even more cameras than the Eastern Bloc, I was able to put two and two together. He's definitely a Zarkov associate of some kind. Anyway, that's about all I've got on him."

Alicia nodded as she sat on the edge of her bed. "I'd say that pretty good. What about mystery man number two?"

"He's a tough one, and to be honest, I'd be careful since this one was a nut I couldn't crack."

She flipped to the image of a large, heavyset man clad in a black balaclava and what looked like mirrored glasses.

"Unlike Petrenko who looked like he went to the warehouse nearly every day, our beefy John Doe seems to only make his presence known Mondays, Wednesdays, and Fridays—always midday arrivals, with evening departures."

"I guess you didn't have time to follow him with all the video cameras—"

"No, I tried. Believe me, I tried." Denny spoke emphatically.

"The man traveled with paranoid precision. He avoided every camera lens in the city like he had a map of their locations burned into his brain. Eventually he'd turn into a zone that was conspicuously empty of any surveillance cameras and I'd lose him. There's only so much I can do from about 5,000 miles away."

Alicia scrolled through the remaining texts and spotted one that looked like a call transcript.

- *Timestamp: 16:07 Kyiv Time*
  - *From: "Unknown Male" (Ukraine Warehouse)*
  - *To: "Mikhail" (Zarkov's network, Russia)*
  - *Language: Russian*

Unknown Male: *The Madonna is nearly ready—final varnish goes on Thursday. Courier still arriving Friday?*

Mikhail: *Yes. And he understands to be cautious. He'll bring the folio.*

Unknown Male: *Don't make the same mistake as you did with the last shipment. I wasted a lot of time and energy on that. Are we understood?"*

Mikhail: *Yes, Maestro. The mistake will not happen again. We too had consequences from the last mistake.*

Unknown Male (Maestro?): *And the other client I told you about? The American. What's his status?*

Mikhail: *He's confirmed. The American's order specs are coming in next week. This will be a bigger canvas this time.*

Unknown Male (Maestro?): *I don't care about the size; I just want to make sure things arrive as they should. Make sure I get the biometric data in that folio. We'll be ready as soon as we can be. Just make sure—*

Mikhail: *No mistakes. We know. There will be no mistakes this time.*

[Call Ends]

"What in the world is this transcript about. Who is this Maestro dude?"

"I really can't tell you much more than what I already sent you." Denny sighed. *"However, I did run an analysis on the voices from that phone conversation. The computers analyzed Mikhail's voice and concluded that he's almost certainly a native Russian speaker, likely born near the Ural Mountains east of Moscow, based on his accent. The results for the other guy are a bit unexpected. It's actually amazing what the computers can pick out, because I listened to the conversation in its original form and they both sounded like Ruskies to me, but the computers say that this Maestro guy is almost certainly an American."*

"American?"

"Yes, but all that really means is that whoever this guy is, he likely grew up in America and picked up Russian afterwards. My ear for hearing accents in a foreign language must be complete garbage, but I ran the analysis on two different systems and they both came back with American at an eighty-plus percent likelihood."

"Okay, that's definitely more than I had to begin with. Anything else you have?"

"No, that's it. I just wanted to give you a dump on what I've managed to collect so far ahead of you doing your thing."

"Thanks Denny, I appreciate it. Speaking of doing my thing, it's that time. If you learn anything else, you know how to get me."

Alicia set the phone down and replayed the conversation in her mind. The one thing that Denny had dug up that helped with her plans was the confirmation that the warehouse was likely where they were creating forgeries on a regular basis.

That and she probably wanted to get there first thing, avoiding the presence of whoever this Maestro was. There were currently too many unknowns about that man for her comfort.

She glanced at Bagel, who was busy licking sardine crumbs from the bottom of his dish. "Okay, it's time for you to earn your keep."

～

Alicia rigged Bagel's sleek black harness with practiced ease, threading the reinforced straps around his chest and shoulders until it fit like a second skin. The modified GoPro—matte black, no LED indicators, and slimmed down with a custom shell—clicked into place with a snug snap beneath the ruff of his shoulder fur. The camera itself rested on the cat's chest, angled to capture a clear view of whatever direction the feline explored.

Bagel shifted under the weight, then looked up at her with

narrowed eyes—equal parts disgruntled and dignified. The feline equivalent of a deep sigh.

"I know," she said, brushing a hand down his back. "It's probably not the most comfortable thing to wear, but at least it'll do the job."

He flicked his tail once in response.

There was a light knock at her door, followed by Tony's whispered voice from the hallway.

She walked over and opened it. Tony loomed large in the doorway. He was wearing black jeans, combat boots, and a charcoal cargo jacket that gave him the rugged look of a seasoned ex-soldier. His gaze swept over her—combat-cut fatigues, dark knit cap, and hands tucked into her coat pockets.

"Nice getup," he said, nodding with approval.

Alicia smirked and reached one hand beneath her coat to adjust the strap of the concealed shoulder holster hugging her ribs. The matte-black Ruger rode snug under her left arm, hidden beneath the canvas folds.

Tony raised a brow, lips curling into a grin. He pointed and said, "I see you've somehow managed to find a new toy."

Alicia gave a sly smile as she zipped her jacket halfway up, concealing the weapon entirely. "I have one for you as well."

She reached into a hidden inner pocket inside her coat and pulled a slim, black pistol wrapped in a small microfiber cloth. Alicia handed it to him grip-first.

"It's a Sig P229." She reached into her duffel and tossed him a fitted in-waistband holster for the gun. "You think I'd have us walking around this city without a little something extra?"

Tony chuckled as he undid his belt to thread the holster.

"Hey, I'm not paid to think too much on this job—that's your department. I'm just the muscle."

He popped the magazine out of the gun, pocketed it, and then racked the slide. Catching the chambered bullet as it was ejected, he gave it a quick look and nodded. "Good, a nine-millimeter will do the job." Topping off the magazine, he slammed it back into the gun and holstered it.

Alicia smiled as he adjusted his clothes, making sure the gun didn't print through his shirt. The man had spent his life on the streets as a mob soldier—Tony would be a reliable backup if things went sideways.

She slipped on a pair of black gloves. "Are you ready?"

Tony nodded.

Alicia shifted Bagel into his sling, the cat's head poking out just above the zipper line. His golden eyes scanned the room with soldierly alertness.

She pulled up the GoPro app on her phone, activated Bagel's device and immediately saw the live video feed—an angled view of the hotel room wall as the cat stretched in his sling.

"All right," she said, brushing a strand back beneath her cap. "Let's go see what's really happening at the warehouse."

∼

The Kyiv morning had grown no warmer as Alicia and Tony followed the cracked sidewalk into the warehouse district. The air reeked of damp concrete and engine oil, thick with the hush of industry. Their breath came out in visible puffs as they approached the building.

The warehouse sat hunched at the end of a narrow street, its silhouette bleeding into the morning haze like an afterthought. It was a large, flat structure—single-story, windowless except for a few high-set panes that reflected nothing but a dull gray sky. The exterior was an unremarkable patchwork of soot-streaked concrete and faded industrial paint, blending seamlessly with the other buildings around it. Nothing flashy. Nothing to draw the eye. Exactly the kind of place you'd overlook if you didn't already know what went on inside.

The air was sharp with the bite of cold and the copper tang of nearby train tracks. Somewhere in the distance, a dog barked. Closer, a smoker's cough echoed from behind a loading dock, then silence again. Their footsteps crunched over frost-slick gravel, the sound loud in the early stillness.

Alicia slowed her pace.

Something wasn't right.

It wasn't anything she could name—just a tension in the atmosphere, like the building itself was holding its breath. Her fingers twitched near the hem of her jacket, where the slim weight of the pistol tucked into her shoulder holster pressed against her ribs.

"This could go sideways fast," she said under her breath.

Tony walked a half step behind her, his hands tucked into the pockets of his cargo jacket. He didn't speak, but when she glanced at him, he gave a small nod. Then, without fanfare, he patted his waistband—the subtle, practiced gesture of a man double-checking his concealed weapon.

They kept walking, boots scraping against frostbitten concrete. At this hour—just after 8 a.m.—the city was still waking up. Somewhere overhead, a pigeon beat its wings against an iron fire escape.

Alicia adjusted the sling that held Bagel, who shifted with a soft grunt, ears flicking forward. The cat was silent, but alert.

She let out a slow breath, eyes fixed on the squat metal door ahead.

"Let's hope they buy my story," she said.

Tony gave her one last sidelong glance. "And if they don't?"

Alicia's smile didn't reach her eyes. "Then the fun begins."

She adjusted the sling across her chest. Bagel shifted slightly inside, his gold-flecked eyes wide but silent, his camera rig snugly secured around his chest. She paused at the rusted door of the warehouse, turned to Tony, and gave a sharp nod.

"Let me do the talking. Not a word."

Tony nodded once, his eyes scanning the surroundings.

She pulled at the handle, half expecting it to be locked.

The metal door groaned open into a cavernous space soaked in artificial light and the acrid sting of solvents. The scent of linseed oil, wood dust, and aged varnish coiled in the air. Fluorescents buzzed above like anxious insects.

A single desk sat near the entrance, manned by a balding man in a cable-knit sweater and a quilted vest. He was flipping through a ledger, pen tucked behind his ear. When he saw her, he paused, his brow furrowing.

This was the same man she'd seen pictures of on her phone. Maksym.

Alicia walked straight toward him, confidence in her posture, Russian on her lips.

"I'm here on behalf of Zarkov," she said evenly in Russian.

"There's been a concern with one of the recent orders. I need to review a piece currently in progress."

The man blinked, clearly caught off guard. He stood slowly. "You're one of Zarkov's people? We've never had a client come here."

She shrugged. "We received a complaint from a buyer and wanted to resolve things in person. The quality didn't meet expectations."

His face drained a shade, his gaze flicked over to Tony and back to her. "That's... odd. The Maestro hasn't mentioned anything to me. No one said there was an issue."

"Not yet," Alicia said, folding her arms. "That's why I'm here. We'd prefer to handle this in person, so that no further incidents occur."

The man hesitated, tilted his head and asked, "The Maestro isn't in right now, but maybe I can help. Can you tell me which order it was that had the mistake?"

Alicia shook her head. "The mistake is done, I'm more concerned about the project you're working on now. I want to make sure things are going as planned, and I want to see what's being done for myself."

The man stood, then motioned her forward. "Follow me."

As they moved deeper into the space, Alicia took in every detail—the rows of canvases stacked in drying racks, the polished easels, the faintly humming dehumidifiers in the corners. She kept mental track of every open and closed door.

From inside the sling, Bagel shifted. Alicia didn't look down, but her hand settled briefly on the cat's back.

That was it.

Showtime.

∽

Halfway through the maze of art paraphernalia, Bagel suddenly leapt from the sling. The desk clerk startled.

"He probably saw a mouse," Alicia said smoothly. "He'll be back."

The man led her to a wide worktable lit by a pair of articulated lamps. Resting on its surface was a half-completed painting—lush with color and masterfully done. A woman was sitting at the worktable, brush in hand, looking up from her work. "Yes?"

Maksym explained something to her quickly in Ukrainian.

Alicia's earbud picked up the words and translated the conversation in real-time.

"She has questions about the art. Just answer truthfully what you know."

Alicia took a step closer, eyeing the crackle patterns in the paint, the gold leaf gilding, the tension in the canvas.

"Do you recall who the original artist was?" she asked.

"This is attributed to Domenico Ghirlandaio," the woman said in Russian, pride in her tone.

Maksym added, "This is the next commissioned piece your people requested for us to ship to a buyer in the U.S."

Alicia nodded and circled the table. "What medium is being used?"

"Tempera and oil, traditional blend. Rabbit-skin glue base," the woman responded. "The canvas is new but treated with historical gesso layering. The frame's reclaimed oak, late 19th century."

This woman almost certainly knew the craft better than Alicia did. She pressed further, draining the queue of questions she'd trained herself to ask—pigment sourcing, drying time, brush types. She answered each with the calm precision of someone deeply invested in her work.

"And when is this due for delivery?"

"Another week or two," Maksym responded, "depending on final inspection."

"Inspection?" Alicia asked. "What kind of inspection?"

The man hesitated. "Our Maestro checks everything before it leaves."

"What exactly does he look for?" she asked, tilting her head.

The man gave a dry laugh. "You'd have to ask him. I just keep track of needed supplies and the artists paint."

"And where is the Maestro now?"

The man gestured to a closed steel door on the far side of the warehouse, its surface scuffed and flecked with old paint. "Normally he's in his office. But he's not due for another couple hours."

Alicia nodded once and gave the door an extra second of scrutiny. Heavy frame. Reinforced hinges. She filed it away—just another detail for later.

They began the walk back through the maze of canvases and

solvent-stained floors. Alicia let her gaze wander without being obvious, tracking every security camera, every closed door, every corridor they passed. The deeper they'd gone, the more the place felt like a honeycomb—spacious and open in some parts, but pocked with quiet corners and blind spots.

A sudden skitter of motion drew her eye—Bagel, padding into view from behind a column of stacked lumber, his tail held high like a flag. His black fur was matted with dust, and one ear bore a clear streak of yellow paint. He slunk toward her like he'd been somewhere he wasn't supposed to be.

The warehouse attendant blinked. "I see he found his way back to you."

"Told you," Alicia said, tone light. She crouched and lifted the flap of the sling. Bagel hopped in without hesitation, turning a tight circle before settling into a loaf, one eye still half open, watching.

The man gave a faint chuckle, uneasy but polite. "Interesting cat."

"You have no idea," Alicia murmured. "I appreciate the quick visit and the artist—I didn't catch her name."

"Helga."

"Well, Helga was very helpful. I'll report back to my superior and thank you again for your assistance."

Maksym wrung his hands nervously. "Is there anything else you needed?"

Alicia shook her head. "No, we're done here."

The fluorescent lights buzzed overhead as they stepped past the work area and back into the entry. Alicia gave the attendant a nod and a quick thank you, then pushed open the main door. The hinges creaked again, and a blast of cold air spilled in like a wave.

Outside, the silence of morning had given way to the distant thrum of trucks somewhere in the district. A diesel engine roared from a nearby loading dock. Alicia tugged her jacket tighter and pulled the sling's flap over Bagel, shielding him from the wind.

She stroked the top of his head as they moved away from the warehouse, her eyes never leaving the entrance behind them.

"That went well," she murmured.

Tony walked alongside her and asked, "Okay, so is that it with the warehouse?"

"No, not even close." Alicia laughed.

"So this was just us casing the joint, eh?"

She looked up at Tony and grinned. "It sounds like you've done this kind of thing before—surveillance and such."

With his hands stuffed into his jacket pockets, Tony shrugged. "You call it surveillance, I call it other things, but either way, I'm thinking you're wanting to get into that metal door we both saw."

Alicia pressed her lips together as they continued walking toward their hotel. Tony may look and sound like a musclehead at times, but the man was smart and very aware of his surroundings. Almost like he was a yin to her yang.

Bagel let out a chirp-like noise and Alicia rubbed the top of his head.

"First let's see what Bagel's scouting mission delivered and we can work out the next steps."

Bagel's ears twitched. His body was warm against her chest,

but his quiet stillness had a tension to it—like he'd been listening to the conversation and wasn't thrilled with what he was hearing.

"Did you find anything interesting?" she murmured.

Bagel let out a low growl, reached out and began tapping her chest with his paw.

Alicia's smile vanished. She did the translation in her head.

"Bad. Very bad."

Alicia picked up her pace but remained silent.

What could he have seen to react that way?

CHAPTER FOURTEEN

He didn't usually do this kind of thing.

He was a runner—Hill contracts, mostly. Documents, catered lunches, the occasional vanity box from lobbyists with just enough charm to make security ignore the rules. Nothing serious. Nothing weird.

But this one... yeah, this one had a little itch to it.

The guy who handed him the box was clean-cut, no accent, and no real tell--dressed like every other staffer on K Street. But what stood out wasn't the pitch—it was the money. Half of it.

A torn hundred-dollar bill, crisp down the diagonal, folded into the corner of a route manifest. It was a good chunk of change for a simple delivery, and he wasn't born yesterday. The guy was probably someone who didn't want a picture to be taken with him handing something to a senator. Probably something shady, but shady crap happened all the time in this town, and he wasn't about to judge. The guy hadn't said much:

"She'll be walking from Hart to Russell at 7:45. That's your window. No detours. No questions. Just make the handoff. If she takes it—you'll get the other half."

So here he was. In D.C.'s underbelly—the Senate tunnels—where the ceilings were low, the lights buzzed with decades of nervous energy, and the air always smelled like old stone and wet paper. Marble and modernity upstairs, steam pipes and politics down here.

He checked his phone. 7:38 a.m. Game time.

He was dressed right. Gray slacks, blue shirt, red lanyard with a fake tag that said "Virginia Agricultural Council." Nobody looked twice at him. Not in this hallway.

The box under his arm was light—matte-finished walnut, maybe cedar. No wrapping. Just a clean black stencil across the top:

"Montpelier Chocolatiers – Artisan Reserve – Handcrafted in Culpeper, VA"

Even had a foil seal in the corner, like it came from a farmer's market with a PR budget.

He turned the corner into the main artery of the Hart-Russell connector, just in time to see her coming—Senator Elaine Carrington, flanked by a pair of aides and still mid-conversation. She didn't move like most of the senators—no stiff posture, no sense of superiority. Just direct, grounded. Sharp eyes that made you want to blink first.

He stepped forward, just two paces off her path, and held the box out like it was something he did ten times a day.

"Senator Carrington," he said, just loud enough to be heard but not draw eyes. "From the Montpelier folks. Specialty drop."

She slowed. Not stopped—just slowed—and glanced at the box. One of her aides gave a quick look, as if running a silent risk matrix in his head.

She took it. That was all. One hand, confident grip. Her eyes flicked to the stencil, then to him.

"You with Agricultural?" she asked casually.

He gave a half-smile, short and respectful. "Just the runner, ma'am. They said it was time-sensitive and for you only."

She nodded once and moved on, box under her arm, talking again before she hit the next junction.

With a surreptitious aim of his phone, he snapped a picture of the receding senator with the package and smiled.

He turned without pausing, took the tunnel stairwell, and only let out the breath he'd been holding when the echo swallowed the sound of her heels.

He reached into his pocket. The burner phone buzzed once. Unknown number. Text only.

He answered, and a voice asked, *"Did she take it?"*

"She did."

"Good, I'm sure she'll be thrilled with it. Meet me at the same spot. The other half is yours."

The line disconnected and he felt the folded edge of the torn hundred in his hand. He slipped it back into his pocket and smiled.

Not a bad hour's work, he told himself.

∼

Kyiv, Ukraine

Premier Palace Hotel – Room 514

Alicia sat on the edge of the bed, phone in hand. Bagel was curled against her thigh like a loaded spring. She'd told Tony to get some rest—their op would be just after midnight.

She'd reviewed the warehouse feed Bagel had captured and felt a growing unease in her gut.

She tapped out a message to Mason.

"Hypothetical: What if I confirm I've got the guy who killed Calloway in my sights? What's the goal?"

Three dots appeared.
    Then vanished.
    Then came back.

"Take him out. Let us know. Cleanup crew's already on standby. Don't get yourself dead."

Bagel blinked up at her. She didn't smile.
    Was the Maestro the guy, or not?
    Alicia knew in her gut—the answer was behind that metal door.
    She locked the screen and whispered, "If he killed the senator, then he deserves it."

Bagel patted out a pattern on her thigh. *"Bad. Very bad."*

Not sure how to read it, her throat tightened. She prayed that she was doing the right thing.

∼

The wind off the Potomac had a bitter edge as Levi parallel parked the sedan on 31st Street. He stepped out, slipped his phone into his inner coat pocket, and scanned the sidewalk. The neighborhood was intentionally forgettable — a few boarded-up shops, graffiti-tagged brickwork, and the faint scent of fryer grease wafting from the chicken joint down the block.

He walked south; his pace unhurried. An old man on the corner barked a request for food, but Levi didn't break stride. Just ahead, under a chipped wooden sign featuring a rooster and a longhorn, he paused.

The door creaked open with a practiced pull, and he stepped into a bar that reeked of stale beer and varnish. The lighting was dim, just bright enough to reveal the dust motes hanging in the air. Behind the counter, the bartender didn't speak, just gave Levi a nod.

Levi returned it and approached the man in the tailored gray suit seated at the bar. Pale eyes flicked toward him. Mason tapped a coin against the bartop and offered it to him.

He grabbed the other half of the coin and almost instantly a tiny LED flashed green. Mason pocketed the coin.

Mason gave him a sidelong glance and said, "Brice just beat you here."

Levi nodded as he stood by the bar and asked, "What are you doing here so early?"

The compact Director of the Outfit shook his head. "It's not early, I just finished up the prior day's work and figured I'd nurse a beer."

Levi patted Mason on the shoulder and said in a whispered tone, "And this is also why I never wanted to be full time with you guys. I like having some time to myself."

Mason shrugged and said, "Say 'hi' to Alicia for me."

"Will do," he lied and made his way to the men's room at the back of the bar, opened the door, and stepped inside.

Three stalls. Two urinals. One "Out of Order" sign.

Harold was already there—perched on a stool, cleaning his glasses with a hand towel like hanging out in the bathroom was the most natural thing in the world. He gave Levi a glance but didn't speak. Just offered him a folded towel.

Levi took it. Familiar weight. No need for confirmation.

He stepped into the marked stall, shut the door, and pressed the towel to the flushing lever.

One flush. The floor dropped.

The world shifted.

The brown-paneled stall was gone, replaced by descending walls of gray concrete. The soft whirr of hydraulics accompanied the ride down, along with a faint vibration underfoot. When the lift finally stopped, Levi stepped out into a small, sterile chamber with a handprint scanner beside a single reinforced door.

He placed his hand on the panel.

A blue line swept beneath his palm. Green light. Audible click.

Three locking bolts slid free. The door swung open.

He entered.

The corridor beyond was pure concrete—unadorned, antiseptic, humming with hidden energy. Bright LEDs lit the way. At the end of the hall, another security check blinked silently. Levi leaned in for the retinal scan. Green light again.

He passed through.

The space beyond expanded into something vast—not in opulence, but in scope. Two stories below, a grid of cubicles buzzed with silent activity. Analysts, operatives, technicians—each working on tasks that ranged from the mundane to those that were key to national security. Digital feeds flickered on massive screens suspended from the ceiling: satellite images, heatmaps, headline clips scrolling from across the world.

From the catwalk above, Levi descended into the heart of the Outfit's headquarters, heading toward the dedicated space that Brice occupied. Office C3 was one of the few badge-access offices where the site's quartermaster and technology whiz kid resided. A place not unlike Denny's hidden lair.

He approached the metal door and pressed the button on the door frame.

It took a couple seconds before Levi heard the sound of metal sliding against metal as the lock disengaged and the door opened with the whoosh of hydraulics.

Levi entered, Brice was there — sleeves rolled, a coffee in hand as he watched text scroll quickly on one of the overhead monitors.

"Levi," Brice said, standing. "My systems are all almost done rebooting with the latest IT update."

Levi nodded once and the door behind him closed on well-oiled hinges.

∼

Washington, D.C. – Outfit HQ
Office C3
07:50 a.m.

The steel door slid shut behind Levi with a muted thud. Brice's office was dominated by a large workbench filled with soldering irons, gadgets, and miscellaneous gear the electronics whiz was tinkering with for the Outfit.

The bespectacled head of all gadget-like things turned in his chair and motioned impatiently for him to take a seat. "Okay, your call last night about doing some legwork ruined whatever sleep I was going to get last night. What exactly did you mean by that? Is this about Senator Calloway's case or something else?"

Levi plopped into the chair and rolled closer to Brice. "It's related, and to be honest, I'm not sure if it's a wild goose chase or not, but I'll need your research talent to help me figure out if there's any connection to what I've learned."

Brice stretched his arms to the ceiling, his knuckles popped as he flexed his fingers. "Let's do this." The technology whiz turned to the terminal at his desk and the keys clacked noisily as he typed. "What have you got?"

"Well, I sort of went on a date last night with someone named

Kendra Holstrom," Levi said, wheeling himself next to Brice and watching the overhead monitor.

"Okay, what do you want me to do with—"

"Her father is a Senator, and into artwork as well. Let's just say that I have a hunch he may be on someone's shit list along with that Calloway guy, and—"

"Got it!" Brice's fingers became a blur as the keys made a rapid-fire clacking sound. "Let's see who this Holstrom guy is. The name rings a bell."

Brice's screen flashed again, populating with rows of committee assignments, subcommittee logs, and briefing schedules pulled from closed Senate calendars and leaked federal registers.

"Okay," Brice said, tapping the keys with more urgency. "This guy is not just some junior senator from the cheese state, he's got to have friends in the right places."

Levi's gaze narrowed as he stared at the screen.

Brice let out a low whistle. "Senator Raymond Holstrom is most certainly a currently-elected member of the Senate. He's the senior senator from Wisconsin. He's in his fourth term and sits on some big-boy panels."

He flipped one window to full screen.

Levi nodded. "So, he's on the appropriations committee, I'm guessing that's a plum position?"

Brice let out a chuckle and nodded. "Most senators would give their left testicle to get on one of those appropriations committees." He began counting out the various committees Holstrom was on:

"It looks like he's on two senate appropriations committees, the subcommittee on Defense, the subcommittee on Energy & Water, which happens to oversee NNSA and nuclear weapons R&D."

"Brice, I'm not a D.C. nerd like you, what's the NNSA?" Levi asked.

"It's the National Nuclear Security Administration. Part of the DOE and it's as critical as it sounds."

"Okay—"

"Wait, there's more," Brice interrupted. "Holstrom's on the senate armed services committee and the select committee on intelligence. And here's the kicker," he said, hitting a key and pointing up at the screen. "Guess who else was on the Defense Subcommittee before he dropped dead in his home office?"

Levi leaned back in his chair and stared at the face and brief bio of a familiar image. "Calloway."

"Yup. And not just that. From what I can see here, they were both looped into closed-door briefings on SAPs—Special Access Programs. I can do some digging to crack open what programs they read into, but that might take a bit of time depending on the nature of the access control." Brice turned to Levi and asked, "We know they worked together on some potentially heavy stuff, but how does that help us track down Calloway's killer? Are you even sure Holstrom was a target?"

"Fairly sure..." Levi nodded as his mind raced. "What I'm not sure about is that knowing this has gotten us anywhere. It was a long shot, I suppose. These D.C. politicians all work together on a million things at once."

"You don't know the half of it, Levi. A lot of these guys who play at being at odds with each other in front of the cameras are buddies in private, and some of the ones you'd think are friends because they're in the same party, they can't stand each other. It's all shenanigans 24/7 in this town."

Levi rubbed his jaw, thoughts churning. Then, without looking up, he asked, "Is there anything more you can dig up on Calloway's death? I know I got that intel packet from Mason, but it felt light on details."

Brice tilted his head, already typing. "Yeah, what specifically are you after?"

Levi leaned back in his chair and studied the contents on the screen. "The artwork. The frame. How the hell did something that dangerous make it into a senator's office without raising alarms? That painting should've been screened, tagged, flagged —*something*."

Brice nodded, already flipping through secure server caches. "You're not wrong. Here's the kicker though: Calloway liked to work from his home office and not at the Capitol."

"Wisconsin?"

"No, he was leasing a real swanky place at Kalorama. Multi-million-dollar homes, extremely private, secure, and discreet. The senator was not hurting for funds, it seems. The place he'd rented had a registered pre-approval from the Senate Security Office and the Office of the Director of National Intelligence as a TSF."

"TSF?" Levi said and made a rolling motion with his hand.

"Sorry, it's a Temporary Security Facility, kind of like a SCIF, but on private grounds. Anyway, it took some doing to scrub that place after his death."

Levi narrowed his eyes. "So, there was no Capitol security screening for incoming packages."

"It seems like there wasn't. If the painting had been delivered to his Senate office, it would've gone through the standard checkpoint—a mix of x-rays, swabs, random physical inspection. That might've caught something… or maybe not."

"Maybe not?" Levi frowned. "Explain."

Brice pulled up a file and pointed up at the screen. The screen was filled with technical details of what was found. "I'll summarize: The artwork arrived sealed inside what looked like a high-end plastic security bag. We sometimes use similar things for diplomatic pouches. Even though the bag may have looked normal, it wasn't normal plastic—it was in effect a biometrically-locked Faraday bag. A bag made of plasticized steel mesh. Anyone trying to open the bag would have found it a pretty interesting challenge. You couldn't slice it open with box cutters, and about the only thing that would have gotten you through was a decent pair of bolt cutters. It looks like the bag was after-the-fact run through x-ray scanners and anything inside would have registered as a low-density unknown object, which usually would pass through without raising much suspicion. Overall, the package looked like a high-value object being transported professionally."

Levi frowned. "And you said this thing was biometrically locked? Fingerprint, I'm guessing? Tell me more about the lock."

Brice smiled, pulled open a drawer and pulled out a sealed clear bag with an evidence label on it. "Here. This is what was used to secure the bag."

Levi held the weighty black metal object and studied it. It was the size of his palm, had two reinforced eyelets at either end where a steel cable would be looped through. Centered on its face was a thumb-sized, glassy panel-slightly recessed, rimmed in a dull chrome ring.

Something about the lock bothered him. Something was missing...

Levi's brow furrowed and he handed the bag back to Brice and asked, "Is this some custom thing or do they make these en-masse nowadays? Also, how would this thing have Calloway's thumb print programmed into it?"

"It's an off-the-shelf part, so it's built for easy programmability." Brice pointed at the edge the lock and said, "See this port? Basic USB-c is good enough to transfer data to and from the lock, and that's how someone can program it." He put the envelope back in his desk drawer and said, "It's an off-the-shelf thing. I took it apart and I can say that this model was made in Poland. And before you even ask, there's no serial numbers on these things so there's no way of tracking it back to a purchase order or anything like that. It was made within the last three years, that's about all I know, and the factory that made them made about 50,000 more of these exact same things, so that's a bit of a dead end."

Levi frowned as his mind wandered back to another time and place.

In his mind's eye, he was in the safe house with Alicia.

He spotted the crate that had killed Vito and Carmine. He saw it as if it were right in front of his nose. It was a medium-sized wooden box, battered, with Cyrillic stenciling on the front: *Red Horizon Transport*. The edges were splintered, nails protruding at awkward angles—it had been resealed in a sloppy, rushed way.

Levi replayed how he'd opened the lid with a crowbar, bubble wrap emerged from the crate.

His mind flashed to the way Alicia peeled back the layers… "Brice, was there bubble wrap?"

The technologist turned back to the keyboard, hit a key sequence and searched for "bubble" and the monitor refreshed with updated information. "Yup. That stuff was all over the floor of the office. Do you need to know how much?"

Levi shook his head as he replayed how Alicia had carefully swabbed and peeled each layer of the protective wrap back, eventually revealing the painting.

There was no bag or biometric lock.

His attention returned to the shoddy way the box had been slapped together and he stood, retrieved his phone and walked away from Brice. "Be right back."

Levi tapped a key and within seconds a voice echoed in his ear. *"Yeah?"*

"Frankie. Who cleaned up the first delivery from Zarkov and brought it to the safe house?"

"Jesus Christ, Levi. It's barely even 8 a.m., I haven't even had my first espresso. Hold on, let me get my head on straight." Levi heard movement on the other end of the line, it was quiet for a couple seconds and then Frankie said, *"I'm pretty sure it was Sally who did cleanup on Zarkov's delivery, why do you ask?"*

Levi knew Salvatore Marchesi from the old neighborhood… before the Bianchi family had moved uptown. He was one of the family's cleaners, whether it was the disposal of bodies or evidence, it didn't matter. He was a no-nonsense professional. "Can you get him on the phone for me, I've got a quick question for him."

"Hold on, I think he's probably still in his apartment. Give me a second."

Levi heard a click on the line and after about ten seconds of silence, a light buzz came on the line.

"Levi, you there?" Frankie asked.

"I'm here—"

"Sally, you there?"

"Yeah." A familiar voice filled with grit and age came on the line. *"What's up, Levi? What can I do you for?"*

"Do you remember the cleanup at the Red Hook Terminal over in Brooklyn?"

"Yeah, two of our guys and a package."

"Exactly. My question's about the package. What do you remember about it. What was there, on it, around it. Tell me everything."

"Bubble wrap was scattered all over—like they tore into it quick. Painting was leaning against the crate when I got there. Looked untouched, just sitting there staring like it was proud of itself."

He paused, then added, *"Everything else—bolt cutters, crowbar, busted lock—left like they dropped it mid-job. Whatever hit 'em, it hit fast. They didn't even have time to panic."*

"Do you remember any details about the lock? Was there anything else other than the bubble wrap?"

"Yeah, I remember the lock," Sally said. *"It was dull black,*

about the size of a wallet. Had two metal loops running through the bag—cable-style. They'd already sliced it with bolt cutters. No keyhole, just this little glass pad, size of a large grape." Sally paused. *"Now that I think on it, there was some empty plastic bag nearby, kind of heavy for what it was. Why do you ask?"*

Levi shook his head. "No reason. You gave me everything I needed to know. You don't by chance still have that lock or bag, do you?"

"Aw, shit. No, I got rid of everything, like I'm supposed to. You know how it is."

Sally knew that the only way he'd get in trouble was if there was evidence left to point back at anything the family had done.

"I do." Levi grinned. "I just figured I'd ask. Thanks for confirming some stuff for me. Go have breakfast with Martha."

Levi pocketed his phone and returned to Brice. "Well, I confirmed something I wasn't totally sure of before."

"What's that?" Brice asked.

"Holstrom was in the same crosshairs as Calloway."

"So he's a target. And what are you going to do with that information?"

"I've got an idea." Levi smiled.

Suddenly a red light began flashing in the far corner of the room and Brice's eyes widened. "Oh, shit."

"What's going on?" Levi asked as Brice turned to his terminal, his fingers a blur on the keyboard.

Levi looked up as the monitor flashed an alert banner across the top of the screen.

"I'm not sure, but the Russell building has gone into lockdown."

CHAPTER FIFTEEN
08:11 a.m.

Washington, D.C
8:11 a.m.
Hazmat Dispatch: Capitol Police, Level Two Alert
Russell Senate Office Building – Room 318
Office of Sen. Elaine Carrington – VA

Captain Marcus Delaney was halfway through his second cup of black coffee in the command van just off Constitution when the dispatch call hit his tablet. A Level Two wasn't routine—but it wasn't a red line either. What raised his eyebrows was the tag: *medical emergency involving a senator.*

Then came the kicker.

"Capitol Med-1 responder collapsed on scene. Hazmat requested. Unknown vector."

Delaney slammed the tablet into its dash cradle and barked to his crew.

"Two teams—one with me, one staging at Dirksen connector for evac support."

He yanked open the side door, boots hitting pavement, and the team was already suiting up in the rear of the truck—Tyvek suits, overpressure masks, medical trauma kits, air-monitoring gear. The Russell Senate Office Building loomed across the street, all marble and civility—masking a potential CBRN scene behind its ionic columns.

They moved fast—across Constitution, through the southeast personnel gate, and down the access ramp into the Russell basement corridor. Delaney tapped his radio.

"Dispatch, confirm: Senator Carrington's office?"

"Affirmative. Office 318. Medical emergency ongoing. Secured at outer corridor. Building status just went to soft lockdown—internal doors sealed, no building-wide evac yet."

They were at the elevators in seconds, but none were at their level. Too much time to wait. Delaney waved the team to the stairwell. "We hoof it."

Three flights up, adrenaline pumping, the team burst through the third-floor access into a hallway that reeked of panic and bureaucracy. Staffers backed against walls. An Aide with a clipboard was crying. A Capitol Police officer red-faced and sweating as he flagged them toward the door.

"Inside. It's bad. It's—"

They were through before he finished.

Chaos.

The senator's outer office was in complete disarray—papers

scattered, chair overturned, a woman on the floor convulsing violently near the reception desk.

"Seizure! Diazepam, *now!*" Delaney called behind him.

The room pulsed with tension. His air monitor spiked as soon as they crossed the threshold—VOC trace, acrid signature. Ammonia? Singed plastic? Could've been cleaning agents. Could've been something worse.

Delaney pushed into the inner office.

Dead silence.

Senator Elaine Carrington was slumped in an armchair, eyes open but glassy. Her lips were blue. Skin already pallid.

To her left—another body.

Medical responder. Med-1 vest, eyes wide open, froth at the lips. No visible trauma.

To her right, a second figure. A man in a suit—likely her chief of staff. Face down on the carpet, hand still clutching a phone.

"Jesus Christ," Delaney muttered, eyes sweeping the room. He keyed his shoulder mic.

"Command, this is Hazmat One on-scene. Confirmed three down inside: one Capitol responder, one male, one senator—unresponsive. Secretary outside seizing. Unknown agent. Beginning containment protocol now."

He nodded to his second.

"Scrub this room—air monitor, temp, volatile detection. Check for any packages, recent deliveries, open containers. I want everything bagged, swabbed, and photographed. And don't touch *anything* until we know what we're looking at."

He turned to the body of the responder. No wounds. No bleeding. No trauma. But the foam at the lips…

"Neurotoxin?" someone whispered.

Delaney didn't answer. But his stomach turned cold.

The senator's office was immaculate—bookshelves, a Virginia flag, a desk covered in briefing papers—and one unusual item:

A small wooden box, tipped over near the senator's side table. No label. No card.

"Check that first," he said tightly. "Don't open it. Just photograph and bag."

Outside, a second medical team arrived, starting treatment on the seizing secretary. Her pulse was erratic. Pupils blown.

Delaney moved fast. If this was chemical, it was contained. If it was biological, they were already late.

But if it was something else—some delivery system buried in that box—they'd just stepped into a weaponized office in the heart of the U.S. government.

He keyed his mic again, this time to Command.

"Level Two upgrade to Level Four. Lockdown Russell. Get the FBI WMD task force on this frequency. Now."

∼

Quantico, VA
FBI WMD Response Lab – Containment Bay Bravo
08:52 a.m.

Nate Carrington exhaled slowly into the soft positive pressure of his Level A suit, the SCBA regulator clicking once as the air valve cycled. The HUD strip inside his visor pulsed: Suit integrity – Nominal. PAPR flow – Normal. Temp: 70.2°F.

He hadn't worn one of these since Kandahar.

The JSLIST ensemble, reinforced for biohazard applications, wasn't exactly graceful. But when the call came in about two dead—including a senator—and a first responder who'd dropped like a sandbag, there wasn't a debate. You suited up or you stepped aside.

Nate hadn't stepped aside. Not even after retirement. Not after that call came in from a name buried in a genealogy chart: Elaine Carrington. Second cousin.

They'd never met. And now he'd never have the chance.

He keyed the inner airlock panel with a gloved hand. The decon chamber cycled. The inner doors to Bay B hissed open.

The wooden box sat alone under dual-arm halogen lights, centered on a stainless-steel workbench bolted to the floor. A single evidence placard: #R318-01A. He stepped closer.

It looked almost… quaint.

Matte-finished walnut, dovetail joinery, brass hinges. A black-ink stencil across the lid:

"Montpelier Chocolatiers – Artisan Reserve – Handcrafted in Culpeper, VA."

It had tested negative for radiological, chemical, and biological agents during initial field triage at the Russell Building, but he'd insisted on full secondary containment for lab-level follow-up. Because this wasn't normal. Not for candy. And definitely not in D.C.

The chocolates themselves—bagged and tagged—were being analyzed in Lab D for trace toxins and particulate residue using GC-MS, LC-MS/MS, and Fourier Transform IR spectroscopy. But the box had raised other flags.

He crouched beside it, boots creaking slightly against the rubberized flooring.

The interior tray had been removed. But what remained was stranger.

Three hand-etched grooves—cut with a rotary engraver, not a CNC router—tight sweep angles, shallow burrs on the left edges. These were channel tracks. Something had been slotted inside them, and it wasn't artisan truffles.

And then there was the biometric latch.

Almost missed it at first—disguised as a decorative brass inlay in the corner. But it wasn't. It was a polycarbonate fingerprint reader, recessed slightly beneath a lens with a chrome ring. The wiring was buried in the wooden frame.

Who the hell seals chocolate with a biometric lock?

He took out a sterile polyester swab and carefully passed it through the grooves—first dry, then with a light trace solvent. He labeled each sample:

R318-01A-G1 / G2 / G3

Dropped them into Tyvek-lined forensic envelopes, sealed and initialed.

"Bay B to Command," he said through the comm mic. "Sample swabs from groove interface logged and prepped. Also recommend latent print lift attempt on the biometric panel—can you flag AFMES for microprint and residue evaluation?"

A voice crackled back. *"Copy, Carrington. Flagged and scheduled."*

He took one last look at the box.

There was no bomb. No vapor trace. Nothing bleeding or pulsing or glowing.

But he'd kicked in doors where people had said the same thing. What made him itch wasn't the contents. It was the container. The elegance. The *engineering*.

This wasn't for smuggling. This was for targeted delivery.

He stood and keyed the intercom.

"And get me the full list of registered biometric locks sold through known vendors in the past five years. Start with anything manufactured in Eastern Europe." Nate tilted the box slightly, eyes narrowing behind the face shield. "I recognize some of this manufacturing. The laminate coating's a poly blend we flagged back in a customs seizure at Dulles—a modified courier pouch smuggled in from Gdańsk. Same weird solder pattern too—widespread beadwork, not machine-tight like the Korean imports. And this USB-C port isn't milled to U.S. spec—it's recessed at a slope I've only seen on Polish OEM batches. This is black-market export gear, no doubt."

Nate's brow furrowed. He didn't like what his instincts were telling him. He set the box back onto the containment cradle and peeled a fresh Tyvek seal pouch from the wall unit. With deliberate care, he slid the wooden case inside and zipped the tamper-lock channel shut. The adhesive strip lit red across the seam.

"Tag this for secondary containment and flag the Joint Tasking Center. If this thing came in from Poland—or worse—

we're going to need eyes from CBP, ODNI, and maybe even DTRA."

He scribbled his initials and timestamped the label.

"And nobody opens this again unless they're wearing something rated for nerve agent fallout. Just in case."

The airlock hissed shut. Behind him, the room hummed with the quiet tension of a box no one understood—yet.

∽

Washington, D.C. – Outfit HQ
Office C3
09:04 a.m.

The room smelled like solder and burnt coffee. Brice leaned forward in his chair, fingers dancing across a split keyboard as three monitors flickered with feed windows, packet logs, and a secure tunnel into an FBI backchannel.

Levi stood behind him, arms crossed, silent. Watching. Waiting.

The Russell lockdown had hit the newsfeeds ten minutes ago. Nothing public. Not yet. Just "senate building incident," and the usual "precautionary measures in place" fluff that meant something inside had gone sideways.

"I'm scraping every internal repo I can find," Brice muttered. "Capitol Police firewalled most of their traffic after Level Four went active, but a few labs didn't rotate credentials yet. I'm listening to half a dozen feeds from Quantico, DHS, and JTF-CBRNE."

"I have no idea what you're talking about. Is there any ID on the senator?" Levi asked.

Brice hesitated. "Yeah. Elaine Carrington. Virginia." He didn't look up. "Active on the same appropriations cluster as Holstrom and Calloway."

Levi's eyes narrowed. "That's three."

"Uh-huh."

Brice clicked open a side-channel labeled FBI-WMD-Audio 3, and a low-fidelity lab feed came through—two voices arguing over a chromatography calibration setting. Background noise—centrifuge hum, clatter of trays, someone muttering about diethyl ether.

"Useless," Brice said, switching channels. "Next."

Another window opened—a live transcribe overlay slid into view. A chemical analyst was dictating test results into a lab reporting system. Half of it was clutter—residue on a stapler, half a protein bar under a desk, fibers from a blazer.

"*...trace amounts of benzoylecgonine detected on Desk Sample 7B—*"

"That's coke." Brice translated, glancing over his shoulder. "But if that was the threat, half of Capitol hill would be dead by now."

Levi didn't even blink. "That's not what triggered a lockdown."

Brice toggled audio up a notch.

"*...swabs from interior wood grain of item 01A show no active volatile residue, but post-sample derivatization confirmed presence of ethyl N,N-dimethylphosphoramidocyanidate—*"

Levi's brow furrowed.

The voice on the feed kept going, suddenly sharper. *"—yes, sir. Confirmed. That's a GD-series compound. Organophosphate nerve agent. Extremely low quantity, likely microdose configuration. Might've been enough just on skin contact."*

The line went silent.

Then, another voice—older, controlled—spoke on the same feed. *"This doesn't leave the room until we know chain-of-custody. Get me full analysis on delivery method and security context. Pull every inch of metadata off that package."*

Brice was already typing. "Pulling metadata now—got access to one of the lab reports before it got sealed. Here—"

A PDF slid onto the central monitor.

Brice scrolled through the preliminary report and pointed up at the screen. "Check out what this says."

Evidence label reads: R318-01A.

Description: "wooden box, walnut, marked as artisanal chocolates—Montpelier brand."

Brice snorted. "Classy packaging for an assassination device."

Levi's eyes darkened. Chocolates. Of course. Innocuous. Precise. He continued scanning the report as Brice scrolled.

NOTE: Biometric locking mechanism confirmed. Fingerprint scanner embedded in latch architecture. Likely Polish-origin construction. Parallels courier equipment seized in 2019 Dulles incident. Further tracing underway.

Levi's eyes locked on the sentence.

Biometric lock.

"You don't put a biometric lock on a gift unless you know who's opening it," Levi muttered. "That wasn't candy. That was a weapon."

He stepped back from the monitor like someone had just fired a shot.

"That's all I need to know," Levi said, voice low.

Brice swiveled in his chair. "You think this is related to—?"

"It is," Levi cut him off. "Same as Holstrom. Same as Calloway. We're not looking for some psycho with an art fetish. This is someone looking to even a score." He nodded to the screen. "We now have three names. Can we triangulate what they might have in relation to each other?"

Brice cracked his knuckles, already tapping into the Senate's historical vote tracker. "These guys didn't even share a political party. Holstrom was a Republican, Calloway was an old blue-dog Democrat, and Carrington's a fairly liberal Democrat."

"Good," Levi said. "So look for common ground. Where did all three of them vote the *same* way?"

"I'm betting Calloway was a swing voter, at least on national security stuff." Brice raised an eyebrow but filtered the query. "These three rarely voted the same. Give me a sec."

He scrubbed the database, whittling down thousands of Senate votes.

"Here we go," Brice muttered. "Over the last seven years, only *six* instances where all three voted identically. Some were procedural, a couple bipartisan resolutions... but this third one—hold on."

He clicked it open, and the monitor filled with text.

Amendment 1427-B – Reallocation of classified research appropriations under DARPA and the Department of Energy's NNSA program.

Proposed reductions: 11.2% from baseline. Target: duplicative or unsupervised defense research entities.

"So, if I'm reading this right, it looks like it was budget cut of some sort, right?"

Brice nodded. "A significant one. These parts of the government rarely get squeezed."

Levi leaned forward. "Can we see who got affected?"

Brice opened the attached impact memo. A massive spreadsheet unfolded. Hundreds of redline entries. He highlighted a column and clicked a few buttons.

"Two hundred seventy-three positions," he read aloud. "Cut from USAMRIID teams, CBRNE liaison units, and Tactical Biochem labs. Here—look."

He pointed at the screen. "This is just some of it."

. . .

Facility: Fort Detrick – Biodefense Division, Experimental Materials Group
   Status: Project Terminated. Personnel: 36 released.

Another entry.

Facility: Dugway Proving Ground – Tactical Biochemistry Testbed
   Status: Defunded. Personnel: 17 reassigned. 12 released.

Levi exhaled slowly, eyes narrowing.

"These three senators were part of the reason a couple hundred bioweapons experts got canned," he said, almost to himself.

Brice caught the change in his tone. "Levi...?"

But Levi didn't respond. His mind had already left the room. Ukraine. Alicia was out there. And if he was right—if this was what he *thought* it was...

A chill raced up his spine. Letting her go without him had felt strategic.

But with a bioweapons expert bent on revenge likely waiting for her...

Now it felt like a mistake.

He clenched his jaw and refocused. "Who else was on that vote?"

Brice ran the roll call.

"Twelve more senators voted the same way," he said, scanning the names. "Seven aren't in politics anymore. Two died in the last couple years—natural causes, from what I can tell. But one..."

He stopped.

Levi stepped closer.

Brice turned slowly toward him. "One of them's now the Vice President."

Levi stood still, breath shallow. His hands balled into fists at his sides.

"Jesus..." Brice whispered.

Levi was already moving toward the exit, phone in his hand.

"Where are you going?" Brice asked.

"I've got somewhere to be."

He paused at the door, turned back. "In the meantime, let Mason know—this isn't some pissed-off art dork. We've got a trained military-grade bioweapons expert out there—someone who thinks these people destroyed his life."

Brice's face went pale.

Levi's voice dropped to a growl. "And the vector for the threat? Anything between *artwork and candy*. Which means everything's a threat. Art. Candy. You name it." He met Brice's eyes.

"D.C.'s going to go nuts if they learn what's really happening."

Levi paused, his hand on the door handle. "I suggest keeping this as a need-to-know exercise."

"No, shit."

CHAPTER SIXTEEN

Kyiv, Ukraine
Premier Palace Hotel – Room 514
7:12 p.m.

The smell of dill and garlic lingered in the air, blending with the crisp scent of fresh linen and polished wood from the Premier Palace's hotel room. Alicia sat cross-legged on the plush bedspread; her open laptop next to her. In front of her was a plate of steaming *vareniki*—delicate dumplings stuffed with mashed potatoes and caramelized onion, swimming in golden butter and a dollop of sour cream.

Tony leaned back on the tufted armchair, spearing another forkful of *holubtsi*—cabbage rolls filled with spiced pork and rice—carefully balancing his plate on his thigh while adjusting himself with a look of discomfort. "I swear, the cabbage here has some kind of ancestral grudge. This stuff hits me like a freight train."

"Just try to control yourself," Alicia muttered through a mouthful of crusty dark rye dipped in *borscht—so thick* it looked like molten garnet. "We don't need to get fogged out of this room." She wiped her lip and gestured toward the open GoPro interface on the laptop screen. She shifted the screen so they could both see it and said, "Let's look at Bagel's feed, see what our guy managed to discover for us."

Across the room, Bagel sat on the carpet in a regal loaf, audibly crunching dried sardines from a porcelain bowl—smuggled in from a pet boutique down the block. Every few seconds, he flicked his tail and gave Alicia a sidelong glance, as if to say *finally, some recognition for my genius.*

Alicia clicked play. The screen flickered.

Bagel's head-cam feed sprang to life.

They watched in silence as the footage showed the cat springing up on top of a shelf and with a graceful leap, he landed in the rafters of the warehouse—silent, sure-footed, the padded GoPro mount catching every detail in infrared-enhanced black-and-white. The warehouse was a chaotic sprawl of easels, crates, and half-draped canvases, each angle sharp with shadow and movement.

There were at least a dozen art stations, but only three of them had been occupied this morning. Bagel slunk through the rafters like a ghost.

Alicia forked another dumpling and said through a mouthful,

"Look at him, the little professional. Bet the KGB wishes they had one of him."

Eventually, Bagel tired of the rafters and silently leaped down to the ground level again.

Alicia studied his movements on-screen and wondered what was going through his head as he explored, seemingly with purpose. As he crisscrossed the space, it suddenly dawned on her: Bagel was marking off a grid pattern. He was going up and down the various logical rows, purposefully surveying whatever was near him, and weaving around obstacles to finish each row of the grid.

Amazing... animals don't just know how to do that, do they?

Bagel paused near a low table stacked with tubes of paint. He sniffed the air, then swiveled. The GoPro picked up the sound of a faint drip... drip... from somewhere off-camera.

Tony swallowed a bite of *deruny*—pan-fried potato pancakes—and leaned forward. "Pause it. What's that?"

Alicia rewound a few seconds and let it roll again.

Bagel approached a canvas on the floor. He sniffed again. The audio caught a faint snort of feline distaste, and then a short, protesting *meep*—he'd brushed against something wet.

"Idiot," Alicia said fondly.

Bagel blinked slowly from his sardine pile.

The footage jumped to him shaking his head violently—then, a bright smear appeared on the lens for a split second. Paint. On his ear.

Alicia sighed and stood, heading to the sink with a warm towel and a bar of soap. She crouched beside the cat and began gently scrubbing the dried ochre streak from the tuft of his left ear.

Bagel grumbled but allowed it.

After she was done, Bagel licked his paw and rubbed at his ear that she'd mussed with, as if reclaiming his dignity.

Back on-screen, the video resumed—smudged with flecks of paint. Less than ideal.

Alicia examined the GoPro, which was now hooked up to her laptop, and carefully flaked the paint off the lens. Thankfully it came off without a problem.

Shifting her attention back to the video on the screen, the cat had moved deeper into the warehouse maze. One corner revealed a narrow metal door to the outside—simple bolt lock, no camera, no obvious alarm wires or magnetic triggers on the doorframe.

"Wait, wait," Alicia said, leaning forward to pause the video.

Tony's brow furrowed as Alicia pointed to the screen.

"That's our way in tonight," Alicia said. "No way this is some side room. That's an outside door."

"That looks unlockable," Tony nodded. "I'd tend to agree. If I'm not mistaken, I think that's literally the opposite side of the warehouse from where we entered. And the lock looks manageable."

Alicia glanced at Tony and chuckled at his look of revulsion. "What's up with that look?"

The big man shook his head and shrugged. "I'm not sure which disgusts me more, how my stomach is reacting to this food or how pathetic that lock is. I wouldn't put that on the shed at my uncle's farm."

"Well, let's hope looks aren't deceiving." She leaned forward and resumed playback.

Bagel kept pacing out his grid, and eventually he approached what had been described as the Maestro's office door.

It was a metal door, but given its location inside the building, it was obvious the door was leading into another room.

Bagel crept closer to the door—and froze.

Both Alicia and Tony leaned forward.

On the concrete floor, dimly visible in the dusty IR illumination, were three—no, four—small, still shapes.

"What the hell is that?" Tony asked.

Alicia's nostrils flared. "I think those are rats."

Tony nodded. "Those things are either dead or asleep, and to be honest, I don't think I've ever seen a rat asleep, so I'm thinking dead."

She tilted her head as she stared at the scene unfolding in front of her. "I don't see any traps... what, does this guy collect dead animals?"

The creatures were all in various stages of rigor mortis, their bodies curled in positions that suggested spasms—or death mid-convulsion.

On the video, Bagel inched closer, ears low, whiskers vibrating like antennae.

He didn't touch the bodies. He didn't even sniff—just stopped, his whole body suddenly still, tense. As if he were evaluating what he was seeing.

Then, a faint vocalization came through the speaker—low and growling.

"Did he just—" Tony started.

Bagel, in the footage, backed away a step and gave a small, deliberate hiss.

In the room, the real-life Bagel had frozen mid-bite. His tail curled low. He let out a matching hiss.

Alicia and Tony exchanged a look of concern.

On-screen, the camera caught Bagel turning once to glance back—toward the main room—then toward the rats again.

A deep, rumbling meow came through the speaker.

And then, with a deliberate series of paw taps, he tapped out a pattern Alicia translated instantly.

"He's warning us—'bad.'"

Tony was staring at the video, eyes wide. "Very bad."

The screen went still.

So did the room.

Bagel shifted his attention back to himself, licked the last sardine scale off his paw and stared back at Alicia with unblinking eyes.

Alicia met his gaze.

"Yeah, buddy," she whispered. "It does look bad."

Tony exhaled slowly, still leaning forward in his chair, the plate of half-eaten *holubtsi* balanced on one knee. "You see any cameras in there?"

Alicia didn't answer right away. She scrubbed a finger back through the video timeline, watching Bagel weave through shadows and cluttered workbenches. Nothing blinked. Nothing panned. No red dots. No wall-mounted domes. Just easels, boxes, and paint-streaked concrete.

"Not a single one," she said at last. "Not even a busted one hanging from the ceiling. You?"

Tony shook his head. "Nope, and I was looking. And you'd think a place like that—stuff that if it were real would be worth millions—they'd have at least one motion sensor or IR trap."

Alicia glanced toward the corner of the room, where Bagel was now curled into a sphinx-like loaf, eyes golden and unreadable.

She narrowed her gaze. "Bagel..."

The cat's ears flicked.

"You see any cameras?" she asked.

He blinked once. Then, with deliberate slowness, he turned his head side to side in a small, unmistakable no.

Tony gave a half-laugh. "Well. That settles that."

Alicia leaned back against the headboard and ran her hand down her face. "Of course there isn't any cameras, duh... That's intentional. No cameras means no digital evidence trail."

Tony pursed his lips. "Ah, you're probably right. The kind of operation that doesn't want to answer for what goes down in there."

"Exactly," Alicia said. "No prying eyes. Nothing for some junior cop to find later. Just shadows and paint and maybe poison."

"Almost certainly poison." Tony muttered.

Bagel made a small, grumbly noise and shifted on the carpet, pawing at the side of his bowl as if to say this conversation was beneath him now.

Alicia gave a tired chuckle. "Alright, we've got our route in, and we know the Maestro's door. I guess we know our next steps."

Tony looked at her. "You thinking tonight?"

She nodded. "Two a.m. should be well past foot traffic. Too early for the dedicated drunks, too late for the cops. Well, at least the American cops. I'm kind of counting that the Ukrainian ones aren't that different."

Tony stood and stretched, groaning. "Great. Remind me again why we don't do this kind of thing at brunch?"

Alicia reached for the GoPro and began unhooking cables. "Because I don't think this Maestro is going to give us permission to look through his stuff."

"Speaking of that," Tony's expression turned serious. "Now that we have a pretty good clue who the poison lover is, what's our goal?"

Alicia met his gaze and said with as calm a voice as she could muster, "We need to verify this guy is responsible for the deaths of Vito and Carmine. I'm figuring that information is going to be in the Maestro's office."

Tony tilted his head and looked at Alicia with a somber expression. "I should probably tell you that Mr. Bianchi gave me specific instructions on what to do if we found Vito and Carmine's killer. You might not want to be in the same room when that happens."

Alicia stared blankly at Tony. For the first time it dawned on her that Tony's role with her had always been of a dual-purpose. Sure, Uncle Vinnie wanted him to keep her safe, but the big mafioso who she truly considered a friend was also a professional killer.

She let out a giggle as a weight lifted off her shoulders.

"What's so funny?" Tony asked with the slightest hint of a smile.

She patted Tony roughly on his upper arm, like she'd seen her father do countless times and said, "I've got my own instructions as well. We might have to flip a coin to see who ends up taking care of business."

Tony's eyes widened and he let out a belly laugh. "You know what, from one of you Yoders, I'll believe just about anything." He walked to the window, pulling back the blackout curtain just enough to see the city lights blinking across Kyiv.

"Two a.m.," he said. "Let's make it clean."

Alicia nodded. "And quiet."

∼

Kyiv, Ukraine
Warehouse District – Rear Alley
01:53 a.m.

The cold in the alley felt personal. It sliced down Alicia's neck, slipped under her collar, and settled between her shoulder blades. Her breath coiled in the air, tight and sharp, fading just as quickly as her confidence in this part of town.

The warehouse loomed ahead—just a box of shadow broken only by the flickering stutter of a dying sodium streetlamp. It gave everything a jaundiced tint, a sickly orange that pulsed like a failing heartbeat above the rusted freight door. She felt Bagel press against her calf, his body a tense line of muscle and fur. His tail flicked once.

They were close now.

Alicia crouched beside a warped steel drum slick with

condensation, one hand instinctively resting on Bagel's back to steady them both. Across the street, slouched on a bench under a half-collapsed bus shelter, was a body. Almost certainly male. Wrapped in an olive drape of clothing that could've been a coat or a tarp. Hard to tell. His presence itched.

"Drunk," she whispered. "Bench."

Tony had already seen him. She didn't have to ask—he just nodded and peeled off toward the street, coat brushing against the concrete like a whisper of imminent danger, a promise of violence.

Alicia stayed low.

Tony moved like a man used to dark places—efficient, quiet, utterly unbothered. She watched him cross, observed his silhouette lean over the man on the bench. Bagel shifted beside her, head tilted, muscles coiled but still.

Tony prodded. Waited.

Then he stood and came back, shaking his head.

"Guy's marinated in vodka and piss. Barely breathing. He's practically dead from alcohol, not a watcher."

Alicia exhaled slowly through her nose. Good.

If there was one thing the Outfit had hammered into her was to always be paranoid. If you can avoid it, ensure nobody's watching.

She turned her attention to the warehouse's back door. From ten feet away it looked like nothing—no label, no keypad, no obvious camera. Just a recessed steel rectangle trying to be invisible.

She stepped forward and crouched. The ground soaked through the knee of her pants instantly. Ice-cold, gritty. Bagel followed, sitting beside her like a quiet sentinel. His eyes gleamed—deep gold in the alley light.

Alicia peeled back her coat flap and unrolled her tool kit across her thigh, the familiar leather settling against the top of her boot. The lock in front of her was blackened steel—worn at the edges, pitted slightly. Someone had replaced it about a decade ago or so. It didn't look like a high-quality lock. Then again, this area was a low-rent district. Not a place where you'd find cash or jewels or anything worth the bother. And this lock looked like it belonged in this neighborhood.

"Let's see what you are," she murmured.

She let her gloved fingers rest against the bolt, feeling its weight, its shape. Cheap hardware. Not a deterrent. Not to someone with even a halfway decent amount of practice.

Bagel let out a tiny, warbling trill.

She smiled without looking at him. "Yeah, I know. We're almost inside."

The metal felt dry and brittle under her touch. If it weren't for the noise, she'd have Tony just kick the door in and the lock would probably snap.

She selected a tension wrench, then a hook pick. In another life, this would've been a parlor trick.

Tony stood a few feet back, body angled so he could scan both ends of the alley. His hand was inside his coat, palm likely resting on his weapon. Always ready.

Alicia focused her attention back onto the lock.

She was listening—to the wind rattling an unseen vent high above. To the scrape of her pick against tumblers. To the way her breath slowed as the world narrowed to steel on steel.

Bagel didn't move. Just stared.

This lock wasn't meant to stop someone like her.

"Almost…" she whispered.

And then she smiled again. Not because it was open.

But because she could feel it.

It was about to be—

The tumblers would wait. She paused.

∼

Kyiv, Ukraine
Warehouse District – Rear Entrance
01:58 a.m.

Alicia stood facing the weather-pitted steel door, her breath fogging in the cold. The alley was silent, save for the occasional distant groan of a trolley and the wind threading through rusted gutters above. The kind of quiet that made your bones remember every decision.

She pulled out her phone, the screen lighting her face in soft blue. Her thumbs hovered a moment, then tapped quickly:

Going in the back way.

All quiet. Tony and Bagel with me. If you don't hear from me by 3, assume the worst.

—A

. . .

She stared at the message, then hit *Send*.

For a moment, she waited—not exactly expecting her father to respond, but she stared for a few long seconds at her phone, just in case something came across the airwaves.

Nothing came.

Alicia slipped the phone back into her coat pocket, jaw tightening.

Time to get this over with.

She pulled in a deep breath and let it out slowly. It was something she'd seen her father do a million times. Evidently, he'd been taught that in Japan a lifetime ago as a way to calm the nerves.

All she knew was that it worked.

She knelt beside the steel door, her breath steady, heart slowed to a deliberate cadence.

Alicia once again peeled back her coat flap and unsnapped the fold-down panel on her right thigh, revealing her Outfit-issued lockpick kit—burnished black leather, soft from wear, and weighted like a prayer book.

Inside were the tools of her quiet trade... well, was it actually her trade? Her father would say this was what a second-story man does. In her mind, she didn't even know what to call what she does, but at this moment, it didn't matter as she took inventory of her tools:

– Bogota rakes of titanium steel, triple-hump and single-spine

– Half-diamond picks, polished to mirror sheen

– Sparrows SSDeV hooks, coated for low-friction response

– A torsion wrench set, thin and thick, curved and straight

— And the holy grail—her electric pick gun, cradled in neoprene like a scalpel

But this wasn't the time for brute force or noise. This called for finesse.

She rolled her wrist, stretched her fingers, and let the door tell its story.

In her mind she replayed the weeks of practice she'd had with professional locksmiths, those folks had their industry lingo that took a lot of getting used to, while her father's "associates" that he'd hooked her up were much more practical with their language and slang.

As she studied the door, she felt like she was back in Quantico having an FBI agent run her through some tests. The lock in front of her was a Euro-profile cylinder—Schlage clone, three-pin wafer, pin-tumbler style with a horizontal keyway and signs of oxidation on the outer housing. The kind of hardware you find in half of Eastern Europe: deceptively basic—until you push a pin too far and the whole cylinder binds like a bear trap.

She gave the knob a slight nudge. Deadbolt confirmed. No give. No sound.

"Tony," she murmured, not looking back. "Keep your eyes peeled."

"Copy."

Alicia pulled out a tension wrench—medium-width, slightly curved at the tip—and slotted it gently into the base of the keyway. Not deep. Not shallow. Just firm enough to apply counterclockwise torque.

She rolled a half-diamond-shaped pick between her fingers

next and slipped it into the lock with the care of a surgeon threading a vein.

"Start at the back, feel for binding."

Her voice was barely a breath. She was repeating lessons taught in low-lit basements by Outfit men who could open safes faster than she could type.

Pin one—springy.

Pin two—nothing.

Pin three—*click*.

There.

She eased the half-diamond pick out. Reached for a shorter hook. Something stiffer. More tactile.

"Don't trust the sound. Trust the *set*."

She probed deeper this time. The pins weren't machined evenly. Pin two had an overset lip—probably a security spool. Designed to fake a false set and ruin your torque.

She backed out, released tension.

Reset.

Applied it again—softer this time.

Hook in.

Pin one—moved.

Pin two—resisted.

She applied feather tension. Not pressure—*feedback*.

There.

Pin two set with a clean, sharp tick that traveled through her bones.

Pin three—already good.

Pin four—*gritty*, stubborn.

She changed tools. Went to her short hook. The pin wouldn't budge.

It almost felt like the inside of the lock had partially succumbed to the weather.

"I know your game," she muttered. "You're a shallow false set."

She rolled her pick under the pin and gave it a microscopic nudge. Not up—*out*.

The pin slipped into place with a soft snick. She felt the plug rotate—half a millimeter.

Her heart skipped.

Set.

Pin five—barely there. Light touch. It set with a sigh.

Then the tension bar moved. Not a full turn. Just a *pulse*.

Alicia shifted her hand, braced her thumb against the faceplate, and rotated the plug fully.

The bolt retracted with the slow, hungry sound of metal unseating from decades of rust.

She exhaled—just once.

Then turned to Bagel.

The cat blinked.

"We're in."

Tony stepped closer, checking both ends of the alley with a tight nod. "No sound, no movement. You're clear."

Alicia pulled the door open a hair—just wide enough to let Bagel slink through ahead, his GoPro already turned on.

No alarms. No buzzers. Just darkness.

She pocketed her tools in reverse order, every motion practiced, every item accounted for. Then she reached back into her pack and unzipped a narrow side compartment.

Out came a compact headset—military surplus, retrofitted for IR. Not top-tier gear, but functional. She clipped the harness into place, flipped the sensor unit down over one eye, and toggled it on.

She heard Tony mimicking her movements just like they'd practiced.

A soft pulse of infrared illuminated the doorway in pale static hues.

Then she whispered, "Here goes nothing…"

Alicia stepped inside.

∼

Kyiv, Ukraine
Warehouse District – Interior
02:07 a.m.

Alicia swept the infrared monocular along the rafters, each heartbeat punctuated by the faint whir of the lens motor. The warehouse was hollow, cathedral-like in its silence—just the groan of winter wind pressing through rusted vents and the distant clink of metal as Bagel leapt from beam to beam overhead.

"Clear left," Tony said in a low voice, hand resting near his sidearm as he stepped over a broken easel.

"Nothing on IR," Alicia murmured, scanning through the monocular. The ghost-lit scene glowed in washed-out green—

crates, canvas, motionless shadows. "No movement. No reflections. Looks clean."

She pulled a compact RF scanner from her thigh pouch and swept the area. The device chirped once, then cycled through bands—static across the board. "Signal dead zone. No Wi-Fi, no RF bleed, no active cams."

They moved methodically through the warehouse, checking each blind corner and workstation. Alicia knelt by a ventilation grate and angled a micro-inspection mirror inside—dust, cobwebs, and oxidized mesh. Not a single micro-lens or motion detector.

Whoever the Maestro was, he didn't want to *record* anything in the warehouse. Probably wanted *plausible deniability*.

Alicia returned to her gear pack and unzipped it with a practiced pull.

The hazmat suits came out first—Outfit-issued Level B+ lightweight polymer with multi-layer barrier coating. Black matte exterior, charcoal PAPR units with 40mm NATO filter ports, rated for low-pressure aerosol threats.

Alicia unrolled hers across a clean tarp and began stepping in, every motion practiced. "Fifteen-minute max exposure window once we cross threshold," she said. "We break seal, we run the clock. Full filter integrity confirmed?"

Tony was already pulling the legs of his suit up, tugging the zipper halfway. "Suit fits fine. No obvious holes or issues on my end."

They both worked in tandem, sealing one another in. Wrists. Ankles. Zippers triple-checked. Tape tabs snugged. Pressure equalized.

Before locking her mask in place, Alicia pulled the IR monocle from its foam pouch and tested the alignment one last time. It was clunky—army surplus—but the eyepiece slotted just inside the mask viewport. A tight fit. Not elegant, but workable.

"Monocle's mounted," she said. "IR check."

Tony slid his in place and gave a confirming nod. "Everything's still okay."

Bagel landed beside the crate stack, tail flicking once, then again.

Alicia bent and touched his head gently. "We need you as eyes in the sky."

Bagel twitched his nose as if questioning the request.

She pointed skyward. "Rafters. No one in. No one out. If anything twitches, you give us a signal."

Bagel gave a quiet *mrrp*, turned, and padded silently up a utility ladder, vanishing into the shadows like a ghost with golden eyes.

Alicia turned back to Tony. "Weapons."

They each pulled their Kyiv-issued weapons from retrofitted Kydex rigs bonded to the suits' outer thighs. The holsters were entirely external—tactical, friction-fit, and heat-resistant—allowing clean draw and reholstering without compromising seal integrity.

Alicia ran through her final suit check. She sealed the neck ring, checked the PAPR fan cycle, and gave a thumbs up.

Tony mirrored her.

Together, they moved deeper into the heart of the warehouse—boots muffled by anti-slip soles, flashlights cut to minimum beam.

The entrance to the Maestro's office stood about fifty feet from them: a windowless steel-paneled room elevated on a concrete slab. No markings. Just one door. Just one lock.

As they got closer, it became obvious to Alicia that this lock was of a different make than the previous one.

With a quick sweep of the dead rats with foot, Alicia crouched in front of the door. The locking mechanism was flush-mount, rectangular, with a magnetic seal strip running the vertical edge. No keyhole. No tumbler. No brand mark.

She frowned.

"Not just any deadbolt," she said. "This is a cam-electro hybrid. Polish, maybe Czech. Could be one of those distributed magnet systems—rare as hell."

Tony crouched beside her, watching over her shoulder.

Alicia reached down and unlatched the external pouch clipped to her suit's thigh—unzipping it just enough to withdraw a slim pick set with gloved fingers, every motion deliberate through the suit's exterior shell.

She drew a slim pick set from her hip pouch—tools burnished steel with rubberized grips. She selected a tension bar no thicker than a piece of wire and a torsion probe with a modified rake head, angled for a low friction feel.

She began gently probing the lower seam.

No give.

She shifted upward, found a notch just behind the outer panel.

Click.

Alicia exhaled. "There it is. Mechanical override port."

Like most electronic lock mechanisms, there was almost always some keying mechanism as backup.

She slid in the probe, delicately teasing each micro-cam into alignment—each movement no more than a degree. The lock resisted—not with force, but with complexity. A twisting array of magnetic sliders rotated behind the faceplate, each needing to be tilted and set in sequence.

Every pick taught her something—resistance, flex, false set.

One mistake, and she'd have to start the sequence again.

Tony stayed still, breathing slowly behind his mask.

Finally—after five silent minutes—she felt it: a fractional movement, like a breath inhaled.

The lock's outer plate clicked softly. A faint green LED pulsed once behind the housing. The magnetic seal stuttered.

Alicia froze, hand hovering near the latch.

She didn't open it yet.

She waited.

And the room waited with her.

∽

Kyiv, Ukraine
Warehouse District – Maestro's Office
02:19 a.m.

Alicia didn't speak. Just shifted back enough for Tony to know. "I got it."

He advanced beside her—weapon up, posture tight. Their suits crinkled with every motion, layers of plastic and rubber resisting every step. The exterior thigh rigs kept their weapons accessible without compromising the integrity of the suits—no slits, no breaks in the seal. Not perfect for speed, but functional. And that was all that mattered. Not tonight.

Above, Bagel crouched in the rafters, tail flicking once.

Alicia pulled the handle.

The door creaked open—just a sliver.

Through the IR monocle, the interior glowed in faint grays. No motion. Shelves. A worktable. Canvas racks.

They stepped in.

Two feet.

SSSSSSSSSHHHHHT—

A sharp hiss exploded from the far corner of the room. A high-pressure vent, tucked near the ceiling. Directional.

Alicia saw the mist erupt—Tony caught the brunt of it first.

The billowing cloud enveloped Tony in seconds. He staggered backward, coughing violently, arms flailing for balance—then went down hard against a desk.

She heard the pain in his voice as he shouted, *"Get out!"*

"Back out—now—" she barked, heart pounding.

Too late.

She couldn't even see him under the thick blanket of whatever it was.

The chemical cloud hit her mask like a slap of acid. Her skin beneath the suit went cold, then *hot*.

A sudden chemical sting hit her forearms—like needles through rubber. The suit was leaking.

Alicia dove forward, dropped to her knees, found one of

Tony's legs splayed out on the floor, the hazmat suit practically melted off of him.

She grabbed him by the ankles as her skin felt like it had caught on fire.

He was dead weight.

She didn't think. Just pulled.

One dragging step. Then another. The rubber of her gloves had gone slick—everything felt wrong, off. Her throat burned. Eyes watered.

The suit had failed.

With a surge of adrenaline, she yanked herself and Tony from the billowing fog and collapsed just past the threshold of the Maestro's office.

The mist hadn't followed—but the damage was done.

Her lungs felt like they'd been replaced with fiberglass insulation. Her pulse roared in her ears.

Bagel let out a low, panicked growl above.

Alicia tried to suck in air—but nothing came.

Her hand, the glove had melted off of it, was still clutching Tony's leg.

The edges of her vision shimmered. The ceiling tilted.

She mouthed his name—Tony—but no sound came.

The gray came down like a curtain into blackness.

CHAPTER SEVENTEEN

Kyiv – Interior, Warehouse – Late Afternoon

Dust hung in the shafts of winter light slanting through the broken windows of the warehouse's upper panes. Plastic sheeting still fluttered near the skylights where Brice's team had entered during the sweep the night before. The air smelled of oil paints, varnish, and the faint trace of vinegar—the tell-tale sign of one of the Outfit's cleanup crews that had come and gone.

Brice led Doug Mason down a long corridor flanked with repurposed gallery lighting and unfinished canvas racks.

"This place seemed to keep the lights on by churning out Old Masters to various clientele," Brice said over his shoulder. "We counted at least fourteen incomplete canvases in here. All of them good enough to fool a collector at a glance—maybe even under scrutiny, if the varnish had been aged correctly."

Mason said nothing. He moved with his hands in his coat

pockets, eyes sweeping the open space with measured calculation.

Brice stopped at one of the makeshift art stations: easels, pigment trays, infrared lighting rigs, and a faint whiff of turpentine. A woman sat on a worn drafting stool, shoulders hunched, knuckles white around a ceramic mug.

She looked up.

Late twenties. Ukrainian. Frail, despite the warm coat she'd been given. Her face was pale from sleeplessness and stress, and her eyes darted between Brice and Mason as they approached.

"This is one of the artists," Brice said quietly. "Name's Kateryna Mylenko. Born in Kharkiv. Passport checks out. No priors. She was in the middle of restoring a 'Ghirlandaio' when we breached."

Mason nodded once, then stepped forward. He switched to fluent Ukrainian.

"Good day, Kateryna," he said gently. "You are safe. I need some help. What is this place?"

She looked down into her mug, then back up, hesitant. Her voice cracked.

"Studio. We... painted. Restored sometimes. Copied."

"Who ran it?" Mason pressed.

She licked her lips. "Maksym. He organized supplies. Paid us in cash. But... he didn't make decisions. The other man did."

Mason narrowed his eyes. "Name?"

She shook her head. "No name. Everyone just called him... Maestro."

The name sat in the air like a curse.

Mason continued, quiet and precise. "Did he come often?"

"No," she whispered. "But when he did, Maksym was the only one who he talked to. They spoke in English, which I understand very little of."

"Where are they now?"

Kateryna's hands trembled. "Gone. Maksym was the one who opened the warehouse for us to work every day, and I haven't seen him since before the police came with the other Americans." She nodded in Brice's direction. "Mister Brice asked me to come in today, but I'm not sure for what. Was it to talk to you?"

Mason patted the air and gave her a warm smile. "Yes, that's probably the reason. I'm sure you'll get compensated and go home soon."

She glanced at Brice. "I don't want trouble. I just wanted to paint."

"You're not in trouble," Mason said. "Trust me, there's a lot of things wrong in this world, but you're not one of them. You're fine." He turned to Brice, switching back to English and said, "I think I've got what I need from her. Make sure she gets paid for her time here."

Brice nodded and motioned toward the hallway. "Come on," he said. "Let's go take a look at the office."

Mason took a step, then paused. "How's Alicia?"

Brice's expression tightened. He gave a small shake of his head. "I'm not sure. I haven't been able to get anyone who knew anything specific about her case since she got medevac'd to Ramstein. All I know is that the guys who first got here said she was barely breathing, and dead guy who was really chewed up by the boobytrap this Maestro guy set."

"Do we have an ID on the deceased?" Mason asked.

Brice nodded. "A known member of the Bianchi crime family out of New York. I'm guessing one of Levi's guys maybe acting as muscle for Alicia."

Mason nodded. "That would be my guess as well. I'll follow up on Alicia." He frowned. "I ended up calling Levi when I learned things had gone sideways here. Believe it or not, he'd just landed in Ukraine."

"Oh, shit. He was probably coming in to back her up, but a little too late." Brice winced. "That had to have been an interesting conversation."

Mason shook his head. "You don't even want to know. I just hope she pulls out of this."

Brice said nothing more, and the two men continued toward the Maestro's office in silence, boots echoing off the concrete as the question lingered in the space between them.

How was Alicia?

∼

Kyiv – Warehouse Interior
Maestro's Office

The room still reeked of scorched metal and something worse—something chemical and sour that clung to the air even days after the detonation. Mason stepped carefully over shattered tiles and blackened remnants of office furniture, much of it looked like it had been eaten away by some kind of acid.

Brice stood near the remains of a desk, holding a sealed

evidence bag containing a warped fragment of circuitry and a corroded housing unit. He didn't look up as Mason approached.

"The bioweapons team finished the decontamination and neutralization process a few hours ago," Brice said. "We cleared forensics to start cataloging. Most of the paper records are now trash, but some of the hardware survived." He held up the bag. "This is part of the booby trap Alicia encountered."

Mason crouched, surveying the damage. "Tell me more about this booby trap."

Brice pursed his lips and frowned. "This was a nasty piece of work, and whoever set it up knew what they were doing."

He walked to the center of the room and pointed upward. A jagged skylight filtered pale daylight across a ruined floor in uneven concentric patterns.

"It looks like Maestro designed this room with a two-stage security mechanism. Most of this place was still wired like a 1950s bunker—only the heater and lights pulled any power. But inside this office things were a bit different. I was able to pull together the warped fragments of some custom-designed circuits and I think I've reconstructed how it worked."

He raised the circuit board again. "This was one of the triggers. Radio frequency receiver, probably tied to a short-range fob —something Maestro carried to disarm the trap when he entered."

"A key fob?" Mason asked.

"Exactly. Like a garage opener. Basic. Untraceable. But here's the catch—*it wasn't enough on its own.*"

Brice gestured up toward the skylight, then picked up another evidence bag containing a flat, wafer-like circuit. "This photovoltaic cell was the second part. It acted as a passive light sensor. The system was wired so that *both* conditions had to be met to disarm the trap: the fob signal *and* the presence of daylight hitting this panel—presumably from the skylight."

"So no light..." Mason said slowly.

"No disarm," Brice confirmed. "We've gone over the wiring —without both inputs, the trap defaulted to armed. Maestro had it set up so the room could only be safely entered during daylight hours, and *only* by him. We also have surveillance records from outside the warehouse and it showed this guy only arrived and left during daylight hours."

Mason's expression darkened.

"She entered at night."

Brice nodded grimly. "The moment she crossed that threshold, the system treated her like an intruder; it dumped a pressurized vapor mix from ceiling-mounted reservoirs."

He stepped toward a blackened vent now covered in corrosive scoring.

"Aerosolized acids—fluorosulfonic compounds, hydrogen halides, plus an oxidizer cocktail we're still analyzing. Hot enough to chew through seals, shred respirators, and ruin any Level B suit in under a minute."

Mason scanned the destruction. "She was in full hazmat."

"Didn't matter. This stuff wasn't designed to kill by chance— it was designed to kill by inevitability. And it did a hell of a job wrecking what was in here."

"Any trace of biological agents?"

Brice nodded. "We found precursors. Not a finished payload, but everything you'd need to cook a series of dirty bioweapons—

ricin derivatives, vesicants, even stabilized alkaloids in trace form. The Maestro was using this place as more than a forgery front. This was a lab."

Mason exhaled, jaw tight. "Prints?"

"Plenty. We lifted dozens from embedded surface points—hinges, drawer rails, tool handles. The cleanup wasn't as clean as he thought."

Mason looked away, eyes fixed on a strip of wall where melted vinyl had run like candle wax.

"Do we have an ID?"

Brice shook his head. "Forensics team just left with the data dump. They'll run it against every NATO and Interpol biometric grid. Could be hours. Could be longer."

Mason was quiet for a beat.

"When we get a hit," he said finally, "I want it first."

Brice tilted his head. "You planning to send a team?"

Mason's voice dropped, each word measured and cold.

"No team."

He turned toward the doorway.

"I'm giving it to Levi."

Brice didn't speak, but the meaning was clear in the tightening of his jaw.

Mason let the silence stretch, staring into the skeletal remains of the Maestro's sanctum. "He'll want to bring the bastard to justice."

He turned; voice as cold as the antiseptic haze floating in the air.

"And this time I'm not going to stop him."

Ramstein Air Base
Medical Wing – ICU, Three Days After Extraction

The beeping of the vitals monitor was steady now, but Levi didn't trust it. Machines lied. He'd watched too many people die with perfect EKGs humming right up until they flatlined.

He stood motionless beside Alicia's hospital bed, the overhead lights dimmed to spare her what remained of her vision. Her face was turned slightly to one side, and even in sleep, the tension in her brow hadn't fully released. Her skin, though still patchy and mottled, had lost the blistering crimson that had first greeted him. Antibiotic gels coated her arms and shoulders like a second skin. A thin tube traced from her nose. A heart monitor cable looped over her clavicle like a misplaced necklace.

She looked like a battlefield survivor.

But that wasn't what Levi saw.

Not right now.

In his mind's eye, he was back in this very room—three days ago.

The door had opened. He'd stepped in.

And his heart had simply... stopped.

Alicia was unrecognizable. She was attached to a ventilator, her chest rising and falling in rhythm with the machine's hissing breath, a breathing tube secured to her mouth like a lifeline. Her face—his beautiful, fierce, smart-ass daughter's face—was beet red, blistered, swollen in uneven patterns of trauma, as if someone had tried to redraw her in pain. Her arms were wrapped in gauze but it was her scalp that undid him. Patches of her long black hair were missing, entire strips chemically burned away, exposing raw, inflamed flesh beneath.

It was as if someone had tried to erase her.

A voice beside him—clinical, too calm—began speaking.

"The extent of her burns covers approximately seventy-one percent of her body," the doctor had said. "She's on life support to relieve the strain on her system. We've kept her in a medically induced coma—midazolam, with propofol drips to manage pain and suppress activity. But with dermal layer destruction that extensive, infection is nearly—"

"—inevitable," Levi had finished quietly.

The doctor nodded, clearly grateful not to have to say it again. "We'll do what we can to stabilize her for grafting procedures, if she makes it through the next forty-eight hours."

If.

The word sat on Levi's chest like a weight. He'd been in rooms like this before. With strangers. With people who didn't have his last name. But this was different. This was *her*.

And then the blur hit.

A streak of black fur zipped past his leg and launched itself onto the foot of the hospital bed. Bagel. Soaking wet from rain or sewer runoff—Levi had no idea how the damn cat had gotten into a restricted military medical wing, but there he was. Tail flicking. Eyes like coals.

The doctor stepped forward, a frown creasing his face. "Animals aren't—"

Levi's arm moved faster than thought. His hand planted squarely on the doctor's chest, stopping him cold.

The nurse behind him let out a breath. Levi didn't turn to look at either of them. His voice was low, flat, final.

"If either of you touches that cat... or tries to remove him..." He turned to face them, his eyes, normally unreadable, now glinted like blades.

"I'll kill you."

No raised voice. No threat.

A statement of fact.

Bagel climbed up toward Alicia's shoulder and curled into a crescent moon of damp fur. He didn't meow. He didn't purr. He just watched her.

So did Levi.

And the machine kept breathing for her.

CHAPTER EIGHTEEN

Ramstein Air Base
Medical Wing – ICU – Day Six

The pneumatic hiss of the ICU door opened like a breath held too long. Two doctors entered, one in his early thirties, the other older—grizzled, bespectacled, and clearly in charge. The younger man hovered by the monitor; the senior physician went straight to the wall-mounted light box, a patient folder tucked under his arm.

Levi didn't move from his chair.

The older doctor clipped two large X-ray sheets into place and flipped the switch. A dull hum filled the room, and a white glow lit the skeletal images from behind.

"Mr. Yoder," the doctor said without looking back. "I'd like to show you something."

Levi stood silently and walked over.

Having learned how to read x-ray images, he didn't need the doctor to tell him what he was looking at.

The first image—dated six days ago—was a mess. Lungs clouded with fluid. The faint outlines of alveoli shredded, collapsed. Rib shadows overlaid with scarring and striation.

"This was Alicia when she arrived," the doctor said. "I've seen soldiers with mustard gas exposure in better shape."

The doctor then pointed at the second film on the light box.

It looked like another person's lungs.

The chest looked normal. There was no fluid buildup. The structural recovery defied explanation.

"We repeated the imaging this morning. No signs of internal inflammation. External recovery is—frankly—a miracle. No grafts have been applied. There's been no infection. We've removed the respirator, and other than a brief dip in her oxygen saturation—which quickly corrected—her vitals have stabilized."

He paused, glancing at Levi.

"There's no longer any justification for keeping her under. We're stopping the sedation now. That said, it may take twelve to forty-eight hours for her to regain consciousness. There's no precise timing when it comes to waking up a body that's been that close to shutting down. A lot of it has to do with the person's metabolism."

The doctor stepped to the head of the bed and tapped the screen on the infusion pump. The gentle whirr of the machine ceased. A moment later, he disconnected the line from the propofol reservoir and capped the port.

"That's it," he said quietly. "She's off the sedation."

He looked to Levi. "We'll monitor her vitals, but if she stays stable... she'll wake up when she's ready."

Levi didn't answer. He simply nodded once and returned to his seat by her bedside.

The doctor left, leaving him alone with Alicia, and Bagel was curled up against side, eyes closed, sucking on the tip of his tail.

She looked better—less like a casualty, more like someone healing. Her face had regained some of its shape, though pink and raw in places. The worst of the swelling was gone. Hair was still patchy where it had burned away, but her breathing was her own. No machine fed her air anymore.

He rested his elbows on his knees and let out a slow breath.

Then, he began to speak.

Not to the doctors.

Not to himself.

To her.

"In a hole in the ground there lived a hobbit," he said softly.

No book. No hesitation.

He recited the words from memory, each line as clear as if it had been printed in front of him. He could hear her young voice echoing them back from decades ago, her tiny fingers gripping the edge of a blanket as he sat beside her, reading through the Tolkien classic.

"Not a nasty, dirty, wet hole, filled with the ends of worms and an oozy smell..."

His voice was calm. Steady. The machines beeped. The room breathed.

Time passed.

Then—

A twitch.

Her left index finger shifted, just barely, enough to pull the sheet a fraction of an inch.

Levi leaned in.

Her lips parted. A faint groan emerged—dry, strained, but unmistakably hers.

He was on his feet instantly, the chair scraping behind him.

Alicia's eyelids flickered.

She was waking up.

And, as always, she was doing it her way—not on the doctor's schedule, but on a schedule that she alone dictated.

∼

Ramstein Air Base
Medical Wing – ICU

Levi didn't know when she'd started crying. One minute she was blinking awake, pupils sluggish, jaw slack from disuse. The next, she was clutching his shoulder, hot tears soaking into his shirt.

Her voice had rasped like gravel, the words barely forming—but her first coherent question hadn't been about her condition. Not about the pain. Not about the missing patches of hair, or the scarring, or the quiet beep of a monitor behind her.

She'd asked about Tony.

And now, she was shattered.

"He didn't make it?" Her voice was so small.

Levi couldn't speak right away. He held her tighter, Bagel curled on the bed beside her, purring so loudly it vibrated through the frame. The little black cat nudged her unbandaged hand with his head and stayed close, as if he understood that the physical warmth of his presence mattered more than words.

Levi swallowed hard. "No. He... didn't."

She broke then. Her shoulders trembled, her breath came in halting gasps, and Levi let her cry it out against him, hand cradling the back of her head where fresh peach-fuzz now sprouted from newly healed skin. The sobs weren't loud. Just raw. Tired. Hollow.

The door opened.

The doctor entered, glancing down at his clipboard—then froze like he'd stepped into the wrong room.

"What...?" he blinked, adjusting his glasses. "How the hell are you sitting up already?"

It had only been two hours since they'd stopped the pump delivering her sedatives.

Alicia wiped at her eyes but didn't look away from her father. Levi finally helped ease her back against the pillows, though she was still upright.

The doctor moved quickly, scanning vitals on the monitor and manually checking her pulse and pupils, his expression ping-ponging between disbelief and cautious fascination.

"Well," he finally said, his voice trailing into a disbelieving chuckle, "your vitals are... exceptional. Resting heart rate, oxygenation, even your inflammatory markers—everything's been dropping faster than we'd ever expect. You were on full life support when you came in. Burn damage across over seventy percent of your body. Inhalation trauma. We didn't think you'd make it through the first twenty-four hours, let alone sit up in less than a week."

Alicia blinked. "I'm starving."

The doctor smiled at that. "That's a good sign. A very good sign. You'll be cleared for light solid foods shortly. If things keep going the way they are, you'll be out of here in a few days. We're still trying to understand how your case seems to have turned so quickly. Honestly, in my thirty years of practice, I've never seen anything like it."

Levi felt her glance at him.

He turned, met her gaze.

They didn't have to say it aloud.

The nanites.

Their mutual curse.

Their miracle.

The doctor packed up his clipboard and gave Bagel a bemused look before slipping out of the room. The door whispered shut behind him.

Alicia ran her fingers gently through the soft fur along Bagel's spine. He rumbled in response, purring like an overloaded generator.

She didn't look at Levi when she spoke.

"Do you still think this is a curse?" she whispered. "It sounds like I should be dead… or most of the way there."

Levi looked at her—his daughter, battered, reborn, surviving yet again—and found he had no answer.

She shifted her legs to the side of the bed.

"Hey—slow," he said, rising, arms ready.

She stood, legs wobbling like a newborn deer, then immediately grabbed his forearm.

"Okay, okay," she admitted, swaying. "How about a compromise?"

He arched a brow.

"I sit in that chair…" she pointed with a trembling finger, "…and you get me something to eat."

He didn't move right away. "What do you want?"

"Everything," she said. "I'm *freaking starving*. These nanites don't run on air, you know. And they've still got work to do." She winked.

That was all he needed.

Levi turned without a word and strode toward the door, boots moving with purpose.

Behind him, Bagel curled tighter against her leg and purred louder, like he was daring the universe to try her again.

∼

Ramstein Air Base
Perimeter Walkway

The cold German air bit at Levi's cheeks as he stepped out of the medical wing and onto the concrete path that curved around the main hospital building. His breath ghosted out in short, sharp plumes. Beyond the fence, the airfield hummed with distant activity—C-130s being prepped, fuel trucks gliding like shadows in the mist.

His phone buzzed once. Mason.

Levi answered without slowing his stride.

"What've you got?"

Mason didn't waste time.

"We got a match. Latent fingerprints from the warehouse came back this morning. One of the prints wasn't Ukrainian. It belonged to a U.S. citizen. Former military."

Levi's jaw tightened. "How former?"

"Name's Derrick Antonov, formerly Captain Derrick James Antonov. Army. Bioweapons division. Fort Detrick. He ghosted during a restructuring audit in 2018. Slipped off the radar before anyone realized he'd taken a truckload of proprietary formulas with him."

Levi exhaled slowly. "And now?"

"He's in Germany."

Levi stopped walking.

Mason continued. "We tracked him because thankfully this guy made a stupid mistake. When Alicia tripped the booby trap, it executed a sort of phone home feature. Two phone numbers were pinged—brief uplink, point-to-point signal. One of the numbers belonged to Maksym, the front man for the art warehouse. The other was Antonov's."

"Let me guess," Levi said. "Neither of them showed up at the warehouse the next day."

"Nope. They were out of Kyiv before dawn. That's when Brice stepped in."

Levi resumed walking.

"Mason, it sounded like Brice was on scene almost immediately, how the hell did he even know Alicia was there?"

"It turns out Alicia needed weapons when arriving in

Ukraine, so she called him, and that's all it took for Brice to start connecting the dots. A little remote observation and it didn't take much for him to figure out the warehouse was her target. Set up a listening post two buildings down, thermal and RF tracking. When the trap went off, he caught the cellular handoff signature. The key was Antonov wasn't using a burner phone. That call went to his normal phone. Unfortunately, six hours after arriving in Germany, the phone was tossed or turned off. We lost his signal, but not Maksym's. They travelled together from Ukraine."

Levi's voice dropped. "Where's Maksym now?"

Mason didn't hesitate. "Augsburg. Bavaria. He's staying at a nondescript hotel outside the old town district. Been there two days. We've got eyes on the building but they haven't moved. I waited until Alicia was stable before bringing it to you."

Levi's fingers clenched tighter around the phone.

"And Antonov?"

"Gone to ground. No new digital trail. At least not yet. But if anyone knows where he is—it's probably Maksym."

Levi was already turning back toward the hospital, boots grinding on frost-slick concrete.

"Send me everything."

A pause. Then Mason said, "Levi... this doesn't have to be just you. I can send a team to back you up."

"There's no need."

Another pause.

"I figured as much," Mason said, the edge of resignation in his voice. "Good luck. And be careful."

Levi ended the call without replying.

He slid the phone into his coat pocket and looked out across the fog-drenched landscape. Somewhere out there, the man who had nearly killed his daughter was breathing borrowed air.

That wouldn't last.

∾

Ramstein Air Base
Medical Wing – Discharge Room

Levi didn't need to read the doctor's face—he could see the hesitation in his hands. The way the man kept glancing at Alicia, at her vitals, back at the screen, then at Levi.

"Her recovery is unprecedented," the doctor finally said, folding his arms. "I'd prefer to run at least a dozen more scans. Cellular regeneration at this rate—it's... well, it's medically impossible."

Levi held his tongue. He'd heard the same thing years ago about his case of so-called terminal cancer.

"She can walk," Levi said flatly. "She can breathe. She's coming with me."

"Provisional discharge," the doctor muttered. "Against recommendation."

Levi signed the paperwork.

In the hallway outside, Alicia was already pacing—still pale, still too thin, but with a fire in her that Levi hadn't seen since she was a teenager who thought she could fight her way through anything.

"You're leaving without me?" she snapped the moment he stepped into view.

He kept his voice calm. "Yes."

"The hell you are."

He blinked. "You're barely on your feet."

"I'm standing," she shot back. "And I'm not missing this. You're going after him, aren't you? The one behind the trap. The one who killed Tony."

Levi didn't answer.

Alicia stepped in close, eyes locked with his, her voice low and razor-sharp. "I *need* to be there. When the life fades from his eyes—I want to be there, so I see it myself."

He exhaled slowly. "Fine. But don't get it in your head that we're running this your way."

"Fine." She tilted her head, triumphant. "So, I'm good to go with you?"

Levi frowned. "I suppose if you're going to do something stupid, it might as well be with me. Fine—you can come."

A grin spread across her face as she balled her fists and did a clumsy little jig. If he hadn't grabbed her shoulder, she would've landed flat on her ass.

"You won't regret this."

"I already do."

∼

Ramstein Air Base
Parking lot outside the hospital

Alicia showed him a still frame from the grainy video one of Brice's people had gotten from outside the warehouse. It was

Maksym. Mid-thirties. Gaunt. Rat-faced with a permanent look of nervous guilt.

"This is him?" Levi asked.

"Clear as we've got."

Levi stared at the image for three full seconds and burned it into memory.

Brice's app was already live on Levi's phone, fed by a service monitoring the pings from Maksym's phone. The signal was good enough to triangulate the location within fifty to one-hundred-and-fifty meters. It had been moving, but now was stationary, pinging from a fixed location outside Augsburg.

~

Outskirts of Augsburg

The car was a matte black Škoda borrowed from one of the Outfit's embedded assets at Ramstein. Levi had no idea who he was, other than he was a Captain in the army, and as he passed them checking out of the hospital, he veered over to Levi, shook his hand in greeting, and departed just as quickly, leaving a key surreptitiously placed in the palm of his hand. On the key was taped a license plate number.

Alicia sat beside him, riding shotgun, a navy ski cap pulled low to hide the disaster that had become her hair. She hadn't said much since they left the base. Her focus was locked on the phone in her hand—his phone, running the tracking app Brice had remotely installed. She hadn't let go of it once.

Bagel was curled in the footwell of the passenger compartment, his head resting against Alicia's shin, fast asleep.

"Almost there," she said. "Signal's strong. He hasn't moved in ten minutes."

Levi said nothing, eyes on the narrowing road. The trees thickened as they entered a cul-de-sac, the gravel lane flanked by scattered homes with sloped roofs and wood-paneled siding. Patches of frost clung to the grass, untouched in the late afternoon shade.

Alicia pointed. "There."

A two-story cottage sat tucked into the trees at the end of the lane, curtains drawn tight. No lights. No movement.

Levi eased the car to a stop just short of the driveway, tucked it behind a stand of evergreens. His eyes lingered on the house—no motion, no vehicles, no heat shimmer off the windows.

He'd worried triangulation might be a problem—easy to be uncertain of the target in a city packed with apartments. But out here, in the open, no such issue.

He'd been worried that the triangulation's accuracy might have been a problem, and it would have been in a city full of dense apartment blocks. But out here in the hinterland, with wide open spaces between homes, there was no such problem.

He turned to Alicia. "You stay here."

She immediately opened her mouth, a protest forming.

"He's seen you," Levi cut in. "He'll recognize you. He won't recognize me."

Her jaw tightened, the gears clearly turning behind that defiant look. After a beat, sense won out over stubbornness. She gave a reluctant nod. "Once the scene is cleared…"

"I'll bring you in."

"Be quick," she said through clenched teeth.

Levi stepped out, shutting the door with a soft *click*. The chill hit him immediately, but he barely noticed. The weight of the pistol inside his coat pocket was cold and familiar, his fingers brushing the grip as he moved. Not drawing—just ready.

He moved toward the cottage with quiet precision, boots whispering over the gravel. His senses sharpened, tuned to the low electric buzz of instinct. Something about the silence here felt engineered.

He knocked.

The door creaked open.

The man behind it matched the image Alicia had shown him—Maksym. Thinner in person. Paler.

Maksym blinked, clearly not expecting anyone. He opened his mouth, maybe to ask a question—

Levi's fist snapped upward in a clean arc—an uppercut honed by repetition and necessity. Maksym's eyes went wide for a fraction of a second before his body folded. The back of his skull hit the floor with a sickening crack.

Silence.

Levi stepped inside.

CHAPTER NINETEEN

Augsburg – Cottage Cellar

The air in the cellar pressed against Alicia's skin like a damp, heavy cloth—clinging, suffocating. Stone walls wept with condensation. The exposed bulb overhead flickered as if unsure whether to illuminate the scene at all.

Alicia stood still, arms crossed tightly against her chest—not for warmth, but to control the tremor in her hands.

She was still recovering.

Not that she'd admit it out loud.

Her skin itched constantly, stretched too tight across healing muscle. It took every ounce of will power she had not to scratch herself raw. And though she'd eaten two full meals—more food in one sitting than she'd ever touched in her life—*she was still hungry.* Starving, in fact. Not a normal hunger. This was something deeper, it was almost like her bones ached she was so hungry. It felt like her body was burning fuel faster than she could eat it.

She knew what it was.

Her father called it a curse.

But it wasn't.

Not to her.

The hunger was a tax. A price to pay for having survived something that should have killed her. She imagined being able to see the tiny miracles crawling through her veins, repairing tissue, rebuilding her strength, dragging her back from the brink. She wasn't whole yet.

But she would be.

Soon.

Her gaze shifted to the figure shackled to the chair— Maksym. The rat-faced little man who had played frontman for the Maestro's operation. His skin was clammy, his eyes swollen, and he reeked of old sweat and panic. Stripped to his underwear, his ribs heaved with each breath.

She'd hit him twice. Hard. And it wasn't enough. She hadn't rattled him. One way or another, getting someone to talk required a deft hand. It was a skill; one she needed to master.

But as she backed away from Maksym, her father approached the prisoner.

What would he do to crack him?

She watched her father move, and something in her gut turned—not from fear, but from the *effortless precision* of it. Gone was the warmth, the dry humor.

This wasn't the man who had raised her. This was the version of him she'd only ever caught glimpses of.

And it scared her how much she admired it.

He radiated confidence and danger. Even after a lifetime beside him, she didn't understand how he could shift so completely—like flipping a switch no else could reach.

"Don't misunderstand me," Levi said softly as he drew the knife.

The steel whispered as it cleared the sheath. Alicia couldn't help but follow the line of it—gleaming, narrow, impossibly steady in his hand.

Maksym's body locked. He whimpered before the blade even reached his face.

Levi stepped in close, eyes like winter glass. The knife hovered a hair's breadth from Maksym's right eye. The man couldn't even flinch for fear of skewering himself. There was nowhere to go.

"You talk," Levi said, voice low, "or you don't leave this cellar alive."

Alicia didn't blink. She couldn't.

"But first," Levi said, his voice low and calm, "I'll make sure you *want* to die."

Each word hit like a nail driven into wood.

"I'll start with your teeth. You wouldn't believe how much pain a manual extraction causes without anesthetic. And when we run out of teeth, we'll move on to breaking things.

"The little bones first—fingers, toes. Then we go upstream. Hands. Feet. You'd be amazed how quickly human flesh starts to resemble rare roast beef. Almost appetizing, for some of us."

He took a breath, then added, almost gently, "And don't worry—you won't die right away.

"I'll make it last. I'll keep you hollowed out, give you blood transfusions just to keep you alive and awake. And when the pain finally breaks you mind... I'll still be there."

The slap came so fast Alicia barely saw it. Her father's open hand cracked across Maksym's face with bone-crunching force, snapping his head sideways with a sickening thud.

Maksym began to shake violently. Alicia smelled the urine before she saw it pooling beneath the chair.

"I'll talk," he sobbed. "Please—just don't kill me."

Levi stepped back. The blade, which had been in his hand the entire time, vanished into its sheath in one smooth, practiced motion—no theatrics, just the cold certainty of command.

Alicia exhaled, slow and steady.

She felt the familiar hunger gnawing again, like some primal force chewing at her from the inside. The itch crawled up her spine beneath her clothes. Her skin didn't fit quite right yet.

Her healing was nowhere near complete, yet.

She moved forward, eyes cold, voice sharp. "Good," she said. "Start with where he is."

Her father melted into the shadows, letting her take center stage.

She looked into Maksym's eyes—the broken, bloodshot things staring back at her—and she knew he'd give her what she wanted.

And as she stood there, something inside her hardened.

She didn't know whether to fear what she was becoming.

Or to embrace it.

Augsburg – Cottage Cellar – One Hour Later

Levi stood over the crumpled form of Maksym, the flickering bulb above casting an unkind light on what Alicia had left of the man. His face had swollen grotesquely, blood caked beneath his nostrils, a split along his cheekbone leaking slowly into the corner of his mouth. He wheezed through what might be a set of broken ribs from the kick she'd landed, but his eyes were still tracking. He was still lucid.

That was what mattered.

Alicia leaned against the far wall, one boot propped up, rubbing her knuckles absentmindedly. He didn't miss the faint swelling there—the quiet satisfaction she tried to bury behind her professional mask. She'd gone harder than he wanted. A little too far.

But they'd gotten what they needed.

Levi crouched beside the battered man and slipped a photograph from his inside coat pocket. It was an old image—seven years, maybe more. A personnel file photo, pre-disappearance. The man stared out from the paper in stiff military posture, face still sharp, eyes confident.

Derrick James Antonov.

Levi held it in front of Maksym's swollen face. "Is this him?"

Maksym blinked through the blood, then nodded quickly, the motion wincing with pain. "Yes," he croaked. "That's him. He looks... older now. Thinner. But it's him."

Levi's voice remained calm. "Are you sure the location you gave us is where he is?"

Maksym swallowed hard, blood dribbling from the corner of his mouth. "Yes. Yes, I swear. He's meeting that real estate broker guy—same one I told you about—at three. In the warehouse district."

Alicia stepped forward; eyes locked on Maksym like she was sizing him up for another round. He flinched.

Levi stood, slid the photo back into his coat, and nodded once to her. Time to go.

Maksym's voice trembled behind them as they turned toward the cellar steps.

"You said... I'd be let go," he whimpered. "You said if I talked... I'd be set free."

Levi paused at the base of the stairs and looked back at him.

"You were only promised freedom *after* we get Antonov," he said evenly. "Once that task is done—you'll be freed."

"I told you everything! Please!"

Levi's expression didn't change. "Then you have nothing to worry about."

Maksym wilted, sagging into the chair like a marionette whose strings had been cut.

Levi and Alicia climbed the narrow steps. He pulled the heavy cellar door shut with a quiet finality. The lock slid into place with a metallic *click* that echoed too loud in the silence.

They walked toward the car, the air thick with moisture and the sharp scent of cold pine. Though the sun hung high in a cloudless sky, winter had already taken hold of the countryside, its chill biting through the light.

Alicia broke the silence as they neared the vehicle. "Are we really going to set him free?"

Levi opened the driver's door without looking at her.

Bagel yowled at the indignity of having been left behind and leaped into Alicia's lap as she settled into the passenger's seat.

"There are many ways to set someone free," he said, sliding in behind the wheel.

He met her eyes briefly as she climbed in beside him.

"I'm just not sure Maksym will appreciate *my* interpretation of freedom."

He started the engine.

∼

Levi steered the Škoda onto the A99 loop, muted gray sky above and the industrial skeleton of Munich's western edge rising like a series of broken teeth ahead of them. Alicia had pulled up the nav on his phone, now docked to the dash, since the car's onboard system was about as intuitive as a Soviet-era microwave. The destination: a specific warehouse address near Aubing, west of the city.

It was 11:58 a.m. They had just over three hours before Antonov's suspected meeting.

Levi hit the call button. Brice picked up on the second ring.

"*GPS is telling me that you're en route.*" Brice's voice buzzed with ambient noise—somewhere loud.

"Yup, I'm just outside Munich. I sent you the target address. You have anything for me on it?"

"*I'm working on getting some surveillance feeds up, give me a bit. In the meantime, I've got a contact waiting near Lochhausen for the two of you. It's a safehouse of sorts buried behind a freight yard off Bodenseestraße. It's ten minutes west of the target site. I'll send you the details. Hey, Alicia, you there?"*

"Yup." Alicia leaned closer to the phone as she stroked the top of Bagel's head. "You're on speaker."

"First, I'm really glad to hear you're in one piece. Also, we managed to extract your laptop and whatever was left in your hotel room back in Kyiv, so we'll have it waiting for you when you're back in the States. When you get back you should have a replacement for the phone that got cooked. When you get a chance let me know what other equipment got hammered and we'll figure something out."

"I appreciate that, Brice. And thanks for being a nosy bastard and having people nearby, I probably owe you my life for that."

Brice laughed. *"No worries. I'm sending the instructions over to you, Levi and then getting my ass working on surveilling your target location."*

"Roger that," Levi said, ending the call. His phone beeped with an incoming text. It was Brice's instructions on how to get to the safehouse. He leaned over, scrolled to the end of the message, and put his eyes back on the road.

Alicia looked over at her Levi and said, "Speaking of lost items, I have no idea what happened to Denny's contact or his earbud that I was wearing in the warehouse. They probably got chewed up in the chemical spray."

Levi nodded. "It happens. Let's not worry about that right now. I need to make sure I don't take a wrong turn. Never been in this part of Germany."

She nodded, resting her hand over Bagel's sling. The cat was curled into a tight ball of fur, the occasional ear twitch betraying light sleep.

They swung off the main road, threading into the outer reaches of Freimann Industrial Park—gray warehouses, gravel lots, and low metal buildings that all looked like they'd been dipped in soot. Chain-link fences sagged under frost. Smoke puffed from a chimney stack nearby, and the heater in the car—which dragged in all of the smells from outside—caused Alicia to wrinkle her nose.

This whole place stank of diesel and other petrochemicals.

A turn brought them into a side road flanked by decaying shipping depots. Half the street signage had been defaced or stolen.

"This place is delightful," Alicia muttered.

"It's a warehouse district, it's exactly supposed to be," Levi replied, slowing to a crawl.

Then he saw it—just as Brice's text had described. A narrow alley, barely wide enough for two people shoulder to shoulder. On the right, a brick building with rusting iron brackets clawing out of the wall like broken fingers.

Levi pulled over, killed the engine, and stepped out into the biting air.

"This is it?" Alicia asked, following behind.

He pointed to the alley. "Let's find out."

The passage was darker than it should've been, even at noon. Something about the angle of the buildings blocked the sunlight, turning the air thick with rot, old motor oil, and wet iron. Puddles reflected overhead drainpipes, their drips echoing like a leaky metronome.

At the base of the wall, Levi found the stub of a rusted iron bracket. He counted up—thirteen bricks—and pressed his palm flat against the spot.

It felt like any other brick. Cold. Solid.

He maintained pressure against the wall for a full three seconds and then—*click*.

Something faintly metallic clanked behind the wall, and the section beneath his hand shifted—then swung inward with a pneumatic hiss. Nearly seamless, the hidden door revealed itself with quiet finality.

Alicia raised an eyebrow. "Seriously? A hidden brick wall? It feels like the Outfit's ripping off Rowling's Diagon Alley."

Levi gave his daughter a look. "Who? What?" He waved her comment away. "It doesn't matter, let's do this."

They stepped through.

The panel sealed shut behind them, cutting off all sound from the alley. Fluorescent lights snapped on overhead, buzzing faintly.

The corridor stretched ahead—sterile, metallic, bunker-like. At the far end stood a steel door flanked by glass walls. Behind each pane, a uniformed soldier in German Bundeswehr fatigues leveled an MP5 through a waist-high firing slot. Each of them with their finger not far from the trigger.

"One at a time, place the palm of your hand on the panel to the right of the door until a green light appears." the soldier barked in German.

Levi didn't flinch but relayed to Alicia what he'd just said.

Alicia nodded. "You first."

Levi stepped forward and placed his hand flat against the chest-high cool, metal panel next to the door.

After a heartbeat's wait, a green light flashed. *Click.*

Alicia followed, doing the same.

The hydraulic hiss of pistons retracting echoed up the corridor, and the heavy door in front of them yawned open on greased hinges.

A calm, pre-recorded voice spoke over the intercom in crisp *Hochdeutsch.*

"Welcome to The Supply Room."

CHAPTER TWENTY

Munich – Outfit Safehouse
"The Supply Room"
12:42 p.m.

The metal door hissed shut behind them, sealing Levi and Alicia in a temperature-controlled chamber that smelled faintly of gun oil and ozone.

Fluorescent panels hummed overhead, throwing stark white light onto rows of matte black lockers, reinforced cabinets, and modular weapon mounts lining the walls. It was equal parts armory and vault—a temple to cold efficiency.

Alicia scanned the room and muttered, "You'd think we walked into a Bond villain's walk-in closet."

Levi smirked. "This *is* the Outfit."

From a recessed doorway near the far wall, a man emerged—tall, rail-thin, dressed in a charcoal gray waistcoat and pressed slacks. His silver hair was slicked back with surgical precision, and a monocle—yes, an actual monocle—rested against one eye like it hadn't gone out of fashion since the Kaiser.

"*Guten Tag*," the man said, bowing slightly. "I am Helmut. Please forgive the… ambiance." His English was crisp, his accent faint but deliberate. "I believe you're in need of supplies. My role here is to help ensure your selection process is… both efficient and bespoke."

Alicia raised an eyebrow. "We get a sommelier for weapons?"

Helmut gave the faintest of smiles. "Think of me as your concierge of applied lethality."

He turned and gestured for them to follow. "Right this way."

They passed through a short tunnel into a wide chamber that opened like a bunker showroom. Behind a thick pane of ballistic glass stood an array of weaponry—everything from collapsible submachine guns to long-range precision rifles, displayed like haute couture in a private atelier.

Helmut motioned toward a touchscreen console built into a central table. "Let us begin with context. Target type?"

Levi kept it simple. "Human. Dangerous."

"Very good. Urban or rural?"

"Urban. Tight quarters."

"Ah." Helmut nodded, fingers dancing across the console. Panels shifted, revealing an array of compact weapons.

"Close range lethality. Suppressed, I presume?" Helmut's tone was casual, clinical. "Assassination?"

Levi hesitated a beat. "Yes."

"Excellent. Then we prioritize acoustic discipline. You will want a suppressed platform firing subsonic rounds. For reference —" he picked up a slim pistol with an integrally suppressed barrel and offered it to Levi, "—this model produces roughly 122 decibels upon discharge. A standard unsuppressed pistol?" He raised an eyebrow. "About 160. Each 10 decibels doubles the perceived volume to the human ear."

Alicia nodded appreciatively. "So we're shaving the volume down by... three-quarters?"

"Precisely," Helmut said. "Enough to make it sound like a car backfiring rather than a threat. Choose your environment wisely, and you'll never need a second shot."

He moved along the wall, selecting a compact PDW, a suppressed .300 Blackout carbine. Levi tested the balance.

Then Levi's phone buzzed.

He checked the screen. It was Brice.

"Yeah?"

"I've got an update for you," Brice said. *"How's your long game?"*

"Long game?"

"You're good with shots at a distance, right?"

"Oh, yeah sure. That's not a problem unless we're talking excessive distances or weird scenarios, why?"

"Your guy's meeting location is perfect for a sniper shot— single entrance, single exit, completely exposed interior wall. And there are two office buildings nearby. Upper stories give a straight shot, maybe 100 meters. I don't normally give operators my opinion on their ground game, but—"

"You're going to give it to me anyway."

"Yup. Take him from distance. Clean and quiet. This should be as textbook as it comes."

Levi's eyes flicked to Alicia. "You up for a snipe?"

She turned to him with a questioning expression. She posed as if she were shooting a rifle. "You mean this kind?"

"Yup."

She lit up. "Hell yes."

"Okay, Brice. Sounds like a plan. Anything else you want to pass along?"

"Nope, other than good luck."

Levi hung up the phone and then nodded at Helmut. "We need something for a roughly 100-meter shot. Precision. Silenced."

"Very well." The butler's eyes gleamed like he'd just been handed a wine pairing challenge. "You'll want something sub-MOA accurate, integrally suppressed, chambered for subsonic .308 or 6.5 Creedmoor. At 100 meters? I recommend the DSR-Precision DSR-1. German-made. Factory-zeroed. Quick-change barrel system. Adjustable match trigger. Carbon-fiber bipod. Schmidt & Bender optics if you want thermal overlay."

He guided them to a sealed cabinet, unlocking it with a thumbprint and iris scan.

Inside lay a sleek, black sniper rifle that looked more spacecraft than firearm.

Alicia ran her fingers along the frame. "She's beautiful."

Helmut inclined his head. "And deadly, Miss Yoder."

"Do you by chance have two of them?" Levi asked.

A smile grew on Helmut's face, and he nodded. "We do."

Levi stepped forward, assessing the gear. "Alright, Helmut—let's get these packed for travel. I want everything discrete and street safe. Sling bags, nothing flashy."

"Understood," Helmut said crisply.

Levi grabbed a low-profile sling and tucked a spare mag into his coat pocket—just in case. Helmut laid out the rest with efficient precision: custom-fit suppressors, compact optics, and two wireless in-ear comms. "Secure channel," he said. "Tight-band encryption. Low latency. You'll hear each other clean, even during suppressed fire."

They loaded up fast. Alicia slung the rifle across her back, the bulk hidden under a puffy jacket that made her look more tourist than assassin. Levi packed spare rounds into a nondescript canvas bag. Bagel, reading the room as always, hopped into his sling without a sound—alert but calm.

"*Danke*, Helmut," Levi said, securing the last clasp.

Helmut gave a respectful nod. "Godspeed. And do be punctual. German targets have a tendency to arrive... early."

The vault door closed behind them, sealing away The Supply Room's treasures as they stepped back into the world.

∽

Munich – Rooftop Overwatch
2:41 PM

ALICIA

The metal groaned beneath her boots as she dropped prone on the gravel-lined rooftop. From here, the view was perfect. Her vantage was slightly elevated and east-facing, giving her a clear shot of the warehouse's main entrance.

Bagel settled himself into a loaf, supervising her preparation as only a cat could do. He remained motionless, eyes narrowed, tail occasionally twitching.

She laid the rifle flat. Chambered a round. Eased into the scope. Adjusted elevation.

LEVI

Two buildings over, Levi steadied himself behind the DSR-10. The bi-pod legs locked against the concrete lip of the rooftop. He sighted through the scope, west-facing, giving him near-perfect triangulation on the same entrance from the opposite angle.

He tapped the comm unit in his ear.

"Say something."

"You suck at small talk."

"Good. They work."

"I suppose so."

"And now we wait…"

ALICIA

She peered through the scope. The view shimmered slightly with heat distortion from the rooftop vents. She tapped her cheek twice. Her face was getting numb from the cold.

Bagel seemed unbothered as he watched and purred.

LEVI

His scope lined perfectly with the front stoop of the warehouse. Just the right distance. 100 meters. Slight crosswind. He made a mental note. Three clicks left. Subsonic. Closed chamber. Everything about this shot felt right.

"Eyes open," he said.

"Always."

"I've got it at 2:57 PM."

"Roger that... a car just parked nearby at three o-clock."

"I see it."

A figure emerged from the sedan. Large. Broad-shouldered. Moving with purpose.

Levi clicked on the safety and leaned in.

"You seeing this?"

"That's him," Alicia whispered in his ear. *"Couldn't confirm the face from any footage back in Ukraine, but the height, the gait—it's dead on. I know it's him."*

The man's head was covered. Reflective sunglasses. Thick coat. Gloves. A man who instinctively avoided exposing his identity.

"I can't make out his face at all."

"Doesn't matter," Alicia replied. *"Dad, I've got that guy's silhouette burned into my head. That's him."*

Levi watched as the man entered the realtor's office. "Okay. We now know what we're looking at. The moment we see that same corpulent bulk exit through that doorway, take the shot."

"Got it. I've got the doorway in my crosshairs."

He'd always hoped her first kill wouldn't have to matter this much. But here they were.

He steadied the rifle. Breathing slowed.

It had just ticked over to 3:00.

Then five more minutes.

"Just remember, Alicia. This is a game of patience."

"Dad, I know…"

Levi smiled as he continued staring through his scope, waiting.

Ten minutes elapsed.

Levi adjusted the scope. Checked wind again. Focused on his breathing.

"Fifteen minutes." He said and at that exact moment, the door opened.

The same man stepped back into the afternoon light.

Levi's heart didn't race.

He just exhaled.

The trigger break was smooth.

The rifle shoved back into his shoulder as the round left the barrel.

Almost simultaneously—Alicia's shot cracked through the silence from her perch.

The man's head exploded in a pink mist.

His body folded like wet laundry.

Levi held position for one more breath.

"Clean shot," he said.

"That was awesome!" Alicia's voice buzzed in his earpiece, electric with adrenaline.

He heard Bagel purring over the comms.

"Clear out," Levi said, already breaking down the rifle with practiced hands.

He allowed himself a quiet smile.

∼

New York – Gerard's

The lights in Denny's place were low and golden, casting a soft glow over the scratched wood bar and the rows of ancient liquor bottles that no one had touched in years. Jazz trickled in through hidden speakers, just loud enough to keep the place from feeling like a tomb.

Levi swirled the seltzer in his glass, bubbles rising like tiny escapees. Across from him, Alicia mirrored the gesture—her own glass sweating slightly in the low light. No alcohol. Neither of them wanted the headaches. Denny had smirked when they ordered.

"Seltzer? That's turning into a Yoder family tradition it seems."

"Don't knock it," Levi had muttered. "Some of us like to keep our reflexes intact."

Now the two of them sat in companionable silence. It had been two weeks since Munich.

Alicia had changed her hair—dramatically. Most of it was

gone, replaced with a jagged, punkish cut that screamed Berlin back alley more than DC operative. She caught him looking at it and raised an eyebrow.

"Don't say a word," she warned.

He frowned anyway. "You planning to join a ska band?"

"How do you even know what ska is?" She rolled her eyes. "Listen, I'm not a fan of my hair either, but give me a break. Half my scalp was chemically nuked. This is the best I could come up with while I wait for it all to grow out."

He grunted, conceding the point.

They'd each just received an e-mail from Brice with a summary of what the forensics team had put together and what amounted to an AAR, after action report.

They were both scrolling through the e-mail and Alicia smiled. "Seems like we got the right guy."

Levi nodded as he skimmed the text.

The identity of the man they'd put down in Munich was confirmed—Derrick James Antonov, formerly of Fort Detrick. No room for doubt. Dead. Deceased. Case closed.

Levi's and Alicia's phone both buzzed as another e-mail arrived.

Switching to the next e-mail, he scanned it with a nod and smiled as Alicia gasped.

"Holy crap." She said a bit too loudly and a few of the bar's patrons looked over at them.

Alicia showed him the email she'd just received. It was a receipt of the amount that had just been deposited into her account. "This feels like too much." she whispered.

"Baby girl, you paid a high price."

Alicia stared again at her phone, her mouth agape. "I guess…"

Levi smiled. "It's a bit more than what they were going to pay you for a yearly salary, eh?"

"And how…"

"You know," Levi said. "You could still go full time with them."

Alicia frowned and shook her head. "No, definitely not. But…"

"What are you thinking?"

A pause.

"I like the idea of being independent," she said slowly. "Driving my schedule and choices, you know? But…" She bit her lip. "I know this might sound weird… but I really like working with you."

Levi blinked.

She continued, voice quieter. "Tony shouldn't have died the way he did. But I keep thinking… if it had been you and me in that warehouse, instead of me and Tony… maybe things would've turned out different."

He didn't say anything.

She didn't need him to.

Denny appeared beside them with a towel slung over his shoulder. "You two want anything to eat, or you just planning to make the chairs part of your asses?"

Levi looked at Alicia, then back to Denny.

"Tell me something," he said. "Do you think Alicia should go freelance? Do her own thing? Or should the two of us stick together and work as a team?"

Denny leaned back slightly, rubbing his jaw in thought.

"Hmm…" he said with mock gravity. "That is a very good question."

Then he turned his head slowly, smiled, and looked directly at the reader.

"What do you think?"

AUTHOR'S NOTE

Well, that's the end of *Canvas of Deception*, and I sincerely hope you enjoyed it.

If this is the first book of mine you've read, I owe you a bit of an introduction. For the rest of you who have seen this before, skip to the new stuff.

I'm a lifelong science researcher who has been in the high-tech industry longer than I'd like to admit. There's nothing particularly unusual about my beginnings, but I suppose it should be noted I grew up with English as my third language—although nowadays, it is by far my strongest. As an Army brat, I traveled a lot and did what many people do: I went to school, got a job, got married, and had kids.

I grew up reading science magazines, which led me into reading science fiction, mostly the classics by Asimov, Niven, Pournelle, etc. And then I found epic fantasy, which introduced

AUTHOR'S NOTE

me to a whole new world—in fact many new worlds. It was Eddings, Tolkien, and the like who set me on the path of appreciating that genre. As I grew older, and stuffier, I grew to appreciate thrillers from Cussler, Crichton, Grisham, and others.

When I had young kids, I began to make up stories for them, which kept them entertained. After all, who wouldn't be entertained when you're hearing about dwarves, elves, dragons, and whatnot? These were the bedtime stories of their youth. And to help me keep things straight, I ended up writing these stories down, so I wouldn't have it all jumbled in my head.

Well, the kids grew up, and after writing all that stuff down to keep them entertained, it turns out I caught the bug—the writing bug. I got an itch to start writing… but not the traditional things I'd written for the kids.

Over the years I'd made friends with some rather well-known authors, and when I talked to them about maybe getting more serious about this writing thing, several of them gave me the same advice: "Write what you know."

Write what I know? I began to think about Michael Crichton. He was a non-practicing MD, who started off with a medical thriller. John Grisham was an attorney for a decade before writing a series of legal thrillers. Maybe there was something to that advice.

I began to ponder, *"What do I know?"* And then it hit me.

I know science. It's what I do for a living and what I enjoy. In fact, one of my hobbies is reading formal papers spanning many scientific disciplines. My interests range from particle physics, computers, the military sciences (you know, the science behind what makes stuff go boom), and medicine. I'm admittedly a bit

AUTHOR'S NOTE

of a nerd in that way. I've also traveled extensively during my life, and am an informal student of foreign languages and cultures.

With the advice of some New York Times bestselling authors, I started my foray into writing novels.

My first book, *Primordial Threat*, became a USA Today bestseller, and since then I've hit that list a handful of times. With 20/20 hindsight, I'm pleased that I took the plunge and started writing.

That's enough of an intro, and I'm not a fan of talking about myself, so let me get back to where I was before I rudely interrupted myself.

The idea of *Canvas of Deception* came as I was watching a show about art theft—especially as Nazi Germany pillaged much of Europe, and there had been a passing reference of how many famous pieces of artwork had been stolen and returned over time, even items like the Mona Lisa.

Yes… that first scene and the ideas that ensued was directly inspired by a five second quip in some documentary I watched a couple of years ago. And yes, I absolutely kept things as accurate as possible when it came to the details. There was a theft back in 1911 by an Italian handyman and former Louvre employee named Vincenzo Peruggia.

You'll want to check out the addendum for more information. Lots of little Easter eggs.

Regardless of what inspired the story, I hope you enjoyed it.

AUTHOR'S NOTE

As always, I'd love to hear comments and feedback.

Please share your thoughts/reviews about the story on Amazon and with your friends. It's only through reviews and word of mouth that this story will find other readers, and I do hope this book (and the rest of my books) find as wide an audience as possible.

And I guess I would be remiss if I didn't at least talk about the ending, or at least the last couple lines of it.

That's a hint to you, my dear reader.

You get a chance to influence how this series evolves.

Even though everyone says an author shouldn't look at the reviews he receives, I don't believe that. There's often wisdom buried within those reviews, but there are also some head-scratchers without a doubt.

I expect that some of you might have an opinion on whether you want Alicia to go solo or to continue pressing forward with Levi.

Let me know through the reviews or wherever you might see me on the internet or in real life. I appreciate the feedback, because I am easily influenced by a consensus.

However, if the opinions are mostly six of one, half a dozen of the other, then you'll end up leaving it to me.

I really enjoyed putting this story together for you guys, and again, I hope you enjoyed it.

Mike Rothman
May 22, 2025

AUTHOR'S NOTE

I should note that if you're interested in getting updates about my latest work, join my mailing list at:

https://mailinglist.michaelarothman.com/new-reader

For those of you who aren't aware, and because it reads on the question that Denny asked, I wanted to make sure you're aware that Alicia currently does have her own parallel series, but it's at a point of turmoil… the last book in that series literally is where Alicia is starting in this book. She's not sure what to do about her involvement with the Outfit.

That being said, I want to give you a free teaser into that series just so you get a feel for her involvement.

You'll find that the first book, Multiverse, has her more as a second main character: she's a student at Princeton, while the other main character is a professor at the same school. Multiverse does pick up almost immediately after the time of The Swamp.

As a teaser, I will include a preview of both Multiverse, and its follow-on, New Arcadia, which has Alicia as the only main character.

PREVIEW – MULTIVERSE

Michael Salomon lurched into a sitting position and felt a wave of dizziness as he blinked the sleep out of his eyes. His heart raced, and he was having difficulty catching his breath as the gauzy memories of a dream fled from his now-conscious mind.

Something had just happened, and he wasn't exactly sure what it could be.

Definitely not a dream. Not with the growing anxiety he felt. Some kind of nightmare…

He glanced at the clock on his nightstand. It was just past seven. He'd gotten to bed only four hours earlier, but waking up at this time was habit. During the school year he'd be frantically climbing out of bed to go teach physics at Princeton. But it was the summer, and he dedicated all his attention to his research.

That was what had kept him up late last night. A discovery that ended with him leaving the lab after two a.m. in a state of shock.

He had wanted to tell someone. Anyone. But it was late, and he couldn't trust himself to talk to his colleagues until he could verify everything with a clear mind. Triple-check the data. Then, and only then, would he risk his reputation.

He stood up from the bed, only to immediately sit back down with a sudden bout of vertigo. Maybe it was his body telling him he needed more rest.

And then he caught the scent of bacon.

He didn't remember making any bacon when he got home from the lab. He had been too exhausted to do anything but go directly to bed. But when he opened the bedroom door, the scent was unmistakable, wafting up the stairs from the kitchen.

And something more.

Someone was humming.

Standing at the top of the stairs, he was about to yell out an empty threat that he had a gun, but his words were choked away when he saw a woman approaching the base of the stairs, carrying a coffee mug. She had straight dark hair hanging to her mid-back, and naturally tanned skin. And she was very pregnant.

Maria.

Their German shepherd puppy, Percy, followed her every step, his nails clicking on the wooden floor.

Before Michael could say a word, Maria's face lit up. "You're awake!" She held up the steaming mug of coffee. "I was going to bring this up to you and tell you I made breakfast."

He merely stared, not believing that this could be real.

Maria waved for him to come down. "The baby is really moving," she said, putting a hand on her stomach. "Come down and feel her."

The puppy looked up at him and barked joyfully.

Michael's skin felt cold and clammy, like he was on the verge of passing out. But he managed to walk slowly down the stairs, unable to take his eyes off the woman he'd loved for nearly a quarter of his forty-two years on this Earth.

Maria grabbed his hand and put it on her stomach. "Do you feel that?"

He nodded. "What—" He cleared his throat. "What day is it?"

Percy whined for attention.

"You poor thing, you're barely even awake." Maria smiled, handed him his coffee, and scratched the top of Percy's head. "It's Thursday, and you practically passed out the moment your head hit the pillow. You didn't even get undressed."

That part was true. He was still wearing the same clothes from last night at the lab.

Still unbelieving, he pressed his hand to Maria's belly once more, feeling the movement as life stirred within her.

Their baby.

His throat tightened with emotion, and he felt like he was about to explode.

"Ay, *mi amor*. What's wrong?" Maria wiped away an unbidden tear that had rolled down his cheek. She wrapped her arms around him. "Whatever it is, it'll be fine. Did something bad happen at work?"

He kissed the top of her head, a storm of emotions raging through him. "I guess I just had a nightmare."

"What about?"

"I don't want to say it out loud."

"Come." Maria grabbed his free hand and gently pulled him toward the kitchen. "Have a seat, and I'll serve up breakfast. I'm sure everything will look better after you've gotten something in your belly."

Michael sat at the kitchen table and watched as his wife of eight years, pregnant with their child, busied herself in the kitchen.

He watched, knowing it was impossible. Because his memories told him of a cascading set of events that had led to Maria disappearing.

First was the late-term complication with the pregnancy. Their daughter was delivered early, and though she should have lived—the odds were with her—she didn't make it. That was the beginning of the end for their marriage. There were arguments. Bitter and nonsensical fights. And then, one day, Maria left and never came back.

He vividly remembered the pain of waking up and finding her gone. Her clothes still in the closet. Her car in the garage.

He filed a missing persons report with the police. They told him she was an adult and maybe she'd just needed time away.

But Maria had literally *vanished*. Gone from his life.

For years.

Until now.

And then there was Percy. The puppy was now watching his mom prepare scrambled eggs, his tail wagging furiously as she scooped some into his bowl on the counter.

Percy was alive... and still a puppy. He had whined for weeks after Maria disappeared. And then one day he escaped from the back yard and got killed by a car.

But apparently that never happened.

It was all a lie. A nightmare.

Percy hopped from side to side with anticipation as Maria mixed his puppy kibble with the eggs. When she set it on the floor, he dove in and devoured it.

Michael smiled at the sight. His wife was really here with him, and as his gaze trailed down to her bulging belly, it took all of his self-control to not break down and begin sobbing right then and there. Their daughter wasn't dead. She was having a little party inside Maria's belly.

Everything was good. Everything was as it should be.

Maria set down two steaming plates of scrambled eggs and bacon, poured herself a glass of orange juice, and sat down beside him.

He sipped the coffee. It was hot, strong, and black. Just like she'd always made it.

She looked longingly at his mug and sighed. "That's the one thing I do miss. My morning *tinto*."

Tinto was what Colombians called a black coffee.

He smiled, reached under the table, and patted her belly. "It won't be long. Would you prefer that I don't drink coffee while you're pregnant?"

Maria gave him a hard look. "Why, are *you* pregnant? Don't be silly. Besides, the orange juice is good for the baby." She took a sip, then pointed at his plate with her fork. "Don't let your food get cold."

"Yes, ma'am." Michael smiled and shoveled a forkful of eggs into his mouth.

Yet even as he chewed, he felt a nagging sense of wrongness.

But then Maria smiled. He returned the smile as he took a bite of bacon.

Everything was perfect.

∼

It was just past ten, and Michael was driving south on US-1 heading in to work when he saw a cluster of brake lights up ahead. Traffic slowed, and then stopped altogether. He sighed, not seeing any cause for the traffic jam. It was a simple two-lane highway, and never got backed up.

"Someone must have gotten into an accident," he muttered.

As he sat in the car, making no forward progress, his mind drifted back to last night's experiments. His area of research had to do with superluminal particles, otherwise known as tachyons—a niche field that occupied one of the darkest recesses of special relativity. And there was good reason for that: no one had ever detected a tachyon. They were the stuff of science fiction.

Tachyons were particles that could go faster than the speed of light. And if there was one thing that everyone understood—or misunderstood—about Einstein's groundbreaking theory, it was that *nothing* could go faster than the speed of light.

This wasn't exactly true.

To be more accurate, Einstein said that nothing that *initially* moved below the speed of light could be accelerated to move beyond the speed of light. And thus the question arose: could tachyons exist?

Up until last night, that question had gone unanswered.

Michael was roused from his thoughts at the sound of tires

screeching behind him. He looked in the rearview mirror and saw a vintage Cadillac swerving, seemingly out of control. No cars had stopped behind Michael, and the barreling Cadillac was no more than fifty feet away from crashing right into him.

Everything seemed to slow. Michael saw the panicked look on the driver's face as he wrestled with his steering wheel. The driver had clearly lost control of the giant boat of a car. It fishtailed, smoke billowing from the tires.

The professor braced himself for impact.

And... the Cadillac skidded to a stop beside him, facing backwards. The driver was literally within arm's reach.

Under normal circumstances, Michael would have thrown his entire inventory of curse words at the man who'd nearly hit him, and would likely have invented new ones for good measure. But he was shaking with the sudden dump of adrenaline into his bloodstream, and he found he couldn't form a coherent sentence. The world was spinning, and he thought he might throw up.

He needed to gather his wits.

So he turned off into the breakdown lane, moved ahead several car lengths, and pulled into the entrance to a parking lot. It was for some kind of medical complex—a sign read "Rothman Orthopedics." But he barely noticed it. He just needed air.

He parked, got out, and took in a slow, deep breath. He felt as though the ground beneath him was tilting. He'd never passed out before, but he was sure he was about to.

Clinging to his car door to keep from collapsing, he closed his eyes and focused on his breathing.

In his mind's eye he saw a verdant field of grass.

It was more than an image; it was a crystal-clear vision,

unfolding as though he were experiencing a dream through a camera lens.

He saw a man in the distance, kneeling. Michael involuntarily moved toward him, despite the fact that the closer he got to the figure, the more anxious he felt.

The man was in a graveyard, kneeling before a tombstone.

Michael's breath caught in his throat. He recognized the man before him.

It was *him*.

But not exactly him. An older version of him. He was thinner. Too thin. A noticeable amount of gray in his hair. A scraggly beard.

Then Michael looked at the tombstone, and his blood ran cold.

Felicia Batsheva Salomon.
We had you only one day, but know this: If love
could have saved you, you would have lived forever.

Below the inscription were two dates: birth and death. They were the same date.

And the date… was tomorrow.

∼

Michael's tires screeched in the driveway as he parked, jumped out of the car, and rushed into the house.

"Maria!" he yelled.

He heard the dog's bark in response, coming from the back yard.

His heart pounding, Michael raced to the sliding glass door leading to the back yard and yanked it open. "Maria!"

"Honey? I thought you were going into work?"

Maria was sitting on a lounge chair in partial shade from their patio umbrella. She looked uncomfortable.

He rushed over and gingerly scooped up her hand. "Baby, are you feeling okay?"

She shrugged. "I'm feeling very pregnant right now. So, the usual. But also my lower back is really hurting today. I thought this chair would help but... no. What are you doing home?"

Michael couldn't explain. "I—I want to get you checked out by the doctor. You look... overly tired."

"Why today? I already have my appointment set for tomorrow."

He pasted on a smile. "Just do me this one favor. It's your job to be pregnant, and my job to be worried, right? I just want to make sure everything is okay with you and Felicia."

Reluctantly, Maria allowed him to help as she slowly levered herself up from the lounge chair. "I haven't even showered yet."

"No one cares about that. Please, just humor me."

"Fine." She rolled her eyes. "But at least let me change my clothes."

He gave her a quick kiss on the forehead. "Deal."

∼

The ultrasound technician placed warm jelly onto the business end of the wide transducer and then placed it on Maria's belly. "Okay, let's take a look at the little cutie and get some measurements."

Maria gripped Michael's hand as the sound of a rapid heartbeat played through the ultrasound machine's speaker. She looked over at the technician. "Is that Felicia's heartbeat?"

"It sure is. Felicia is a beautiful name. It means 'smile' in Spanish, doesn't it?"

"Close, but not exactly. It's more related to *feliz*, which means happy."

The technician continued moving the probe across Maria's belly with one hand while working the machine's keyboard and mouse with the other. "Do you have a middle name picked out?"

Maria smiled at Michael. "We're not sure yet, but I was thinking about Batsheva. It's his grandmother's name; she passed not too long ago. What do you think, honey?"

Michael nodded, but a chill raced up his spine. That was the name on the tombstone.

Felicia Batsheva Salomon.

The technician stopped suddenly and lifted up the probe, making the screen go black. "Wait here a moment," she said. "I'll be right back with Dr. Sakata."

Though her voice was calm, Michael spotted the look of concern on the woman's face as she got up from the stool and left the room.

Maria squeezed his hand. "I should ask Sakata if there's anything I can take for my lower back. I'm not sure I can handle another eight weeks of this."

Michael gave her a warm smile, but inside, he was freaking out. What had the technician seen? There shouldn't be any big surprises in the beginning of the eighth month; it should be smooth sailing at this point. At least, that's what all those damned pregnancy books said that Maria had made him read.

The door opened, and Dr. Sakata walked in. "Hello, Mr. and Mrs. Salomon. I understand we're doing a wellness check. Did you have any spotting or other symptoms that made you come in today?"

"Spotting, as in bleeding? No." Maria hitched her thumb at her husband. "He's just worried, and wanted me to get checked. The only new symptom I have is back pain. But I guess that comes with the territory."

The doctor sat on the stool. "Well, let's have a look."

As the physician slid the probe across Maria's belly, the ultrasound screen showed various structures that meant nothing to Michael. Still he watched closely, his eyes moving from the screen to the doctor's expression and back, looking for some kind of reaction.

Sakata stopped on one fuzzy image that looked like all the rest, clicked something on the keyboard, and zoomed in. He shifted the angle of the transducer slightly.

The sound of the baby's heartbeat thudded loudly in the room.

"Is there something in particular you're looking for?" Maria asked.

The doctor glanced at her. "You said you're having back pain?"

She nodded. "It's much worse today. I normally don't sleep

on my back, but I fell asleep that way waiting for my husband to get back from work." Maria gave Michael an accusatory glare, then squeezed his hand and blew him a kiss.

Sakata zoomed in on different parts of the image and clicked more buttons, causing small printouts to roll out of a slot in the machine. After about a minute of that, he lifted the transducer, wiped it off, and then wiped down Maria's belly with a fluffy white towel.

"Well," he said, "let's start with the baby. She seems to be under no distress and is about where we'd hope she'd be for a gestational age of thirty-two weeks. That's all good. But it's also good that you came in today." Sakata held up one of the images and pointed at something that was hard to make out. "Maria, you have a minor placental abruption. That means that the placenta has partially torn from the wall of the uterus."

Maria gasped. "What does that mean for the baby?" Her eyes welled up with tears and she squeezed hard on Michael's hand.

"Like I said, it's minor. But I would like to keep you overnight for some tests. We need to check the blood chemistry of the baby and make sure she's still getting everything she needs. It's likely the tests will come back okay, but you two should prepare yourself for the possibility that we may have to deliver early."

All Michael could see at that moment was the birthdate on the tombstone. His voice sounded far away as he said, "But she's only thirty-two weeks…"

Sakata patted the air and tried to smile reassuringly, with minimal success. "A fetus that reaches thirty-two weeks' gestation has a ninety-five percent chance of survival. The important thing is that you're here and we know about this issue. I'm going to prescribe antenatal betamethasone, which is a corticosteroid to help with the baby's lungs. It'll help them mature in anticipation of a possible early delivery."

Maria asked with a quavering voice, "You think we'll deliver early?"

Sakata smiled, and this time it seemed genuine. "We'll do everything we can to keep your little one inside you for as long as possible. We're just preparing for other eventualities." He leaned forward and patted Maria's foot, then shifted his gaze to Michael. "I'll have the nurse give you a list of things to get from the house. I'm going to call admitting and get your wife checked in for tonight."

"How long do I have to stay?" Maria asked.

"At least through tomorrow morning. By then we'll know more. If this is a developing issue that needs immediate treatment, we'll address it then. But it may well be that we can treat this with careful monitoring and bed rest."

"Bed rest, as in *at home* bed rest?" Michael asked.

Sakata nodded. "*If* things are stable, then yes." He gave them both a sympathetic look. "I know this isn't what you wanted to hear. But at least we know about it now, and you're where you need to be. In the meantime, let's try our best not to worry about things that may well not happen."

As the doctor left, Michael could think only of the tombstone.

He leaned down and gave Maria a kiss. "It'll be okay."

"Th-thank you," Maria stammered as she let out a shuddering breath.

"For what?"

Maria began practicing the breathing techniques she'd learned in one of their many pregnancy classes. "For feeling paranoid today. You probably saved the baby."

Michael leaned down and held his wife close so she couldn't see the worry on his face. He wanted to believe her, believe the doctor, and assume everything would be all right.

But he couldn't. His mind's eye couldn't look away from the haunting image of tomorrow's date carved in stone.

Birth... and death.

His fear wouldn't lift until tomorrow had passed safely.

It's only a vision, not a prophecy.

He held his wife tightly and tried to believe it.

PREVIEW – NEW ARCADIA

The mist hung low in the forest, and the agent's footsteps squished through the damp ground, kicking up the aroma of peat moss—an earthy, dark, rich scent reminiscent of wet wool, with a hint of rot. In the distance, he caught sight of a barbed wire fence, the first sign of the high-security camp that wasn't supposed to be there.

Crouching low, the agent continued advancing toward the camp, but froze suddenly upon hearing a crunching and snapping sound underfoot. Dread consumed him when he recognized the sound of children's bones breaking.

The brittle remnants marked another shallow grave just outside the camp codenamed New Arcadia.

Despite the horror of the situation, the agent took another step forward.

He didn't hear the sniper round traveling at twice the speed of sound before it slammed into him.

The world turned black.

～

In a sound-isolated room fifty feet below Fort Meade, Doug Mason watched as two of his specialists worked on a patient lying on a hospital gurney.

One was a neuroscientist monitoring a flatscreen that had a bundle of wires attached to the patient's scalp. The other, a tiny bespectacled man who had been a practicing anesthesiologist before Mason recruited him into the Outfit.

A clandestine government agency that didn't officially exist, the Outfit and its members were an exclusive bunch, hand-picked for their special skills. These two both came from the private sector, and now served a higher calling... one that involved any number of unusual tasks, in all of which national security was at stake. Today was no exception.

Mason shifted his gaze to the head of the gurney. "Jerry, he'll be able to respond to questions, right?"

"Oh, most definitely." The neuroscientist pointed to the monitor, which displayed a variety of squiggly patterns. "We've got a classic EEG signature of unconsciousness at the moment. Mohan's going to chemically immobilize Agent Xiang, and the sedative he's on should give up the ghost. Then he'll wake."

"It's got to be strange waking up and not even being able to blink," Mason said. He'd never witnessed a programming session before, mostly because it had only been done a handful of times, all when he wasn't on the premises.

"It's best that he can't move for a variety of reasons, but the most important have to do with the auditory and visual programming sequences." The neuroscientist adjusted a setting on what looked like a virtual reality headset the patient was wearing. "When we first began experimenting with neuro-programming, the subjects couldn't handle it. The results were miserable."

"What do you mean, couldn't handle it? Was it painful?"

The gray-haired man shrugged. "Hard to say. Before we started inducing paralysis in the subjects, they had an autonomic reaction to the process, flailed uncontrollably, and even when we strapped them to the hospital bed we couldn't get a complete lock on the programming. This is very fidgety, cutting-edge stuff. And the subjects usually don't even realize what's going on during the programming."

The anesthesiologist cut in, his Indian accent thick, yet intelligible. "Let's get things rolling." He cleaned the injection port on the IV with an alcohol swab, then injected a clear liquid into it. "This is Quelicin," he explained to Mason. "The good stuff. He'll be completely immobile. I'll attach an infusion pump to the IV so that he gets a constant four milligrams per minute throughout the procedure."

Mason watched the men work together smoothly as a team. Jerry Caldwell, was a neuroscientist, and Mohan Patel, an anesthesiologist. The two men already had a shorthand between them, and an easy, unspoken calm relationship. He didn't share their calm, feeling uneasy about this whole thing. He understood the necessity of the procedure—the news out of China looked grimmer by the day, and the Outfit needed Agent Xiang for a very special mission—but that did nothing to calm his nerves.

"I pushed a counter to the sedative," Caldwell said. "He

should be awake now." He broke a capsule under the man's nose, and the smell of ammonia permeated the air. "Did he respond?"

"Yup. He's awake, Mohan," Caldwell said, eyes glued to the monitor.

Patel spoke, keeping his voice clear, and his speech measured. "Agent Xiang, this is Doctor Patel. Can you hear me?"

Mason couldn't make heads or tails of what was on the monitor, but it clearly meant something to the neuroscientist, who said: "He hears you."

"Agent Xiang, we're about to start the session. Just relax. You won't remember any of this when this is all over."

Caldwell pulled up a new screen on the monitor, this one flashing a series of patterns.

"Sending a baseline set of signals…"

A buzzing noise leaked from the agent's headset. A 3D representation of the brain appeared on screen, rotating, with portions of it highlighted.

"Do those highlights indicate where you're setting the memories?" Mason asked.

"Yes." Caldwell tapped on one of the highlighted areas of the screen. "This will be programming run one of three."

"Why do you have to do it three times?"

"We've found that repetition helps the memories stick. And it's not just pure repetition. On the third run we induce a slow-wave sleep to consolidate the memory—"

"I thought something like that required REM sleep," Mason interjected.

"No. The slow-wave sleep that comes right after you fall asleep is when memory consolidation occurs. So I induce that state with a slow-wave frequency generator and then trigger delta waves with about ten milliamps of current through the electrodes attached to the agent's forehead and the base of his skull.

"This isn't a great analogy," Caldwell continued, "but conceptually it's similar to when your computer gets an update and you have to reboot before it can process the changes. And sometimes you have to reboot it yet again once things have been configured. The brain has a similar process."

The scientist tapped some things on the screen, and text scrolled rapidly past, along with images of places and people. All the things pertinent to an upcoming mission.

"Okay, Mohan, I've got the signals oriented. I'm about to hit go. Is he good?"

"Blood pressure is at a baseline of 115 over 78, oxygen is at 100%, and heart rate is 45. All good to go."

"Here goes."

A portion of the neuroscientist's screen blurred into streams of unrecognizable character patterns, not unlike the kind shown in the movie *The Matrix*. Mason looked over at the agent and saw Xiang's pale skin turning pink, almost as if he were having an allergic reaction or a hot flash.

The anesthesiologist adjusted the respirator, and its cyclic rate increased, giving the agent more breaths per minute. "BP is now 165 over 80, and heart rate has spiked to 115. We're still okay."

As the programming continued, the agent's skin went from pink to red, and dots of perspiration appeared everywhere his skin was exposed.

"How much longer?" Mohan said, adjusting the respirator

once again, his expression tense. "BP is now 205 over 84, and heart rate is at 185."

Mason clenched his jaw as his gaze panned back and forth between the physicians and Agent Xiang.

"Almost done," Jerry said. "Five... four... three... two... one... done!"

The white noise permeating the room stopped, leaving only the sound of the respirator trying to keep up with the demands of a patient they had put through the wringer.

Letting out a breath he hadn't realized he'd been holding, Mason felt a wave of guilt wash over him. No wonder the subject had to be immobilized for this. What kind of hell was he putting these people through? And was it worth it?

"Patient's stats are dropping back into normal range. BP is 135 over 78 and heart rate is 70. Both are drifting lower."

Mason turned to the neuroscientist. "Can he hear me?"

Jerry nodded.

"Chris? Agent Xiang, this is Director Mason. Are you okay to continue?"

The neuroscientist was watching his screen. "Can you ask your question again? I'm not sure the agent heard it. His brain is still processing the onslaught."

Mason leaned in closer. "Agent Xiang, are you okay to continue?"

The neuroscientist nodded. "EEG waves match the affirmative responses we recorded before the testing began. He's good to go."

Mason took a step back and motioned for the doctors to

continue. There weren't any laws against what they were all doing, but he felt like there probably should be.

All in the name of national security.

~

The fires of hell didn't seem that bad compared to how Alicia's face felt as it burned from the chemicals she'd been sprayed with. She jogged in place and heard the other trainees coughing and struggling against the effects of the pepper spray. Blinking away the chemicals didn't even help; her eyelids felt like flaming hot sandpaper. She could only grit her teeth and try to ignore the pain as she bounced up and down on the balls of her feet.

"Move it, move it, move it!"

One of the instructors shoved her toward the track, and it took everything Alicia had to *not* send a back fist to the guy's temple.

She and a dozen other FBI Academy trainees were on a remote portion of Marine Base Quantico. She'd been integrated into this training class only three days ago. Yet despite the dusty surroundings, the chemicals in her face, and her complete physical agony, she knew there was one thing she *couldn't* do.

Let these bastards get the best of her.

"The more you sweat and suffer here, the less you'll bleed when on assignment. I want one and a half miles from all of you! That's six laps, for you people who aren't all that bright."

Blinking through the pain and tears, Alicia began running.

"Yoder, Sanchez, and Smith!"

Alicia and two other agents turned to the instructor.

He made a counterclockwise motion with his finger. "The other direction, numbskulls."

Alicia pressed a finger against the side of her nose, blew a seemingly impossible amount of snot in the instructor's general direction, and ran to catch up with the rest of the class.

∽

Alicia felt much better after finishing the run—though she still felt a burning sensation in the back of her throat. She hadn't been the first to complete the six laps, but she had finished in the front third of the trainees, which would have to be good enough. Halfway through the run, she had developed a pain in her lower abdomen. It didn't feel like a normal period cramp, but what else could it be? She sure as hell wasn't going to mention it; as the only woman in this class, she wasn't about to allow that to be an excuse.

She had never run with anything more than two-pound ankle weights in college, and she'd never have imagined just how exhausting it was to run in full tactical gear. All the trainees had been completely kitted out, from military-issue combat boots to an advanced battle vest with ballistic inserts, load distribution system, and what the instructor called SAPIs and ESBIs—small-arms protective inserts and enhanced side ballistic inserts. The whole thing probably only weighed fifteen or twenty pounds, but Alicia had felt every one of them over the course of the six laps.

The last two trainees came walking back from the track looking exhausted. Their eyes were bloodshot, and partially dried snot and Lord knows what else was streaked across their faces and into their hair. They looked like hell.

Alicia now knew the feeling—quite well.

When all of the would-be agents had completed the run and settled onto the benches, an instructor stepped in front of the group and spoke.

"Okay, trainees. We've got something special today."

He hitched his thumb toward the training site behind him—a dusty ghost town that had been constructed about a quarter mile away. It had been set up in a grid pattern, with a wide main street splitting it from north to south. Yesterday, when they'd used it to go through various close-quarters combat scenarios, corpses of burnt-out vehicles had lined the street. Today Alicia saw something else out there. Something metal. But she couldn't quite make it out from this distance.

The instructor smiled. "Some researchers out of DARPA have developed a new artificial intelligence unit, and we've plugged it into one of our EOD robots."

EOD was shorthand for explosive ordnance disposal—the bomb guys. And now Alicia realized what the metal object in the main street was. A couple weeks earlier she had worked with some folks from the Army's EOD group, and she'd gotten a chance to operate one of their remote bomb disposal units. It was kind of neat, reminding her of the robot from the cartoon *WALL-E*. It even had arms that she could manipulate through a remote control.

"With this new AI enhancement, the robot is supposed to detect and identify combatants in the field. It's been through quite a bit of testing already, but before it can be put out into the field, it's going to need a lot more work. Today is your turn to see if you can fool the robot. All you need to do is go up to it and touch the thing without it raising its red flag, meaning it saw you. Any questions?"

One of the trainees raised his hand. "Sir? How far can it see?"

"Good question. The robot will analyze anything coming within a thousand-foot radius."

A voice broadcast from what looked like a walkie-talkie on the instructor's utility belt. *"We're ready."*

The instructor spoke into a shoulder-attached mic. "Roger that." He then pointed at the man who'd asked the question. "Smith, since you're the curious type, you can go first."

The trainee launched himself from the bench and jogged north, skirting the edge of the makeshift town, then vanished between the buildings. After a moment the robot turned eastward, sensing him.

Suddenly the trainee raced into view, and the robot's arm shot upward, with something red hanging from it.

"Subject detected," the walkie-talkie squawked. *"Send the next agent."*

The instructor pointed at another trainee. "Darby, you're up next."

Scott Darby, a tall, blond, giant of a man, stood and tapped the shoulder of the guy who'd been sitting next to him. Carl something. "Hey, want to try and tag team Robo-Grunt?"

"Sure."

The two men spoke in hushed whispers, then took off at a

sprint. They split up, approaching their target from opposite directions.

Was one of them going to sacrifice himself so the other could tag the thing?

As they converged onto the town, the robot seemed skittish, scanning back and forth, clearly sensing movement. But the men were ducking behind buildings before the robot could zero in on them.

Then Carl launched a rock past his target.

But instead of following the movement of the rock, the robot turned, raised its arm, then spun, kicking up a cloud of dust.

Alicia wasn't quite sure what had just happened, but the voice on the walkie-talkie said, *"Both agents identified. Send your next."*

"Cortez, you're up."

The man sitting next to Alicia jumped up and raced forward. Like the others, he ducked behind the buildings and thus delayed his inevitable defeat. His tactic was to throw up a cloud of dirt to distract the robot. But the moment he leapt from cover, the robot flagged him.

Damn, that thing is fast.

"Yoder, you're up."

Alicia stood, then tilted her head to the supply shed. "Can I use the mosquito netting?" she asked.

The instructor shrugged. "Whatever's here, you can use."

Alicia unrolled nearly fifty feet of thick mosquito netting from the spool and wrapped herself with it. The instructor and trainees watched with confusion and interest as she created a puffy ghillie suit.

When she tied it off, she checked her shadow. She could barely see anything through the layers of mesh, but she'd created the desired effect: her shadow was round—not shaped like a human at all. Alicia hoped that the AI wouldn't know what to make of her.

Keeping her hands inside the suit, she pushed out the edges of the mesh, making herself look even rounder as she trudged northward.

She didn't bother skirting around buildings. She moved straight at the robot, her heart thudding in her ears as she wobbled forward.

It turned slightly as she got in range.

Alicia kept moving.

The robot shifted back and forth like it was suffering from a nervous tic. It clearly sensed her approach. But would it identify her as a combatant?

Alicia heard the whoosh of the robot's hydraulics. She saw the red cloth clutched in its robotic grip.

It's about to raise its arm.

But it was too late. Alicia bumped directly into it and yelled, "I tagged it!" She felt a wave of triumph.

Two men stepped from the nearest building. They were dressed in street clothes and had picture badges clipped to their collars. One looked annoyed, but the other laughed.

"How did you know that your heat signature wouldn't be able to be detected through that mesh?"

Alicia shrugged. "I had no idea. I just figured if I didn't have a human outline, it might get fooled."

The other man grumbled, "Dumb luck."

PREVIEW - NEW ARCADIA

"No, this was perfect," said the first man. He gave Alicia a thumbs-up. "I'd never have thought of this approach." He spoke into a handheld device. "It seems your trainee found a chink in our armor. We've got some work to do."

"*Roger that. I'll dismiss the rest of the trainees for the day. Yoder, good job. We'll be back in the classroom at 0800.*"

As the scientists began unscrewing one of the panels on the robot, Alicia wriggled out of the layers of mosquito netting. Despite her little victory against WALL-E the Robo-Grunt, she couldn't help but feel anxiety over the training activities still to come. Unlike her classes in college, all of which provided a clear syllabus with what to expect, here she had been given absolutely no idea what the Outfit had in store for her.

She wasn't even completely sure what being an agent at the Outfit even entailed. The training seemed almost random. Last week it was working with some Marines on conditioning exercises. This week it was training at the FBI Academy. And next? Who knew?

She wished she at least had some grades to measure herself against, unsure if she was doing well or poorly. But that might change tomorrow. She had a mid-cycle evaluation with Mason at the Outfit's HQ, and she couldn't help but wonder what Mason would have to say about her performance.

~

It had been three months since Alicia had agreed to join the Outfit—a huge decision for her. It had not only meant moving to a new apartment in DC, it had meant leaving Princeton without having finished her master's degree in neuroscience. The unfinished degree didn't sit well with her, and now, as she drove past Lincoln Park, through the National Mall, past Foggy Bottom, and into old Georgetown, her mind was filled with doubt about her choices.

She placed a call on her phone and transferred it to the car's speakers.

"What's up, baby girl?"

The sound of her adoptive father's deep voice should have taken the edge off of her nerves, but it didn't.

"Dad, what the hell was I thinking? I feel like it was just yesterday that I was taking classes, an ordinary student, and now I'm training to be... hell, I don't even *know* what I'm training to be. Shooting drills, CQB training, and a few days ago they put me through an entire session on vehicle engagement tactics—learning how to drive and shoot at the same time, evasive maneuvers, anti-ambush drills... Dad, this is insane."

Her father chuckled. *"Alicia, take a deep breath. Where are you?"*

She took a deep breath and let it out. It did make her feel a little better. "I'm driving to HQ for my three-month review with Mason. My nerves have me all knotted up inside. Hell, I'm trying not to throw up right now."

"There's no reason for you to be nervous. You've got this. And besides, I've been keeping tabs, and everyone so far has had nothing but good things to say about your progress."

"If you say so. It's not like they would tell *you* if I'm doing poorly. You're Levi Yoder, Super Spy. I'm just... me." Alicia's throat tightened and her heart raced. "Dad, I... I can't remember what made me say yes to this. And I mean that literally—it's like total blanks in my head. I think I might be losing it."

"I assure you, you're not losing it. And those gaps... honey, let's just say that they're there for a reason."

"What do you mean?"

"It's hard to explain. Sometimes when people go through trauma, things get blocked from your consciousness. It's totally normal."

A chill raced through her, and she began feeling lightheaded. "You don't have to explain to me how the brain works—I'm the neuroscientist, remember? Or I was *going* to be. But—what trauma, Dad? Was I"—she swallowed—"was I... raped or something? What am I blocking out?"

"No, no, it was nothing like that. You just... you managed to get mixed up in something that involved the Outfit. You kicked ass, Alicia. But it was hard on you. Mason and I thought you might lose some of those memories of the incident, and honestly, I'm glad you did. You're better off, trust me. And if you're nervous about it, talk to Mason. He'll totally understand."

"Maybe."

"It's your call. But listen—I'm in DC today for a quick meeting. Maybe you could meet me upstairs for a bite to eat? How's noon sound?"

"It sounds great, Dad." Alicia wiped tears of frustration from her cheeks. She took a deep breath in, then let it out slowly in an attempt calm the roiling fear, anxiety, and nerves. "I'm sorry. I'm acting like a baby. I'm just nervous and... freaking out a bit."

"Alicia, you have nothing to worry about." She could hear the smile in his voice.

They ended the call as she pulled into an open spot on the side of the road in old Georgetown. Traffic had been unexpectedly light, and she was an hour early for her meeting, so she tuned the radio to an oldies station and tried to calm her nerves.

Even the sounds of *Earth, Wind & Fire* couldn't banish the feelings pressing in on her. After thirty minutes, she gave up and got out of the car.

"Hey honey, you have any food I can have?"

She turned to see an old man in dirty threadbare clothing yelling at her from down the street. She grinned as she walked toward him. She recognized the "beggar" as a member of the Outfit, and the things he yelled were actually codes to notify anyone approaching headquarters if there was anything amiss. Asking for food was a sign that everything was clear. Had he asked for a drink… well, then Alicia was to leave the area immediately.

Ahead, Alicia saw a familiar sign. It featured a profile of a rooster on the left, and the head of a longhorn bull on the right. This area wasn't exactly upscale, but Alicia had gained some fondness for the dingy street front.

She walked into the Rooster and Bull, and the smells of stale beer and wood polish washed over her. The place was a dive bar… and also an entrance into one of the most secretive organizations in the world.

Dimly lit as always, the place's few tables and booths were all empty at this time of day. Behind the bar, a man toweled a glass dry. He nodded at her as she walked toward the back of the establishment.

Alicia entered the men's bathroom. A white-haired man

sitting on a stool near the sink looked at her over his John Lennon-styled spectacles.

"Back again, little girl?"

She grinned. "Harold, how many pairs of tan slacks and plaid button-down shirts do you own? That's all I ever see you wear."

"Bah!" Harold held out a white towel. "My wife always harped about the same thing."

Alicia took the towel. It looked like an ordinary towel, but she knew it had a string of RFID tags sewn into it, and acted as a key of sorts.

"Sounds like your wife was a smart woman," she said, giving the old codger a wink.

For the blink of an eye, the old grump cracked a smile, then he muttered something unintelligible as he waved her away.

Alicia chuckled as she entered the third of the bathroom's three stalls—the one with an "Out of Order" sign taped to it. She shut the door behind her, then placed the special towel on the flushing lever and flushed the toilet.

Immediately the floor dropped—taking Alicia and the toilet with it. She put her hands on the tank to steady herself as she dropped with frightening speed down an incredibly deep shaft. She'd taken this route dozens of times, yet her stomach still lurched.

After a few very long seconds, the walls fell away and the toilet-elevator slowed nearly to a stop. Alicia focused on regaining her balance as she descended into a featureless room deep underneath old Georgetown. The platform settled softly into a recess in the floor, and Alicia stepped off.

Just as quickly as it had dropped, the toilet-elevator launched back up again, disappearing into the shaft in the ceiling.

Alicia tossed the hand towel in a nearby basket, then walked to the room's only exit: a steel door with a security panel mounted to one side. She placed her splayed hand on the panel, and a blue line passed back and forth. Then a green LED flashed, and a click echoed from inside the wall.

"Stand clear," warned a digitized voice.

Three massive locking bolts slid out of their retaining blocks on the right side of the door, and the door slowly opened outward.

Alicia remembered the first time she'd been brought here, by her father and Director Mason. The place had reminded her of a 1950s bomb shelter, except that no bomb shelters she knew of had a four-foot thick, tungsten-steel alloy door weighing eighteen tons at its entrance.

She walked through the opening, around a corner, and down a hall that ended at another door, this one with a retinal scanner. She put her eye up to the box on the wall, and with a flash of green light, the door clicked.

Alicia pushed it open and stepped into the inner sanctum of the Outfit's US headquarters.

She was in a room larger than most warehouses. Standing on a metal walkway about twenty feet above the floor, Alicia had a clear view of the cubicles arranged in a grid below her, stretching as far as she could see. No matter what time of the day or night she arrived, she always found men and women working like their lives depended on it. And very likely, somewhere out there in the world, someone's life *did* hinge on these people's work.

Four huge display screens, each fifty feet across, hung from the ceiling at the center of the space, displaying information, maps, photographs, satellite feeds, and more, and the walkway she was on continued around the edges of the giant room, leading to offices whose windows also looked down on the central work area.

She was reminded, not for the first time, of the headquarters in the movie *Men in Black*, except there were no aliens—at least, not that she knew of.

She walked down a flight of metal stairs, stepped into the cubicle bullpen, and started the long walk to the far side of the cavern-like complex. When she finally reached conference room C1, where she was scheduled to meet with Mason, the butterflies in her stomach were threatening to come flying out of her mouth.

Despite her early arrival, she found the director already waiting, studying a photograph. She looked up at the wall clock and saw to her astonishment that she wasn't fifteen minutes early, she was forty-five minutes *late*.

"Oh my God, I don't—"

"Daylight savings?" Mason said. "Did you forget the time changed early this morning?"

He stared at her with his pale, silver-hued eyes. He was in his fifties, with light brown hair and a receding hairline. Most men with his looks would have been dismissed by the general public as boring or average. Not Mason. Something in the way he held himself... his presence commanded attention. This man was the Outfit's most senior member in the US—at least, as far as she knew, and here she was showing up almost an hour late for her evaluation.

"I'm so sorry! Do we need to reschedule?"

Mason waved dismissively at her and slid the photo he'd been looking at across the conference room table. "Tell me what you see."

Alicia took a seat across from him and picked up the photo. It looked like some kind of business social. "Well, lots of Asian people, but I don't suppose you needed me to tell you that."

"Do you recognize anyone?"

She nearly shook her head when a woman caught her attention. She was only in profile, and she was a good distance from the camera, but...

"I'm not positive, but I think I do."

She felt a surge of apprehension. Her boss expected an answer—an *honest* answer—but Alicia didn't want to betray this woman's confidence. She was, after all, involved in the shady side of business.

"I... I think my father knows her."

"A very diplomatic way of putting it, young lady." Mason's stone-like expression softened, and he gave her a slight nod. "Very well, I'll talk to Levi in a bit."

He glanced at the wall clock and rose from his chair. "Unfortunately, I have another meeting at the top of the hour, so we'll have to postpone our review. I'll have my admin set something up." He walked to the door, put his hand on the knob, and looked back at Alicia. "And next time, don't be late."

She nodded.

As Mason opened the door, his phone rang, and he put it to his ear. "Hey, Levi. I'll be right up. My office." He looked back at Alicia once more. "This room is free for the next couple hours if you want to use it."

He closed the door silently behind him.

Alicia put her head in her hands. All her life she'd been an overachiever. She was always early for every engagement, meeting, class—everything. She couldn't believe she'd made such a dumb error. The training over the last weeks had been so intense, it had made her completely forget about the outside world... and ordinary things like *Daylight Saving Time*.

She'd been hoping that today's meeting would ease her anxiety. If she could just get some feedback on how she was doing—even if it was bad—she thought she'd feel more at ease. Instead, Alicia was almost an hour late to a meeting with one of the most important men in the entire Outfit. And had she not been wasting time sitting in the car, she'd likely have almost made it in time.

She remembered her father's advice, and took a deep breath.

It didn't help.

— end of preview —

If you're interested in ordering this novel, this link will take you to where you can order it: New Arcadia

ADDENDUM

If you've read my books in the past, you've come to expect this scientist to weave in some science regardless of what genre the book is. I don't like to be predictable, but here we are, once again, at the addendum, and as with most Levi Yoder novels, I've introduced some things that might warrant some explanations.

Nanites: Real of Make Believe?

Let's get this straight: nanites—also called nanobots or molecular machines—aren't magic. They're real science. The word gets thrown around in sci-fi a lot, but the basic concept is this: a microscopically small machine, programmed to carry out very specific tasks inside the human body.

In this story, nanites are doing something incredibly ambitious: continual repair based on a template of an "ideal" human blueprint. That means they don't just fix damage after it happens—they're always working to push the body back to an optimized state. The moment something starts to go off the rails—cell damage, inflammation, chemical burns—they intervene.

Now here's the science part.

Can we build things that small in real life?

Yes. Actually, we already do. A perfect example is modern semiconductor lithography.

The latest chips from companies like TSMC and Intel are built using 3-nanometer process nodes. For context, that means the transistor channels—essentially the on/off switches of your computer—are now smaller than the width of a single strand of DNA.

This kind of precision proves that engineering at the nanoscale is absolutely possible.

So if we can build processors that small, why aren't we all walking around with health-restoring nanobots in our bloodstream?

Because it's not a tech problem—it's a manufacturing problem.

Designing one nanite is like designing a Ferrari with tweezers. Painstaking, but doable.

Mass-producing millions or billions of those Ferraris, cheaply and reliably, in a package that can survive the human immune system and actually perform useful work inside the body?

That's the mountain.

In *Canvas of Deception*, we skip ahead to a world where someone has solved that problem. The nanites exist.

ADDENDUM

They're scalable. And they've been deployed into people like Levi and Alicia.

Which brings us to how they work in the story.

Take Alicia, for example. After the chemical trap in the warehouse, by all accounts, she should have died. Her lungs were destroyed, skin chemically burned off, organ systems collapsing. And yet... she didn't. She stabilized. She regenerated. Her body didn't just survive; it recovered—aggressively, unnaturally.

That's the nanites at work.

Don't get me wrong, that doesn't make Levi nor Alicia immortal in that they can't be killed. It's just that things we couldn't normally recover from, they might be able to. And their ability to recover in general is highly improved.

And it's not just trauma recovery. These machines are also fighting aging, because aging is just slow, cumulative damage. If your cells are constantly being cleaned up, repaired, and optimized, the very thing we call aging becomes... optional.

Of course, there's a cost.

You're always hungry. You itch under your skin. You burn fuel like a furnace. Your body feels like it's being re-engineered on the fly.

And maybe, just maybe, you're not entirely *you* anymore.

That's the tension Levi lives with. He sees the nanites as a curse. Alicia?

She's not so sure.

Because in her case—they saved her life. It's saved Levi's life on more than one occasion, he just doesn't like to acknowledge it.

And that makes the tech more than just a plot device.

ADDENDUM

It's a question:

If you could fix everything that goes wrong with the human body…

What would you lose in the process?

∼

Novichok and the attack in the warehouse, was that stuff real?

So let's talk about something nasty.

Novichok.

Sounds like a spy movie term, right? Unfortunately, it's very real, and worse—it's been used in the real world to kill people. Multiple times.

What Is Novichok?

Novichok (Russian for "newcomer") refers to a family of next-generation nerve agents developed by the Soviet Union in the 1970s and '80s. These were designed to be more lethal, harder to detect, and easier to manufacture from common precursors than older nerve agents like VX or sarin.

They work by disrupting the nervous system—specifically, by binding to an enzyme (acetylcholinesterase) responsible for clearing neurotransmitters. Once that enzyme is blocked, your body goes haywire.

Muscles seize.

Lungs fail.

Heart spasms.

Death follows unless *very specific* and immediate medical treatment is available.

Real-World Use of Novichok
Yes, it's been used outside war zones:

- 2018 – Salisbury, UK: A former Russian double agent, Sergei Skripal, and his daughter were poisoned with Novichok. A civilian who accidentally came into contact with the container later died.
- 2020 – Russia: Russian opposition leader Alexei Navalny was poisoned with Novichok. He survived thanks to quick international intervention and was flown to Germany for treatment.

These are not battlefield weapons—they are assassination tools, deliberately used to eliminate targets while leaving confusion and plausible deniability in their wake.

Why Novichok Still Matters

In the book, the idea wasn't to focus only on Novichok—but to highlight the evolution of assassination tools. From subtle nerve agents to room-scale chemical traps, this kind of tech shows the mindset of operators like the Maestro: don't just kill... erase.
And Novichok?
It's not gone.
It's still in the wild, and the knowledge to make it still exists —along with other compounds just as deadly, possibly worse.

ADDENDUM

That's the chilling part.

Because in fiction and in reality…

Sometimes the weapons don't look like guns.

Sometimes they look like a warehouse with one door, no escape, and an invisible death hanging in the air.

∽

The Mona Lisa Heist – Truth and lies…

Let's talk about the *Mona Lisa*.

Yeah, *that* Mona Lisa—the smirking lady behind bulletproof glass at the Louvre. Possibly the most famous painting on Earth.

But here's what a lot of people don't know: she was stolen once. For real. And it wasn't some high-tech, laser-grid, Oceans Eleven kind of job.

Nope.

It was an inside gig… pulled off by a guy with a mustache and a white smock.

The Real Story: Vincenzo Peruggia

In 1911, an Italian handyman named Vincenzo Peruggia, who had previously worked at the Louvre, walked into the museum in broad daylight… and walked out with the Mona Lisa under his coat.

You read that right.

He *literally* took it off the wall, hid it under a canvas smock, and strolled out.

Security back then? Not exactly Fort Knox.

The museum didn't even realize the painting was missing for a full 24 hours.

Peruggia held onto it for over two years, hiding it in a trunk in his apartment in Paris before eventually trying to sell it to an art dealer in Florence, claiming he was a patriot trying to return the painting to Italy.

Spoiler alert: he got caught.

The *Mona Lisa* was returned to the Louvre in 1913.

The resulting fallout…

The theft turned the Mona Lisa into a global celebrity. Before the heist, it wasn't the most famous painting in the world—it became that *because* it was stolen.

Newspapers around the world covered the saga like a royal scandal. Parisians lined up around the block just to see the *empty wall* where it had hung. Picasso himself was brought in for questioning. (He didn't do it, for the record.)

So yes, the *Mona Lisa* became a legend, not just for who painted her…

…but because someone actually made her disappear.

And in This Story…

If you've read *Canvas of Deception*, you'll notice how much this heist inspired the opening.

The idea that art can vanish—and with it, the truth—makes for great thriller material. Combine that with modern forgery tech, black-market dealers, and a dash of mob paranoia? Suddenly, you're not just stealing paintings...

You're rewriting history.

~

The coin – is the Outfit's coin a thing? Really?

I've never actually sat down to write an explanation of a curious little item that Outfit members use to identify each other— the *coin*—and I think it's about time I did.

On the surface, it looks like a high-end poker chip or commemorative challenge coin. In reality? It's one of the most fun biometric verification tools you'll (n)ever see.

Here's how it works—*and yes*, before you ask, it's based entirely on tech that already exists today.

The Coin as a Biometric Authentication Device

Each coin contains two capacitive touch pads, one on either side. Each pad is wired into an embedded chip inside the coin (think Apple's Secure Enclave or YubiKey's NFC chip), capable of:

- Capturing electrical impedance signatures from the human skin (basically, your unique electrical "skinprint").
- Optionally reading vascular patterns, a.k.a. the unique vein layout beneath your skin (used in palm and finger vein scanners).

ADDENDUM

- Reading temperature, sweat composition, and conductance variability—basically confirming you're human *and* alive *and* matching the expected biometric signature.

So how does it know who you are?
It doesn't—not locally, anyway.

Here's where secure cloud verification comes into play.

Once both users touch the coin simultaneously, it does the following:

1. Presumed that it's been paired with the owner's phone over encrypted Bluetooth LE (yes, that exists).
2. The phone app encrypts and sends the anonymized biometric data from both parties to a secured cloud endpoint—the Outfit's private server farm, naturally off-grid and compartmentalized.
3. The server cross-references the submitted biometric signatures against its internal membership database.
4. Within seconds, the server sends back a boolean result (YES/NO) to the phone, which relays it back to the coin.
5. A tiny LED on the coin lights up:
    - Green = both users are verified Outfit members.
    - Red = someone's a stranger. No go.

ADDENDUM

That's it. Silent handshake, zero spoken words, no passwords exchanged.

You don't even need to know the person's name—just that they're legitimate.

Are there any real-word parallels?

If you're thinking this sounds far-fetched, let's break down where the tech already exists:

- Capacitive biometric sensors are everywhere: your phone screen, your laptop, your car door.
- Multi-factor authentication tokens like YubiKeys and NFC rings already offer secure verification with contact and contactless methods.
- Bluetooth LE + Secure Cloud Apps? Apple Pay, Google Authenticator, even two-factor enterprise badges do this in real time, right now.
- Vein scanners and sweat-based ID systems have been tested by DARPA and Samsung for device locking, and are far more unique than fingerprints.
- Cryptographic anonymization and lookup-only biometric systems? That's already standard in decentralized ID protocols (think: zero-knowledge proofs + blockchain-secured ID).

What *isn't* mass-deployed is cramming all of that into something the size of a half-dollar and making it look innocuous.

ADDENDUM

But that's where fiction lets us push just far enough to let imagination bridge the rest.

Why does it matter to the story?

The Outfit doesn't trust anything that leaves a trail. Phones can be cloned, voices imitated, names dropped. But biometrics embedded in a closed-circuit tool? That's harder to fake.

The coin makes sure everyone in the room is who they say they are—*without saying anything at all*. It's a test of presence. And trust.

And if it glows red?

Well, someone's about to have a very bad day.

ABOUT THE AUTHOR

I am an Army brat, a polyglot, and the first person in my family born in the United States. This heavily influenced my youth by instilling in me a love of reading and a burning curiosity about the world and all of the things within it. As an adult, my love of travel and adventure has driven me to explore many unimaginable locations, and these places sometimes creep into the stories I write.

I hope you've found this story entertaining.

- Mike Rothman

You can find my blog at: www.michaelarothman.com

I am also on Facebook at:
www.facebook.com/MichaelARothman
And on Twitter: @MichaelARothman

Made in the USA
Columbia, SC
31 May 2025